Smith's
MONTHLY

Every Month Original
Novels, Stories, and Articles

USA Today Bestselling Writer
Dean Wesley Smith

I0554015

TABLE OF CONTENTS

Smith's Monthly Issue #13

Introduction
The Christmas Issue

I HAD ALWAYS PLANNED on doing a Christmas issue for this magazine. I didn't last year because of all the start-up stuff of just getting this magazine through the first three issues, but right from last Christmas I knew this fall and winter I would do this kind of special issue.

I have written a lot of Christmas stories over the years. The first three Poker Boy stories were Christmas stories, actually. And for years and years I did a challenge every year with another writer to write five Christmas stories and put them in a booklet and give them to friends as presents. Great fun.

I like writing Christmas stories.

So as this year got to about the halfway point, the sun was shining, people were taking summer vacations, and I honestly hadn't given the Christmas issue any thought. Not a bit. For me, it's difficult to think about Christmas in July

and August. Something about heat and sunshine I would imagine.

But in early July I was asked to contribute a Christmas novel to a story bundle that will come out in late November and early December. I said sure. I love having novels in bundles with other writers. The bundles are always fun and allow readers to find new authors they didn't know about or hadn't read.

But alas, after I said yes, it dawned on me that I didn't have a Christmas novel.

Oops.

But not having a Christmas novel was a problem that could be solved. After all, I write novels every month for this magazine.

But with the deadline for this magazine and then the bundle deadline, if I didn't write a Christmas novel in August, the novel would not be here in these pages first. I always want the novels in these pages to be original to this magazine for at least a month or two. That makes it

Thanks for the Support

Dean Wesley Smith

worthwhile for the wonderful subscribers who support this crazy ongoing journey.

So during the month of August and into early September, I wrote the novel *Heaven Painted as a Christmas Gift* that is in this October issue.

I offset the thinking of snow by setting the novel in Las Vegas, mostly. Tough to write well about cold and snow when the weatherman is talking about ninety degree days and I'm driving everywhere with the air conditioning on.

So with a Christmas novel in this issue, I figured it would be only logical to add in some Christmas short stories. And even a Christmas poem or two.

A couple of the stories in this issue were first published way back in the last century, but are my favorites.

"Jukebox Gifts" was first published in *The Magazine of Fantasy and Science Fiction* a very long time ago. It's my favorite Jukebox Series story. And for those following along, the Jukebox Series stories are actually part of the Thunder Mountain series and the two series will be combined down the road.

The very first Poker Boy story is in here as well. It's called "The Old Girlfriend of Doom."

I also have included a very short story called "Sprinkle on a Memory" that was published first in *Ellery Queen Mystery Magazine*.

And one of my favorite older stories is in here. It's called "The Christmas Escape" and was first published in an anthology in 1990 that came out and vanished. It hasn't been anywhere since.

Plus there are two other stories in here, bringing the total to six short stories this issue. All the stories have Christmas as a theme in one form or another. Granted, a couple of them have Christmas only as a setting, but close enough.

This issue will come out in November. So if you are like me and think the Christmas season doesn't start until after Thanksgiving, catch up on your reading from the other issues first for a month and then dig into this issue in December.

But if you want to start getting into the Christmas spirit right after Halloween, read away.

I hope you enjoy the Christmas treat.

Dean Wesley Smith
September 17, 2014
Lincoln City, Oregon

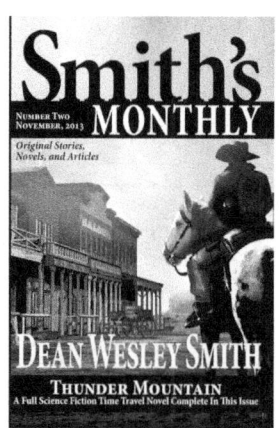

Coming Next Issue in Smith's Monthly
A return to the Thunder Mountain world
in a brand new novel
THE EDWARDS MANSION

Dean Wesley Smith

USA Today Bestselling Writer

Jukebox Gifts

A JUKEBOX STORY

A bar, five friends, and a very special jukebox that lets you time travel back to a memory for the length of the song.

What could go wrong with giving such a special trip and the gift of a second chance to each of your closest friends?

First published in The Magazine of Fantasy and Science Fiction *way back in 1994, this story kicked off my Jukebox Series of stories, even though the first real Jukebox Story was published in* Night Cry Magazine *in the 1980s.*

For those wondering, the Jukebox Stores are tied to the Thunder Mountain series of novels.

JUKEBOX GIFTS
A Jukebox Story

Chapter One

THE STEREO BEHIND the bar was playing soft Christmas songs as I clicked the lock to the front entrance of the Garden Lounge and flicked off the outside light. I could feel the cold of the night through the wood door and the heat of the room surrounding me. I took a deep breath. Christmas Eve was finally here.

I could see the entire lounge and the backs of my four best friends sitting at the bar. I had never been much into decorating with Christmas stuff, and this year was no different. My only nod to the season was a small Christmas candle for each table and booth. Some customer had tied a red ribbon on one of the plants over the middle booth, and the Coors driver had put up a Christmas poster declaring Coors to be the official beer of Christmas. The candles still flickered on the empty tables, but the rest of the bar looked normal. Dark brown wood walls, dark brown carpet, an old oak bar, and my friends. The most important part was the friends. My four best friends' lives were as empty as mine. Tonight, on the first Christmas Eve since I bought the bar, I was going to give them a chance to change that. That was my present to them. It was going to be an interesting night.

"All right, Stout," Carl said, twisting his huge frame around on his bar stool so that he could face me as I wound my way back across the room between the empty tables and chairs. "Just what's such a big secret that you kick out that young couple and lock the door at seven o'clock on Christmas Eve?"

I laughed. Carl always got right to the point. With big Carl you always knew exactly where you stood.

"Yeah," Jess said from his usual place at the oak bar beside the waitress station, "What's so damned important you don't want the four of us to even get off our stools?" Jess was the short one of the crowd. When he stood next to Carl the top of Jess's head barely reached Carl's neck. Jess loved to play practical jokes on Carl. Carl hated it.

"This," I said as I pulled the custom-made, felt cover off the old Wurlitzer jukebox and, with a flourish, dropped the cloth over the planter and into the empty front booth. My stomach did a tap dance from nerves as all four of my best customers whistled and applauded, the sound echoing in the furniture- and plant-filled room.

David, my closest friend in the entire world, downed the last of his scotch-rocks and swirled the ice around in the glass with a tinkling sound. Then, with his paralyzed right hand, he pushed the glass, napkin and all, to the inside edge of the bar. "So after hiding that jukebox in the storage room for the last ten months, we're finally going to get to hear it play?"

"You guessed it." I ran my shaking fingers over the cold smoothness of the chrome and polished glass. I had carefully typed onto labels the names of over sixty Christmas songs, then taped them next to the red buttons. Somewhere in this jukebox I hoped there would be a special song for each man. A song that would trigger a memory and a ride into the past. My Christmas present to each of them.

I took a deep breath and headed behind the bar. "I hope," I said, keeping my voice upbeat, "that it will be a little more than just a song. You see, that jukebox is all that I have left from the first time I owned a bar. Since I've owned the Garden Lounge, it has never been played."

Jess, his dress shirt open to the third button and his tie hanging loose around his neck, spun his bar napkin on top of his glass. "So why tonight?"

"Because a year ago on Christmas Eve I made the decision to buy the Garden Lounge, and try again."

"And I'm glad you did," David said, lifting his drink in his good left hand in a toast.

"Here, here," Fred said, raising his drink high above his head and spilling part of it into his red hair. "Where else could we enjoy a few hours of Christmas Eve before going home to be bored."

All four men raised their glasses in agreement as I laughed and joined them with a sip of the sweet eggnog I always drank on Christmas Eve. No booze, just eggnog.

"It's been a good year," I said, "especially with friends like you. That's why I've decided to give each of you a really special present."

"Oh, to hell with the present," Jess said. "How about another drink? I've got a wife to face and knowing her, she ain't going to be happy that I'm not home yet."

"Is she ever happy?" David asked.

Jess shook his head slowly. "And I wonder why I drink." He slid his glass down the bar at me as he always did at least once a night. I caught it and tipped it upside down in the dirty glass rack.

"I'll fix everyone a last Christmas drink as you open the first part of your presents." I reached into the drawer under the cash register and pulled out four small packages. Each was the size of a ring box wrapped in red paper and tied with a green ribbon.

"Awful little," Fred said as I slid one in front of each man and then put four special Christmas glasses up on the mat over the ice. I'd had the name of each man etched on the glass.

"You know what they say about small packages," Jess said, twisting the package first one way, then the other while inspecting it. "But knowing Radley, the size will be a good indication."

"You just wait," I said.

"Great glasses," David said, noticing them for the first time. "They part of the present?"

"Part of the evening," I said. I let each man inspect his own empty glass before I filled it. The names were etched in gold leaf over the logo of the Garden Lounge. I'd had them done to remember the night. I hoped I would have more than a few glasses left when it was all over.

Carl was the first to get his present unwrapped. "You were right, Jess. It's a quarter." He held it up for everyone to see. "Looks like old Radley here is giving us a clue that we should tip more."

I laughed as I filled his glass with ice. "No. It's a trip, not a tip." I finished pouring his drink and slid it in front of him. "Since you unwrapped yours so fast, you get to go first." I nodded at the jukebox. "But there are rules."

"There seem to be a lot of rules around here tonight," Fred said. Everyone laughed.

I held up a hand for them to stop. "Trust me. This will be a special night."

"So give me the rules," Carl said.

I leaned on the dishwasher behind the bar so no one could see that I was shaking. "On that jukebox is every damn Christmas song I could find. Pick one that reminds you of a major point in your life — some *thing* or *time* or *event* that changed your life. After you punch the button, but before the music starts, tell us what the song reminds you of."

Carl shook his head. "You know, Stout. You've gone and flipped out."

"Sometimes I think so, too," I said. I wasn't kidding him. Sometimes I really did think so.

"Tonight seems to be ample proof," David said, holding up the quarter.

"Just trust me, that is a very special jukebox. Try it and I'll think you'll discover what I mean."

Carl shrugged, took a large gulp out of his special glass and set it carefully back on the napkin. "What the hell. I've played stranger games."

"So have I," Jess said. "I remember once with a girl named Donna. She loved to—" David hit him on the shoulder to make him stop as Carl twisted off his stool and moved over to the jukebox to study the songs.

I watched as he bent over the machine to read the list. At six-two, two hundred and fifty pounds, Carl was all muscle, with hands that looked like he was going to crush a glass at any moment. A carpenter in the real world outside the walls of the Garden Lounge, his small business sometimes employed four or five workers. Mostly he built houses, although his big project this year had been Doc Harris's new office. That had taken him seven months and helped him on the financial side. He had never married and no one could get much information about his past out of him. He had no hobbies that I knew of, and winter or summer I had never seen him dressed in anything other than work pants and plaid shirts. He kept his graying black hair cropped short and never wore a hat, no matter how hard it was raining.

After a moment bent over the jukebox, Carl's large shoulders slumped, almost as if someone had put a heavy weight square in the middle of his back. With effort he stood, turned around and faced the bar. His face was pale, his dark eyes a little glazed. "Found one. Now what?"

I took a deep breath. It was too late to back out now. These were my friends.

"Put the quarter in and pick the song." My voice was shaking and David looked at me. He knew me better than anyone and he could tell something was bothering me.

I took a deep breath and went on. "Before the song starts tell us the memory the song brings back."

Carl shrugged and dropped the quarter into the slot. The quiet in the Garden seemed to almost ring as he slowly punched the buttons for his song. "Anything else?" he asked as the jukebox clicked and the mechanism moved to find the record.

"Just state what the song reminds you of. And remember, you only have the length of the song — usually about two and a half minutes. Okay?"

Carl shrugged. "Why?"

"You'll know why in a moment. But remember that. It might be important. Now tell us the memory."

He glanced at the jukebox and then quietly said, "This song reminds me of the night my mother almost died."

I thought my heart had stopped. This wasn't what I had planned. Why did he have to pick a memory like that? This was Christmas Eve. Most people would have memories of good times. Times they wanted to relive. Damn, it was too late now. "Two and a half minutes, Carl," I managed to choke out. "Remember that."

He glanced over at me with a frown as "I'm Dreaming of a White Christmas" started. Then he was gone, back into his memory.

Chapter Two

THE URINE and disinfectant smells of the nursing home washed over Carl like a wave over a child on the beach. He grabbed the door frame and held on, feeling dizzy, confused. A moment before he had been standing in front of the jukebox at the Garden Lounge, playing a stupid game that Radley Stout, the owner of the bar, had insisted on playing. Carl had that memory firmly placed in his mind, as well as the memories of the last twenty years.

Yet he also had fresh memories of driving to the nursing home this Christmas Eve. Memories of wishing he could go back to college, wishing he could do something to put Mother out of her pain and suffering. And a very clear, very fresh memory of his decision to help her die with some dignity as she had asked.

It had been a Sunday afternoon, right after the second stroke. She had not only asked, she had begged him to help her if another stroke took her mind and left her body alive. That had been her worst fear. Yet he hadn't done anything. The part of his mind that remembered the Garden Lounge knew that she had suffered three more strokes. He had been too afraid.

He squeezed the doorframe until his hand hurt. Christmas music played softly down the hall. "I'm Dreaming of a White Christmas," the same song he had just punched up on the jukebox at the Garden Lounge. How...? This made no sense.

He forced himself to take a deep breath and look around. There was a white-haired nurse sitting behind the counter at the nurse's station. His mother was in her bed across the small room. Slight, wasted remains of the woman she had once been, she no longer recognized him or anyone else from her life. Most of the time she sat in a wheelchair and just drooled, her head hanging limp.

The doctors had said she would never recover from the series of strokes. She would spend the next five years in that bed and chair. He would grow to hate this room, hate his own fear, hate his own inability to do something to help her.

He glanced over at his own hand against the doorframe. It was his hand all right, only young. No scar where the broken window cut it last year. No deep tan from being outside for so long. He was somehow in his young body, his old memories combined with his young ones. He felt dizzy with the conflicting memories and thoughts. His mouth was dry. He could really use a drink.

From down the hall the song reached its halfway point and Carl felt panic filling his mind. Radley Stout and that damn jukebox of his had given him a second chance. An opportunity to do what he had

always wished he had done. Now he was wasting it by doing what he had done the first time.

Nothing.

He took a deep, almost sobbing breath. This time would be different. He checked the hall and then moved across the room and around to the other side of his mother's bed. She smelled of urine. The nurses would change her diapers many times in the next five years, and many times he would be forced to help.

"This is what you wanted, Mom." He swallowed the bile trying to force its way up into his mouth. "I'm doing what you asked."

He pulled the edge of the pillow up and over her face, pressing it hard against her mouth and nose.

"I love you, Mom," he said, softly. "I've learned to be strong. I hope you would be proud of me."

She struggled, trying to twist her head from side to side. But he held on, wanting to be sick, wanting to let go, wanting to let her breathe, but not wanting her to suffer day after day for five long years.

Finally the tension in her body eased and her head became heavy in his hands. Very heavy.

He gently stroked her soft hair as he held the pillow in place for another fifteen seconds. Then he eased his mother's head back into a more comfortable position.

He stood up straight and took a deep breath, never taking his gaze from the face of his dead mother. A feeling of sadness filled him at the same time as a lightness, as if a great weight had been lifted from his shoulders.

"Thanks, Stout," he said out loud as the last faint chords of the song died and took his future memories with it.

Chapter Three

AS THE LAST FEW NOTES of the Bing Crosby song faded into the carpet and booths of the Garden Lounge, the air shimmered as if a heat wave had passed though the room. None of the plants moved. And I felt no heat. But I knew what it meant.

I glanced around the room. Fred was sitting where Carl had sat, and the planter that Carl had built for me under the east window was gone, replaced with two chairs. Carl wasn't coming back, that much was clear.

During the song I had calmed the other three men down, explained that Carl had gone back into a memory. Then, on the excuse of Carl needing a drink when he returned, I took his glass and moved over to the jukebox. I had stood there with one hand on the cool chrome of the jukebox for the last half of the song.

I glanced down at the glass with Carl's name in my hand. So it had worked. Anything I held as I touched the jukebox stayed in this time line after the switch. Good. And because I was touching the jukebox, I still remembered Carl. Carl had changed something in his past and his new future no longer brought him to the Garden Lounge. I hoped it was a good new future for him.

I studied the jukebox to see if anything had changed. Damned if I knew how it worked. I had just taken it from storage in my old bar and fixed it, put a favorite record in, and the next thing I knew I had found myself facing my old girlfriend, Jenny, in my young body.

Scared me so bad all I did was sit there and stare at her. I had wanted to be with her more than anything else, but I had not had the courage or the desire to ask her to stay with me. On our third year of being together she had gone back to college while I stayed in our hometown to work. That semester she met someone else, and by Christmas she was married to him.

The song I had played on the jukebox had been our song. It had been playing the afternoon I had a chance to stop her leaving. And that was where the jukebox took me and left me for the entire length of the song.

The next day I played the song again and the same thing happened again. I did nothing but sit and stare at her.

I didn't play another song on the jukebox until I had all the possibilities figured out, including what would happen if I changed something, as Carl obviously had done.

"What the hell are you doing over there?" David said, twisting his custom drinking glass in his good hand.

"Yeah," Jess said. "You going to tell us what we're supposed to do with these quarters?" He flipped it, caught it and turned it over on the bar. "Heads."

"Play a song," I said. None of them remembered Carl or my explanation of where he had gone or anything he had done, which included playing the last song. He had never existed for them because they had not been touching the jukebox.

I moved back around the bar, dumped the remainder of Carl's drink out and set the glass carefully on the back bar.

"Who's Carl?" David asked.

"Just another friend I wanted to give a glass to."

"So how come you want us to play a song?" Jess asked.

I took a long drink of my eggnog and let the richness coat my dry throat. I was going to miss Carl. I just hoped he was happy. Maybe sometime over the next few days I would look up his name in the phone book. Maybe he had stayed around town. He would never remember me, but it would be nice to see him again and see how things ended up for him.

"You all right?" David asked. All three men were staring at me.

"Yeah, I'm fine. I was just thinking about how songs are like time machines. When you hear one it takes you back to some special moment when the song was playing."

I pointed at the little boxes and the quarters. "Those are for your memory trips. Fred. Why don't you try it? But you've got to follow my rules."

"More damn rules, huh?" Fred said. "Can I at least get off my bar stool or do I have to toss the quarter at the machine from here?"

I tried to laugh but it came out so poorly that David again looked at me with a questioning look. "Go pick out a Christmas song that reminds you of something in your past. Then after you've selected it, stand beside the machine and tell us the memory."

Fred picked up the quarter from the bar and swung around. "I think I can handle that."

"I'll bet that's not what your ex-wife would say," Jess said.

Everyone laughed, and that started the nightly joking about Fred's ex-wife. She was well known to the group because it seemed at times that was all Fred could talk about. Her name was Alice and she and Fred had gotten married young, had one child, and gotten divorced in an ugly fashion about ten years before.

Fred was tall and thin, with about twenty pounds of extra weight around his stomach. He used to have bright red hair that was now sun-bleached because he worked for the city streets department. He said that almost a quarter of his salary every month went to paying child support, even though his ex-wife very seldom let him see his daughter. He claimed he loved his daughter, and one Saturday had brought her in for all of us to meet. Sandy had bright red hair like her father.

"Got one," Fred said as he dropped the quarter into the slot and quickly punched two buttons.

"So what's the memory?" I asked. My stomach felt weak. Was I going to lose Fred, too? Maybe I shouldn't warn him that he only had the time of the song, that if he wanted to change anything, he would have to do it fast.

"The first time I got laid," he said, smiling. "The night Sandy came to be."

God, what was I doing to my friends? What kind of presents were these?

"Stout," David said. "You all right? You're as pale as a ghost."

I nodded and looked up at Fred. "You only have the time of the song. Remember that. Just over two minutes."

Jess laughed. "More than enough time for Fred to get laid, from what I hear."

Fred had taken a step toward Jess when the Gene Autry song started and Fred vanished from the bar.

Chapter Four

THE SNOW BLEW HARD against Fred's face as he dodged across the rush of pedestrians on the busy sidewalk and in the front door of Abraham's Drug Store. The bell over the door jingled as he entered. The store smelled clean, with a faint background of medicine. The tile floor looked slick from polish.

Old man Abraham was behind the druggist's counter in his white smock. Judy, the clerk, was at the cash register waiting on a heavyset man who was buying cough syrup. In the background the song, "Rudolf the Red-nosed Reindeer" played. That was the same song he had punched up a moment before on the Garden Lounge jukebox. How the hell had Radley Stout done this? What was going on?

Fred glanced down at himself. He was young, dressed in his high school clothes. How could that be? Only a moment before, he had been in the Garden Lounge, drinking, eighteen years in the future. This was some practical joke. He'd get Jess for this. And Stout.

He was about to turn and head back into the storm when the younger memories that were mixed with the older ones reminded him of why he was here. He had come to the drugstore to buy a rubber. A condom.

He was on his way to Alice's house. Her parents were at a Christmas party and would be gone for a long time. He and Alice would start out on the couch watching television and work their way naked to the floor. It would be their first time and because he had chickened out and not bought the rubber on the way to her house, she had gotten pregnant and they had gotten married right out of high school. Sandy had followed three months later.

He grabbed hold of the doorframe, then touched a bottle of hair oil on a nearby shelf. Everything felt real. Damned if he knew what was going on.

He turned back to face old man Abrahams who was now watching him. It was no wonder he had chickened out the first time. He had bought condoms hundreds of times in the last twenty years, but right now he felt afraid. But what the hell could the old man do to him? Fred shook his head. He didn't want to think about that.

He took a deep breath and moved up to the counter.

"Can I help you?" Abrahams said, staring down from his high perch. The guy looked like a cross between God and his dad.

"I'd..." His voice broke and he cleared his throat and tried to lower the pitch to a more normal range. "I'd like to buy a..." He glanced quickly around. Judy was watching him and smiling. He'd had a crush on her for years. It was no wonder his younger self had chickened out.

"Well, young man?"

Fred turned back to face Abrahams. He could feel his face getting hot. If he didn't ask now, Alice would get pregnant and they would end up married. That had turned out to be a fate much worse than asking one simple question. Much, much worse. All those years of shouting and the hate and the ugliness their marriage had been. The only slightly good thing had been Sandy. But who knew how screwed up she was going to be because of the ugly marriage he and Alice had had.

He looked up at Abrahams. "I'd...I'd like to buy a condom." There. He had done it.

Old man Abrahams had the good sense not to laugh. But Fred could tell he was holding back a smile. "Well, son, they come in packages of three or six or twelve."

"Six," he said quickly. No point in having to go through this too often. But a dozen would seem like bragging.

Abrahams nodded and rummaged behind the counter. "Now, which brand would you like?"

At that Judy giggled and Fred could feel his face and neck burning. His younger self wanted to flee the store. He'd never be able to face her.

But his older memories kept him there. "I... I... I don't care. Your best."

Again Abrahams nodded. "That would be Trojans." He slid the box across the counter. "Pay Judy."

Damn him. He was doing this on purpose. He had a register. He could take the money. Again Judy giggled as Fred picked up the box and turned. At that very moment he noticed that the song was almost over and he knew without a doubt that his face was as red as Rudolf's nose.

He pulled a five-dollar bill out of his pocket and tossed it on the counter. "Keep the change," he said to Judy and, without looking at her, he sprinted for the front door and the snow beyond. At least now he had the choice to have Sandy or not. He'd have to give this some serious thought.

As the door slammed shut and the song ended, the memories of the choice, Sandy, the marriage to Alice, and the next twenty years faded and were gone.

Chapter Five

WHEN THE LOUNGE finished shimmering I let go of the jukebox and moved around behind the bar. Carefully I dumped what was left of Fred's drink and placed his glass beside Carl's on the back bar. I hadn't felt this tired in years. I looked at the two glasses. "Good luck, guys," I said softly. "I hope life is better for both of you." But now I only had two friends left in the bar. I could stop this at any time, while there was still someone left to talk to.

"So what are we supposed to do with these quarters?" Jess asked. "I got to get home before that bitch of a wife chews my head off."

I glanced at Jess and then at David. He was looking worried. "You play a song. That's all." I motioned at the jukebox. "But find one that has a strong memory with it." I took a deep breath. I might as well give him a real present. "Maybe even one that was during the time that you met your wife."

Jess laughed. "Why the hell would I want to do that?"

"Trust me," I said. "Just find a song." I dropped down onto the counter behind the bar and concentrated on taking deep breaths and not thinking about Carl and Fred.

"You all right? David asked. I looked up into his worried face. What would I have done over the last few years without David's friendship? What was I going to do without it over the next few years if I let him play a song?

"Just suddenly got tired. Nothing big." I stood and moved to pour myself another eggnog and watch Jess pick over the tunes. Jess was the best joker. He said he needed the practical jokes to keep his sanity with his bitch of a wife. But when asked why he didn't just leave her, he always said marrying her was his mistake and he would live with it. That was what he had been taught. Then he would make a joke and change the subject.

"Found one," Jess said. He held up the quarter. "You want me to play it?"

"Yeah. But after you select the song tell Dave and me what memory it reminds you of."

Jess dropped the quarter into the slot and punched two buttons to start the jukebox. "You remember the song, 'Snoopy Versus the Red Baron?'"

David and I nodded.

"That was playing the moment I asked my wife to marry me. Figures, doesn't it?"

David laughed.

But I didn't. I knew I was going to lose Jess also. "Remember that you only have the length of the song. Not one second longer. All right?"

Jess shrugged and started back toward the bar. "Whatever you..."

The song started and he vanished.

"What the hell?" David said, standing and heading toward the jukebox.

I picked up Jess's mostly empty glass and moved around toward the jukebox, too.

David glanced at the two glasses on the back bar and then at the glass I held. Then he looked over to where Jess had been. "You want to explain exactly what the *hell* is going on here?"

I nodded, too tired to argue. "But come on over and touch the jukebox. It's the only way you're going to remember."

Chapter Six

SNOOPY AND THE RED BARON were just starting to go at it on Jess's '65 Ford car radio as Jess found himself face to face with Mary, his soon-to-be bitch-of-a-wife.

"What the...?"

"Is something wrong, Jess, honey?" Mary said, her hand stroking his arm up and down and up and down. She looked more beautiful than he had ever remembered, and she smelled wonderfully fresh,

as if she had been outside in the country all day. But he knew the look and the smell wouldn't last long. Six months after they were married she would gain fifty pounds and a few years later she would level out a hundred over her marriage weight. But now, in this dream or whatever it was, she looked sexy and very trim in her low-cut blue dress.

Jess pulled back away from her and looked around. This was his car all right. The same one he had sold in '71. The same one that he and Mary had first made love in. He rubbed his hands along the steering wheel to make sure it felt solid. They were parked just down the tree-lined street from Mary's house.

So how had Stout pulled this off? This had to be some kind of dream or hallucination. That was it. Stout had hypnotized him and he was still sitting in the Garden Lounge while they laughed at him. He'd get them for this.

Mary scooted over closer to him and rubbed his leg real nice, getting the reaction in his crotch she wanted. "Were you going to ask me something?" she said, looking up at him with her large brown eyes.

"That I was," he said. It was a clear memory that in this exact situation he had asked her to marry him. He knew that's what his younger self had been planning to do. He was currently a second-year law student, and he remembered his classes that Friday morning real well. Yet he also remembered sitting having a Christmas Eve drink with his friends at the Garden Lounge twenty some years in the future. Strange. Too damn strange.

On the radio the Red Baron shot down Snoopy. Stout had said Jess only had the length of the song. Whatever was going on, it was halfway over. Mary rubbed

Jess's leg and waited. Waited, knowing what the question would be. Waited, knowing that she had led him right to where she wanted him.

Well, this time around she would get a surprise, because dream or no dream, this was going to be fun. Hell, after all the years with her, he deserved a little fun.

"I wanted to ask you," Jess said, then paused, trying not to smile.

The Red Baron and Snoopy drank a Christmas toast.

"Yes," Mary said, her voice low and sexy. She had been one beautiful woman on the outside. That had kept him blind to all the ugliness that was just under the surface. Blind until it was too late.

"I wanted to ask you if it would be all right if I slept around with a few other women? You know, sew a few wild oats before I settle down?"

That did it. The sultry look drained from her face like wet makeup, to be replaced by the bitch look he had grown so familiar with. "What did you say?" she asked, her voice low and mean and controlled. He knew that voice real well, too.

He smiled, easing toward her, trying to act romantic. "I was just thinking that for a few years, maybe five or ten, we could have an open relationship. I'd love to sleep with a few other women. It would be good for us. Honest. You know, free love and all." He moved as if to kiss her and she backed away across the seat.

"Wouldn't you like sleeping with other men? Then after we've both got a little more experience we could live together for a few years. Trying on the old shoes, as the saying goes." Jess knew that would get her. She had said a hundred times how much she hated the thought of living together. For her it was marriage or nothing. Damn it was hard keeping a straight

face. He was going to thank Stout for this one. Best Christmas present he had ever had.

"You're sick!" she screamed. "Sick! Sick! Sick!"

Jess tried to look innocent and sad.

On the radio Snoopy flew off singing about Christmas cheer as Mary rammed against the car door, opened it and ran up the sidewalk.

"Thank you, Radley Stout. I've been dreaming about doing that for years."

The song ended.

And so did the dreams.

Chapter Seven

I MOVED SLOWLY around behind the bar, dumped out the remainder of Jess's drink and set his glass beside the others on the back bar.

"Got quite a collection there," David said as he moved over to take his stool. "So Carl and Fred were friends of mine in another time line?"

I took a long hard drink of my eggnog and then nodded.

"Jess," David said, "was sent back by the jukebox to his memory and he changed something that moved his life in another direction. And with that new direction he didn't end up coming in here. Right? And he would have no memory of ever being in here because he hasn't been."

Again I nodded and finished off the drink.

David picked up the quarter in front of him and glanced over at the jukebox. "You know this is a wish that everyone has had at one time or another? How come you've never done it?"

"Oh, I did. Actually twice when I first discovered what the jukebox could do.

But I didn't change anything. Too afraid, I guess. And, I suppose, not that unhappy with this life." I nodded at the three empty glasses. "That is until tonight."

David took a sip of his drink and looked at his name on the glass. "So you gave the gift of a second chance to your friends for Christmas."

I laughed. "Seemed like a good idea at the time. But I didn't expect to lose everyone. Not exactly sure what I expected, to be honest with you"

"I'm still here."

I glanced over at my best friend. He worked as a vice president of a local bank and enjoyed flying his small plane on the weekend. But back twenty-some years ago he and his new wife, Elaine, had been driving home from a Christmas party. David was scheduled to finish flight school that next spring. He had a dream of flying for the airlines.

That night David had had a little too much to drink and the car missed a slick corner and plowed into an embankment. Elaine was killed and David lost most of the use of his right hand. End of flight school. End of dream.

I reached out and slid the quarter at David. "Your turn."

David shook his head. "No chance. There's no way I'm leaving you after what you've done for Jess and those two other guys." He pointed at the glasses lined up on the back bar.

I laughed a laugh that sounded bitter even to my ears. "I don't know what exactly I've done except change their life in some fashion. I can only hope it is for the better. But you I *do* know the jukebox can help." I reached across the bar and patted his ruined right hand. "Go back to before the crash and save Elaine. And yourself."

David jerked as if he had never thought of the possibility.

"You saw it work," I said. "If nothing else, give it a try. You don't have to change anything. Just go back and see Elaine again. It's not a one-way trip if you don't change anything."

He looked dazed. "If I don't change..."

I nodded and picked up the quarter and placed it in his good left hand. "Go say hello to your wife."

Still looking dazed, he slowly stood and moved toward the jukebox. "Is it really possible?"

"Yes," I said. "Now pick the right song."

He nodded and turned to study the song list. His tie hung loose in front of him, his right hand useless against the glass of the jukebox.

My stomach hurt and I downed a little more eggnog. I knew that once he saw Elaine he would be unable to stop from changing the past. I was going to lose my best friend. But maybe someday I would see him again, striding through an airport in his pilot's uniform. That alone would be worth it.

"Found the song," he said and turned to look at me.

"Then go for it," I said.

He paused, as if he wanted to say something. Then he turned and dropped the quarter into the machine and punched the two buttons.

"State the memory," I said. "Got to follow the rules, you know."

He smiled. "This song reminds me of the night my wife died."

I nodded. "Good luck. And say hello to Elaine for me."

"I will," he said." And I'll be back."

"In case you're not, I'll be holding onto your glass and the jukebox."

He smiled. "Thanks." The song started and he vanished.

Chapter Eight

A LIGHT SNOW kept the old Ford's windshield wipers busy as David and Elaine headed down the gravel country road toward the lights of the city.

"Silent Night" was playing on the portable radio on the seat between them. She was singing along, her voice pure and clear, even though a little drunk. The party, just south of town in the foothills, had been a good one and they had stayed far later than they planned.

David looked over at his wife of six months. She had dark brown hair that flowed long and straight down her back. Her eyes were a dark green and her face lightly wrinkled with laugh lines. While David was in school she worked at a dress shop. Her desire was to someday design clothes, and he knew she would be, would have been, good at it.

"Son of a bitch," he said out loud. "Stout was right."

"Who was right?" Elaine said, then went back to singing and watching the beautiful wooded countryside flash by through the snow.

David glanced once more at her and then back at the road. He couldn't let her die. Stout had known that.

David braked the car to a quick stop on the side of the road. He turned off the car, yanked the keys out of the ignition and got out. Then as hard as he could, he tossed the keys into the woods. In the silence of the night he could hear them catch brush as they landed.

That was his only set. Now there would be no way he could drive again tonight.

"David," Elaine said, getting out of the car and coming around to him. "What are you doing?"

"Saving our lives," he said.

He grabbed her and held her tight, relishing in the feeling of her against him after such a long time. He had never remarried because there had never been anyone again he felt this way about. No one woman who had felt this good.

The faint sounds of "Silent Night" drifted from the portable radio in the car. The song was about half over. He didn't have much time.

"Are you all right?" Elaine asked. "Why did you throw the..."

"I'm fine. Like I said, I was just saving our lives. But now, before that song ends, I need to save a friendship. A very important friendship to me. And I'm going to need your help."

Chapter Nine

I LET MY HAND slip off the jukebox as the last strains of the song faded into the empty Garden Lounge. David's glass was in my hand and I looked down at it, feeling its heavy weight.

David must have stopped the wreck.

"Well, Stout," I said to myself out loud just to hear some noise. "Looks as if you've gone and done it now."

I moved slowly around behind the bar and set David's glass beside the other three, name out. "I'm going to have to find some special place for these." I laughed. "To remind me of another life that never was."

The silence seemed to echo in the room. It was going to be a very long, very quiet Christmas.

I refilled my glass of eggnog and moved around to what had been David's favorite stool. The jukebox seemed to call to me. "Come play me, Mr. Radley Stout. Come and see your old girlfriend again. Ask her to marry you. What would it hurt?"

"No," I said, loud enough to echo between the empty tables and booths. I squarely faced the glasses on the back bar and held up my mug in a toast.

"Merry Christmas, my friends."

Then I added softly, "Wherever you are."

The empty glasses didn't return my toast, so I went ahead and drank alone. I had the sneaking feeling I was going to be doing that for a while.

I had finished the eggnog and was about to start closing down when someone knocked on the front door.

"I'm closed," I yelled. "Merry Christmas." I was in no mood for visitors now.

But the person knocked again.

"All right, all right. Hang on a minute." I went around to the back bar and, being careful to not look at the four glasses lined up there like so many tombstones,

retrieved the keys and headed for the front door.

As I unlocked it and swung it open I heard, "Merry Christmas, Mr. Radley Stout."

David and a woman about his same age stood arm in arm facing the door. He wore an airline overcoat and she had on a nice leather jacket.

"David," I said. "How...?"

He unhooked himself from the woman's arm and extended a perfectly healthy right hand for me to shake.

"Your hand," I said as I shook it. "You didn't...?" Again I stopped. There was no way he could know about the wreck and his lame hand if it hadn't happened. And in this world it hadn't.

"This is my wife, Elaine," he said.

"I don't know what to say," I took her hand. I felt as if I was shaking the hand of a ghost.

"Please come in." I stepped back, the feeling of shock washing over me.

David and Elaine moved into the bar. Both of them walked directly to the jukebox.

"But how could you remember?" I asked moving up beside them.

"He doesn't," Elaine said, laughing with a tense sort of laugh. David only nodded and then turned to face me.

"Christmas Eve, twenty years ago, Elaine said I suddenly called out the name 'Stout,' then stopped the car. I then proceeded to toss the car keys into the trees. For what crazy reason, I have no idea."

I laughed. "I do. Pretty smart thinking if you want to make sure you can't drive that night."

"But why would I want to do that?" David said. "And how would you know anything about it? This entire thing has been driving me nuts for two decades."

I waved my hand. "I'll try to explain in a minute. For now please go on."

Elaine reached into her purse, pulled out a few tattered pieces of paper, and handed them to me. "For the next minute after he tossed the keys into the brush, David madly wrote this while repeating your name and the name of this bar over and over again so that I would remember it. He made me promise that no matter what he claimed he didn't remember, we would come to this bar on this Christmas Eve at this time to meet you. Not one minute before or one minute after."

David looked at me and shrugged. "Dammed if I can remember why. It was as if I was possessed."

"In a way, you were," I said.

"You know what else he said?" Elaine asked. She looked at David and he motioned for her to go ahead. "He said it was his Christmas present to you."

David looked at me. "Did it work?"

I nodded, afraid to say anything. But I could feel the smile trying to break out of the sides of my face. And after a moment all three of us were laughing just because I was smiling so hard. I was going to enjoy these new friends.

I motioned for them to take a seat at the bar. "Boy have I got a story to tell you." I scampered like a kid around behind the bar and grabbed the glass with his name on it.

"And for you, David," I said as I held the glass up for them to see. "A very special Christmas present and a toast to friendship."

Some Classic Jukebox Stories
Available at your favorite booksellers.

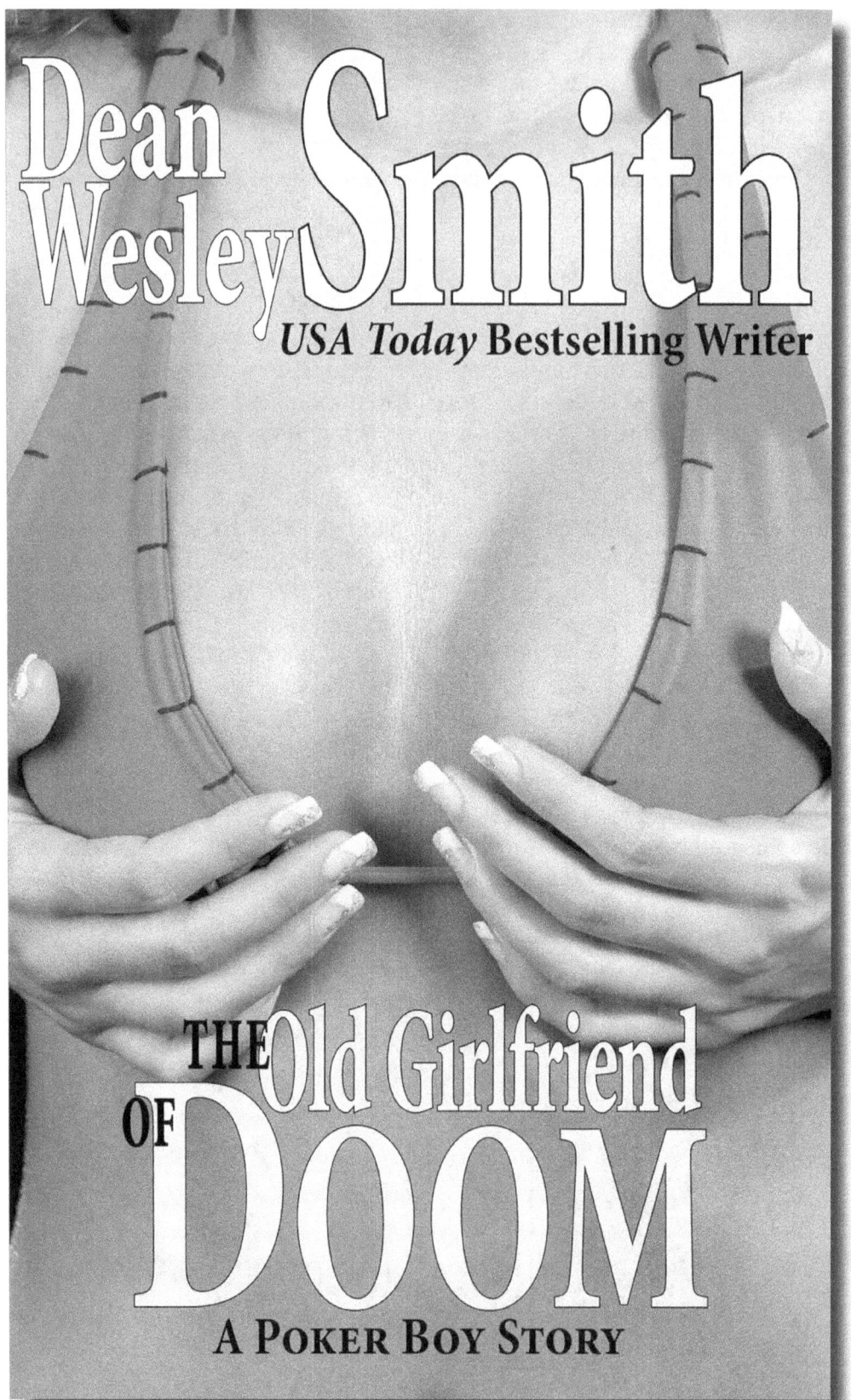

Dean Wesley Smith

USA Today Bestselling Writer

THE Old Girlfriend OF DOOM

A POKER BOY STORY

Even superheroes can't always save the girl.

As one of the greatest superheroes in all of the Gambling Universe, Poker Boy does everything he can to help, but when the damsel in distress refuses to be rescued from her own deadly breasts, what's a superhero to do?

"The Old Girlfriend of Doom" was first published in the anthology Crime Spells *in February 2009 from Daw Books, edited by Loren L. Coleman and Martin H. Greenberg.*

THE OLD GIRLFRIEND OF DOOM
A Poker Boy Story

One

SOMETIMES EVEN SUPERHEROES can't save the day, or the girl, or the dog, and that fact is even sadder when the girl is one of the superhero's old girlfriends.

Honest, Poker Boy, and just about every superhero, once had a childhood, a life as a young adult, without powers. I only discovered my Poker Boy super abilities later in life, after I had lived a fairly regular life until the age of twenty-nine. Little did I know that some day I would put on the black leather jacket and the fedora-like hat and become Poker Boy, savior of blind women, lost husbands, and dogs.

It was Christmas Eve, a holiday for me just about like every other one. I was home, alone, in my double-wide mobile home that I had bought twenty years ago with the money from my winnings in a poker tournament. The green couch and chairs had come with it, and so far I had seen no reason to replace the perfectly good, but dog-ugly furniture. As a national-level poker player, I had more than enough money in a dozen accounts to buy a nice home, and nice furniture, but since I was in poker rooms and hotels more than I was here, what was the point?

Besides I spent most of my time with Patty Ledgerwood, aka Front Desk Girl, in her apartment in Las Vegas. She was working tonight, pulling a double shift, so we had no plans until later in the week.

I was watching some lame Christmas program on television and eating a TV dinner with fried chicken and the really good cherry desert. I had about two hours to get to the casino to sign up for the poker tournament, and I was enjoying the quiet, to be honest.

Then there was knock on my door.

As Poker Boy, I very seldom have the people who need help come to me, but there have been exceptions. And since I wasn't expecting any company, I figured right off this was one of those exceptions.

I opened the front door of my double-wide mobile home and saw my old girlfriend, Julie Down, standing there on the other side of the screen door. Of course, right at that moment I didn't know it was Julie. All I could see was that it was some woman about my age with a nice smile and an over-built chest.

"Hi," Julie said, smiling at me as I stood there, hand on the wooden door, staring at her through the screen.

Now I have a great memory for faces across poker tables. I can tell you the moment a person sits down if I have played with them before, the style of their play, and their poker tells. I won't remember their names, but I know the important stuff and how to take their money.

With old girlfriends, from the life before I became the superhero Poker Boy, I am lucky to even remember going out with them, let alone things like their names, or if we slept together. I assume that any old girlfriend coming to find me years later is someone I must have slept with.

On top of my bad memory, Julie didn't look like the Julie of old. Granted, I'm forty-nine in human years, and Julie and I were an item back twenty-five years before, when she was only twenty. But that said, she just didn't look the same. Not even close.

Julie of old had long blonde hair that had touched the top of her butt. I remember I used to love lying in bed and watching that hair flow over her back as she walked naked around the bedroom. This Julie standing in front of me had tight, short graying hair, curled in a style that made her look older and very business-like.

Julie of old was rail thin, with no real breasts to speak of, and no body fat at all.

This Julie had filled out, as all of us have. She wasn't fat, but she wasn't that light and rail thin either. And she had had a boob job at some point. Or one hell of a growth spurt focused only on her chest. The white blouse she now wore under her open suede jacket made sure that everyone could see the growth spurts and the lace bra trying to hold back the progress.

"Hi," I said in return, at that point not yet knowing who the hell I was talking to. I wished at that moment that I had my black leather jacket and hat on, and was closer to a casino. Then I could use my super powers to help me figure out exactly what this woman wanted to sell me.

Or wanted me to do.

"You don't remember me, do you?" she said.

Okay, I have to admit that those words are the worst words any guy can ever hear from some strange woman standing at his door. I didn't have a clue who she was, yet she remembered me well enough to track me down.

A guy is never allowed to forget a woman.

Ever.

I glanced at her boobs, and since they were new since the last time I saw this woman, they didn't help. And her face rang a sort of bell when I looked right at her, and into her eyes, but not much of a bell. Actually, sort of a faint ding, like an oven timer going off in another room.

If I hadn't been a superhero, who didn't lie unless it was to save a life, or rescue a dog, I would have just laughed and said, "Sure I do, come on in." And then tried to figure out who she was through the conversation.

But she had asked me a direct question, and being a superhero, I couldn't lie. So instead I said, "I can't really see you very well in this light. Come on in."

I honestly couldn't really see her that well in the porch light and through the screen door, so I didn't lie. I just bought a little needed time.

As I swung open the screen door to let her come inside, she let me off the hook.

"It's me, Julie."

For a moment, as she stepped past me, leading into the room with those new growth spurts on her chest, I couldn't remember any Julies in my life either. Especially Julie with a chest the size of the Rockies.

"Julie Down," she said, ending all torture.

"Oh, my god, Julie," I said, "what a great surprise."

Actually I sounded happy mostly because she had let me out of the trap, and not because I was actually glad to see her. The last time we had spoken, she had called me a lazy bum, said I would amount to nothing, and that I should get a life. Or at least a reason for living and breathing.

Actually, at the point she left me, I was a lazy bum, and I really did need a life, but I wouldn't find that life until a number of years later when I became Poker Boy.

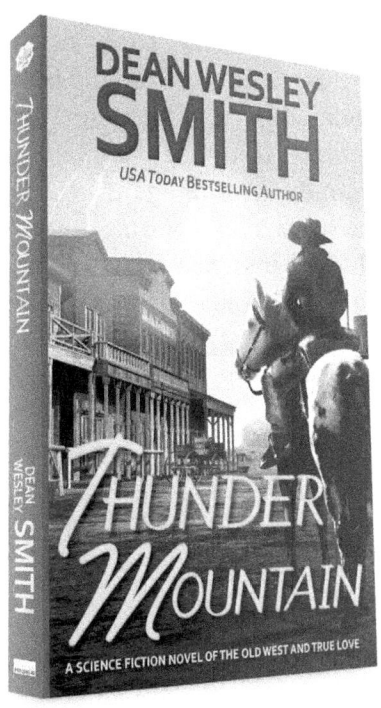

In all, I think we dated seven months, or more accurately, had sex for seven months. I don't remember much else in the relationship with her.

After I gave her the required hug, with her growth spurts holding us apart, she stepped back and studied me, then my abode, like a meat inspector looking over a side of beef.

"You look like you're doing well for yourself," she said.

Even without my super powers I knew that was a lie. I was living in an old mobile home, with old, ugly furniture and a half-eaten TV dinner on the coffee table. I looked like, on the surface, the same guy she had gotten mad at twenty-five years before. If I had not had my Poker Boy identity, and a lot of money in different banks from all my poker winnings, I would have been ashamed that an old girlfriend saw me living like this. But superhero status, and large bank accounts tend to make a guy not care, and I didn't really care what she thought.

"Actually," I said, "I'm doing very well. Can I get you something to drink? Diet Coke and water are the options."

She laughed, a high, soft sound I remembered from our past. Her laugh had been one of the things that had attracted me to her back then. That, and sex.

Now I just wanted to know what she wanted. And the only way I was going to be able to do that with my super powers was get my coat and hat on, and get back into a casino.

My super powers don't work a great distance from a casino. They are powered by the energy of a casino, like a flashlight is powered by a battery. My black leather coat and hat seemed to focus the energy from the casino and make me into Poker Boy.

"Wait," I said, "I have another idea. Let me buy you dinner and a drink at the casino." I pointed to my partially eaten TV dinner. "That just isn't doing it for me."

"That sounds great," she said.

No doubt she was clearly relieved to get out of the old mobile home.

Two

FIFTEEN MINUTES of very, very small talk later, we were seated in the fine dining restaurant at the casino. I had my leather coat and hat on, and was in full Poker Boy power mode.

I knew with a quick scan with my Ultra-Intuition Power that she needed help. Poker Boy's help, actually, which was interesting that she had found me.

My Ultra-Intuition Power is my most used power. With a focused glance, I can tell what a person needs, what they might say next, or even their next action. The information comes to me by "little voice messenger" and I have learned to listen.

I could list all my super powers right now, but that would be a dull monologue, not worth the time since there are so many. Some of the powers I haven't even named.

"Thank you," she said to me after we were settled at a table and the waiter was off getting our drink orders.

"For what?" I asked.

"For being so welcoming, especially on Christmas Eve."

"Poker players are never much for Christmas," I said, shrugging. "The ones with the families miss days and sometimes weeks of play. The rest of us just continue on and mostly don't notice."

"You have no family?" she asked. "And you play poker for a living?" She sounded actually impressed about the second part.

"Right on both counts," I said. "How about you?"

She sighed, and then for the next twenty minutes, through drinks, appetizers, and into the main course, she told me about her family, her parents being sick, her brother being stupid, her last two husbands being abusive.

I wanted to ask her when the growth spurt on her chest had happened, but refrained. Some things you just don't ask a woman, I have learned, and that's one of them.

Suddenly, she stopped talking, afraid to tell me about something. She had been fairly graphic about her past husbands, what they had done to her. Some of it I couldn't believe she would just tell a stranger like me. Granted, we had a past, but after not seeing this woman for over twenty-five years, I was still a stranger.

She studied her salmon, forked it a few times, studied it some more, forked it again, all the time trying to say something. Whatever was now stopping her must be really something. It was, more than likely, the reason she had looked me up.

I used my Ultra-Intuition Power on her again, but could only see blackness.

Deep, deep blackness.

Not good, not good at all.

I needed another super power to help her out, get her to tell me her problem. I focused across the table at her, leaning forward, clicking my mind into a friendly, giving mode. A moment later I felt the super power click on.

Empathy Super Power to the rescue.

I could make her feel better: I could make her trust me. My Empathy Super Power sort of radiated good feelings to another person, so it really wasn't empathy, by the standard dictionary definition, but Empathy Super Power was the only thing I could think to call it. I had tried Feel Better Super Power, but that had seemed silly. And so did Trust Me Super Power. So until I could come up with a better name, it was called my Empathy Super Power.

She looked up at me, her gaze holding mine. "I just feel like I can talk to you, and that you'll understand."

Empathy Super Power working just fine.

"I will," I said, easing my hand across the table between the water glasses and salt shaker to touch her hand.

Touch always made my Empathy Super Power even stronger.

"What's bothering you?" I asked.

She looked embarrassed for a moment, then took a deep breath and blurted out her problem.

"Aliens are trying to steal my breasts."

Three

I KNEW there were no such things as aliens, at least at the moment on the planet. There had been in the past, and I am sure there would be again. They visited all the time. But right now none of them were around that I knew of.

But there were many, many other things that normal people confused with aliens. And there was an entire dark world that existed along with the light world we all lived in. It was against creatures from that dark world that I, and other superheroes, fought so often.

"Aliens?" I asked, keeping my touch on her arm and my super Empathy power turned on. "What do these aliens look like? Have you seen them?"

She nodded. "Gray, short, with long fingers and little round-shaped mouths."

"Big heads?" I asked.

"Yeah," she said, staring into my eyes. "Big for their bodies."

I could feel my stomach twist. She was in even more trouble than I had thought.

"And they want your breasts?"

She nodded.

I sat back, pulling my hand away and shutting off the super power. "You're not dealing with aliens. Those are Silicon Suckers."

"Silicon Suckers?" she asked. "How do you know that?"

"I've had to deal with them a couple of times over the years," I said. "They're not a nice bunch, and you clearly have something they want, or they wouldn't be showing themselves to you."

I knew exactly what they wanted, but I was going to have to work into telling her what it was.

Silicon Suckers are a race of intelligent creatures that have existed on Earth far, far longer than human beings. They live in the deserts, burrow deep under the sand, and have the ability to change their appearance and blend with about anything. In this country, Phoenix, New Mexico, and Las Vegas areas have the most trouble with them.

"Silicon Suckers?" she said. "My breasts are silicon implants." She was clearly starting to understand what the little guys were after.

I almost said, "Really, I hadn't noticed." But I stopped myself before that gaffe and instead just nodded. Then I moved to the next question.

"Where have you been living?"

"Vegas," she said. "I've been working as a blackjack dealer at Circus Circus for the last six years, since I left Bastard Husband #2."

"Good for you," I said, actually impressed. I knew how hard, and how special it was to become a dealer on the strip. "When did you have the implants put in?"

"Twenty years ago," she said. "I did it between Bastard Husband #1 and Bastard Husband #2. But I upgraded them six months ago, and that's when the gray aliens started showing up."

"Oh, oh," I said. "Dr. Doubleday did the upgrade. Right?"

She looked at me as if I had lost my mind, then nodded. "How did you know that?"

Actually, I wasn't reading her mind or using any other super power. I had dealt with Silicon Suckers for a friend of a friend in Vegas five months before, on an adventure that also rescued three dogs. On that trip, I had discovered that Dr. Doubleday had been using a very special silicon mix taken from pure natural sand and then refined down into a very special silicon gel.

The problem was the sand he had been using was from a sacred Silicon Suckers burial site. Julie, my old girlfriend sitting across the table from me, had a real problem. She had dead Silicon Suckers for breasts.

Four

I KNOW because one of the things I do is help people as I travel around the country playing poker," I said.

"I know," she said. "I've heard about you. Some people call you Poker Boy."

Since she clearly looked as if she didn't believe what she had just said, I let it pass and went on. "I helped a previous client of Dr. Doubleday. I assume you tried to go back to him after the Silicon Suckers started showing up and playing with your breasts. And I bet you found him missing."

Now Julie was looking at me as if I was an alien.

I knew for a fact that Dr. Doubleday had given his life for trying to improve his craft and find the most perfect silicon implants. After what he had done to the Silicon Suckers sacred resting place, many of us in the superhero world thought he got off light by only being killed. His body will never be found. More than likely parts of Dr. Doubleday are tinting car windows everywhere.

"How did you know he wasn't there?" she asked.

"Doubleday is dead," I said. "Killed by the Silicon Suckers."

She sat there in silence, first staring at me, then down at her salmon. Finally she said, "Let's assume that I believe what you're saying."

"No weirder than thinking aliens are trying to steal your breasts."

She shrugged. "True. So what do I do?"

I put another bite of steak in my mouth, savored the flavor for a moment. There was only one answer to her question.

"If you're going to want to live, you have to give them your implants back."

"I'm not going to do that!" she said, her hands going to the monsters on her chest as if to protect the big girls.

I kept eating, staying calm. "You have no choice. If you don't have the money, I can pay for an exchange operation for the silicon implants you have now. All they want is those implants. They don't want you to be flat chested."

There was no chance at that point that the rest of her salmon was going to be eaten. She scooted the plate away and stared at me.

"I was *not* flat chested before I had the implants," she said. "You know, you're totally nuts."

I wanted to remind her that she had come to me for help. That she thought aliens were trying to take her boobs, but I didn't. Instead I just gave her the rest of the information, calmly and slowly, keeping my voice level.

"The creatures you are having trouble with are not aliens, but they are after the special silicon Dr. Doubleday used in those implants. If you have the implants removed, I'll be glad to help you give them to the Silicon Suckers in a special exchange ceremony. You give them back what they want and you'll always be an honored guest in their sand castles."

She stared at me like she was seeing me for the first time.

"Sand castles?"

"That's what they call their homes. I've been in a few of them outside of Tucson and Las Vegas. Big, but very dusty and dry."

She stared at me again, then shook her head slowly from side to side.

"I knew better than to come to you," she said. "Even with Suzy's recommendation, I knew better."

She stood and thrust her chest out so far I was afraid she was going to go head-first into my steak. Somehow, she managed to remain standing, although she cast a very dark shadow over the table as her breasts pulled an eclipse on the overhead light.

"These are mine and I paid good money for them," she said, loudly, indicating what did not need to be indicated. "And I'm not letting any little gray alien suckers take them."

The guy at a table against the wall choked, then coughed, clearly trying not to laugh.

"Your choice," I said. "But I'm doing all right with money and I would be glad to pay for replacements. Remember that. No strings attached. You can even make them bigger if you want."

"I'll give it some thought," she said.

"Don't take too long to decide," I said, staring up at her over the monster mountain range between us. "Silicon Suckers are not creatures to be played with. The only way they know how to get into a human body is through the anus, and trust me, taking those silicon implants out that way will not be fun. And more than likely fatal."

She sputtered, started to say something more, sputtered again.

I didn't blame her.

Finally she managed to get those sacred and very dead Silicon Suckers on her chest turned toward the door. Then, with one last withering glance at me, she stormed out.

The guy against the wall was laughing so hard I thought he would go face down in his soup.

For me, it really wasn't a laughing matter. She was in mortal danger.

I wanted to run after her and stop her, but I knew, for a fact, there was nothing I could do at this point. I certainly wasn't going to force her to have an operation. A woman's choice of what to do, or not do, with her body was not something a man, or a superhero, should get involved with. She was going to have to make that choice for herself.

For some reason that I didn't

completely understand, Julie's entire self-image must have been tied up in what the Silicon Suckers wanted back. And replacements might not be enough to matter to her.

I wished I understood Julie's side. I did understand the Sucker's side.

The guy against the wall finally coughed a few times, shook his head, and went back to eating. I stared at my steak for a moment, thinking over anything I might still do to help her. Without butting in on her rights to do with her own body as she saw fit, there wasn't much.

She had come to me for help, then refused it. As those of us in the Superhero business know, there are times you just can't help.

Five

I FINISHED MY STEAK, and just barely made it into the poker room in time for the seven o'clock tournament.

I won the thing and put the money in a jar on my kitchen counter, saved for Julie's operation. But I had a hunch she would never call me, because after the tournament, on the way home from the casino, I found a German shepherd in the ditch beside the road. It had been hit by a car, but was still alive.

I rushed it to the local vet, but the dog died on Christmas morning.

On good adventures, I save people and dogs. I couldn't save the dog, so I had a hunch I hadn't saved the person either in this one.

But that didn't stop me from trying some more.

I tracked down Julie and called her the day after Christmas with the hopes of

Now Available
from all your favorite booksellers
in trade paper and electronic editions.

trying to convince her to change out the breast implants. She heard my voice and hung up.

I called a few friends I knew in Vegas who could be trusted to go talk to her. Both of them said she got rude and angry at them the moment they brought up the subject, or my name.

Julie had made her decision, and by all the gambling gods, she was sticking with it.

Somehow, I had to convince her to change that decision.

I had to keep trying.

That's what superheroes did, usually against all odds and at some cost and danger to their own lives. And trying to convince any woman to change her mind always had danger involved.

So throwing all caution to the wind, I jumped on a plane and headed for Vegas. Besides, I wanted to spend some time with Patty and get her opinion on all this.

Julie wouldn't see me, and had me removed from the Circus Circus when I went up to her blackjack table and sat down. Even my Empathy Super Power couldn't cut through the anger, although it made the guard very nice and apologetic for escorting me to the door.

Since the direct approach hadn't worked, I headed out into the desert, to where I knew the Silicon Suckers had a pretty good-sized village. It was impossible to see unless you knew exactly what you were looking for, and I did. The entrance to this one was hidden right under a billboard beside the highway.

The entrance led to a huge underground cavern cut out of the sand and rock and filled with castle-like buildings. I was welcomed into their castles, as I knew I would be, since I had helped them recover one of Dr. Doubleday's mistakes.

The main leader of this band clicked at me in Silicon Sucker language, and I used what I called my Understand Most Anything Super Power to talk with him, asking him for more time to convince Julie to get their sacred dead off her chest.

He clicked that he would give me two full moons, or something that meant two months.

I thanked him, backed from his castle in a show of respect, and went back to Vegas.

Patty told me what I had feared, that there was nothing I could do unless Julie decided for herself.

I left the message on Julie's answering machine that I had the money for the exchange, had contacted the best doctor in Vegas to do the job, and had prepaid for it. All she had to do was show up. I left the time and date and address of the doctor, the most famous and expensive in Vegas, hoping that might convince her to change her mind.

Nothing. She missed the appointment.

So I pulled some strings in the Casino Gods area of the superhero world, and got the Blackjack God named Danny to talk to her pit boss at work.

That didn't work.

I talked to her friends, even called her mother, then I set up another appointment for her with the great doctor.

Again she missed it.

So one last time, with Danny, the God of Blackjack keeping the pit boss busy at another table, I went in to talk to her.

She was shuffling and didn't see me coming.

When I slid the doctor's business card with a third appointment written on it across the table toward her, she glanced up, the anger in her eyes almost knocking me back a step.

"Why are you insisting in meddling in my life?" she demanded, ignoring the stares from the older couple sitting at the table.

"Because you are in real danger," I said, using every convincing power I could use in my super power collection. With this much energy turned on at a poker table, I could have convinced a world-class player I had a pair of deuces instead of aces.

Julie, on the other hand, was a little tougher. She just glared at me, so I went on.

"I have enough money to help. You won't ever see me again, but please, just do this. It's paid for."

She stared at me as I radiated super levels of good will and empathy and convincing. My superhero powers were on full tilt right at that moment, and for a second I thought she was faltering a little.

"I'm being honest with you," I said. "Your life is in danger. Please just do it, either with this appointment or on your own. It's your life, I know, and your body, but I care about your life."

Then I turned and walked away.

There was nothing else I could do.

I spent the night with Patty trying to sleep, then got back on the plane and went home.

I finally heard three months later that they had found her body face down in the desert, as flat-chested as the day she had come into the world.

I think back and wonder at times what more I might have done to convince her I knew what I was talking about. More than likely nothing. She needed to believe I was still the loser she left for abusive husband hell all those years before.

She needed to believe that those special breasts made her a better person. For her, a certain self-image was more important than life itself.

For me, Poker Boy, I have my hat, my leather coat, and my super powers. What more could I want out of life?

Nothing, except maybe winning every time. But even the best superheroes have to lose once-in-a-while. I learned that lesson on the poker tables, and with Julie.

Still, you have to feel bad for a person like Julie, caught in a self-image nightmare.

And besides, pulling those sacred suckers out of her ass just had to have hurt.

~

USA *Today* Bestselling Writer

DEAN WESLEY SMITH

THE LIFE AND TIMES OF BUFFALO JIMMY

Chapters 37-39

What Came Before...

Nineteen-year-old Boston native Jimmy Gray had been traveling with his parents and older brother, Luke, headed west to find a new home and new riches. Before even reaching Independence, they were attacked and robbed by Jake Benson and his gang. Jimmy's parents were killed, his brother wounded.

In one of the wildest towns in all of American history, Jimmy Gray, a sheltered, educated son of a banker from Boston suddenly finds himself very, very much alone. But then through some luck, he finds other young men about his age and down on their luck who might be able to help him.

Together, the five of them head west after Benson. They end up hunting buffalo as he always dreamed of doing, but then they are hit with a massive flash flood and Jimmy is left alone, his friends more than likely dead. Luckily, they all meet up again and are all safe. So they continue west, knowing that Benson is just ahead of them.

Suddenly they come upon Benson and his men killing a farm family. They manage to get one of the men separated from the others, but in a fall he accidently dies. So they scatter to meet up later at a camp. They managed that but found a survivor of the killings. So one of them had to go back with the kid while the others followed Benson.

They caught him once again terrorizing a small wagon train and managed to scare him and his men off. But then they had to cross the forty-mile desert. And right from the start, things started off deadly. Then, in the middle of the worst part of the desert, they find a wagon train, horses stolen, water gone, only women and children left to die by Benson.

But what can they do? If they try to take them along, everyone will die. They decide they can't leave them and take them, barely making it to the river. Barely. Then, after getting help, they go back into the desert to get the women's wagons and supplies, again risking their lives. They make it and head to Virginia City looking for Benson. They find him, trick him as he comes out of a barbershop, and knock him out.

THE LIFE AND TIMES OF BUFFALO JIMMY

Part Thirty-seven
Trying to Get the Mine Back

BENSON MOANED and tried to push himself to his feet, seeming to realize slowly that his hand was injured and his feet tied.

Jimmy moved over to Benson, who looked up at him from his hands and knees. "Remember me?" Jimmy asked.

Benson blinked a few times, then suddenly he remembered. "The Tyler kid."

Jimmy nodded. "Good, I was hoping you would remember, since you killed my mother and father."

Benson snorted and said, "We're a long way from Missouri, kid." He turned around so that he could work to untie the ropes around his feet.

"Before my mother died from the two bullets you put in her back," Jimmy said, "she told me and my brother it was you. Now I would like my father's gold mine deed back that you stole."

Benson snorted again. "Tough woman, your mother."

Benson kicked the rope loose and tried to push himself to his feet, wincing at the pain in his hand as he braced himself with it.

With all the anger that had built up over the past few months, Jimmy stepped forward and stamped down hard on Benson's gun hand again, smashing it into the ground.

The tough man screamed and fell back into the dirt, clenching his broken hand.

"I'm going to kill you, kid," Benson said through clenched teeth, his eyes closed in pain as he rolled in the dirt.

"Not with that hand you're not," Jimmy said. "So, my father's gold mine deed, please."

"You going to have to kill me before you get that gold mine deed back, kid," Benson said.

"Oh, we're going to do much worse than that," Jimmy said.

Jimmy glanced at C.J. who was standing in the street behind Benson. "Want to help our guest rest for a few more minutes?"

"I would love to," C.J. said, smiling.

When Benson moved to sit back up, C.J. stepped forward and hit Benson from behind on the side of the head with the flat base of the shovel. The clang echoed down the street and the few of the town's people who were watching and listening made laughing noises as Benson flopped out cold in the dirt.

"Remind me that next time we're digging," Truitt said to C. J., "that you're deadly with a shovel."

"Thank you," C.J. said, smiling and pretending to bow like he was performing in a Wild West show.

"Truitt, keep an eye out for this guy's riding companion," Jimmy said.

"Yeah, real good thinking," Truitt said, moving up the street closer to town. He jumped up on a rock so that he could see over the growing crowd.

By now, people were watching from both sides of the street and close enough to hear everything that was said. Jimmy didn't care. At this point, he had nothing to hide.

Zach wrapped the rope around Benson's feet again, and tied it off solid. It would take a knife to get that rope off the next time.

"Remind me to not get you men mad at me," the barber said from his doorway.

Benson's damaged hand was flopped in the dirt. It was clearly broken at the wrist and already starting to swell.

Jimmy, with his mother and father's dead bodies in his mind, stepped forward and smashed Benson's gun hand again with the heel of his boot.

Bone snapped loud enough to echo down the street.

Around them, the crowd made a gasping noise.

"Oh, that's got to hurt," C. J. said.

Jimmy smashed Benson's hand once more, grinding it under the heal of his boot just to make sure the man would never use that hand for anything, let alone firing a gun to kill anyone.

To Jimmy, what he was doing didn't feel good. But it felt right.

Chapter Thirty-eight
A Second Attempt

THE PAIN of the second stamping woke Benson up and he screamed again, clutching his forever-useless hand to his chest and rolling in pain in the street.

Finally, after what seemed like a long time of cursing and shouting, Benson sat up and tried to untie the ropes with his one good hand.

Jimmy kneeled down to face the man who had killed his parents.

"Now, the deed to the gold mine that you stole from my father after you killed him and my mother. Where is it?"

Jimmy made sure his voice was loud enough for anyone in the crowd to hear.

"Never," Benson said through the pain.

"It's all right for you to kill anyone you want," Jimmy said, shaking his head and laughing. "But you can't take a little pain?"

Benson glared at Jimmy.

Jimmy decided to try another way to get the mine. "You know, all those women and children you left in the Forty Mile Desert without water are going to be really happy to see you."

Jimmy made sure his voice was loud. He wanted everyone to know what this man had done.

Benson again just glared at him.

Jimmy went on. "Especially since you gunned down their fathers and husbands and stole all their water and stock. What do you think they're going to tell the sheriff when they see you?"

A couple people in the crowd gasped.

"They're dead," Benson said, trying to spit at Jimmy and missing.

"No," Jimmy said, "actually, they are all alive. My friends and I were behind you, and we saved them. And they are all very willing to tell the sheriff what you did. Now, where is my father's gold mine deed?"

"Never," Benson said. "I said never, kid, and I mean never. You're going to die for what you have done to me."

"Oh, you're going to shoot me in the back like you did my mother?" Jimmy asked, not bothering to hide the anger in his very loud voice.

Benson tried to spit again, but nothing seemed to come out of his mouth.

"Listen," Jimmy said, "you think what we did to you here is bad, in front of all these fine people?"

Benson twisted around, suddenly realizing that a crowd had gathered to listen and watch and no one was helping him.

Jimmy went on. "You'll discover this is nothing. We're going to dog you every step you take, every moment of every day and night and make your life a living nightmare until we get my father's gold mine deed back."

"Just try it, kid. You'll make it easier for me to kill you."

"Just remember I warned you," Jimmy said.

Jimmy stood up as Benson struggled to untie the ropes around his ankles with one hand.

Jimmy nodded to C.J., who smiled and once again hit Benson on the back of the head with the flat of the shovel.

Benson went over sideways in the dirt.

The crowd cheered this time.

"He's going to have one very nasty headache," Zach said, laughing.

Chapter Thirty-nine
Doing the Right Thing

Jimmy quickly searched Benson, not enjoying the feel of touching the man at all, but he had to look for the gold mine deed.

Nothing.

"Search him to see if I missed it," Jimmy said to Zach.

Zach found only a few coins that he pocketed. But no gold mine deed.

"So, we going to turn him into the sheriff?" C.J. asked.

"I think that's what he deserves, don't you?" Jimmy asked. "Then we have to go see if we can catch the women's wagons before they get too far up the Truckee. They will need to stand witness against him for what he did to their husbands and fathers."

"Good answer, kid," a voice said from the crowd as a man stepped forward.

Jimmy turned to see the sheriff of Virginia City walking toward him. He was a tall man, very thin, with rough skin on his face and a scar on his forehead. But the smile on the sheriff's face told Jimmy that he was in no trouble.

"Sir," Jimmy said, "are you willing to hold him until we get the women to come and testify against him?" Jimmy asked.

"We know he's killed at least ten men in Nevada," C.J. said.

Again the crowd gasped.

The sheriff stood over Benson and shook his head in disgust, then turned to Jimmy. "You boys bring witnesses to a crime this man committed and we'll put him on trial. Nevada Circuit Court rides through here in three days."

"Thank you, Sheriff," Jimmy said, smiling.

The sheriff glanced around and motioned for two men to come help him carry Benson. "Better stop at Doc's office to get him to take care of the hand," the sheriff said, smiling. "Looks to me like he caught it between two rocks."

The crowd just laughed.

Jimmy felt very, very relieved.

Jimmy and Zach went back up the street until they found Benson's horse and searched his saddlebags.

They found a few things that would help them, and a little more money tucked down in a hidden pocket.

And in the hidden pocket they found the deed to the mine. Jimmy just stood there, stunned, holding it in his hand.

It didn't bring his parents back, but it meant they had won.

That night, they celebrated around their campfire. Jimmy knew that his brother Luke would be proud of what he had done, the lives they had saved by stopping Benson. It felt very, very good.

Josh made C.J. tell him three times what had happened so that he could write it all down, and then made C.J. promise that the next day he would take Josh into Virginia City to see the area in front of the barbershop, so he could get it right in the story.

Since losing his parents, it was the best night Jimmy had had.

And tomorrow, he would decide what to do next. And it would feel wonderful not chasing Benson.

Now Available
from all your favorite booksellers
in trade paper and electronic editions.

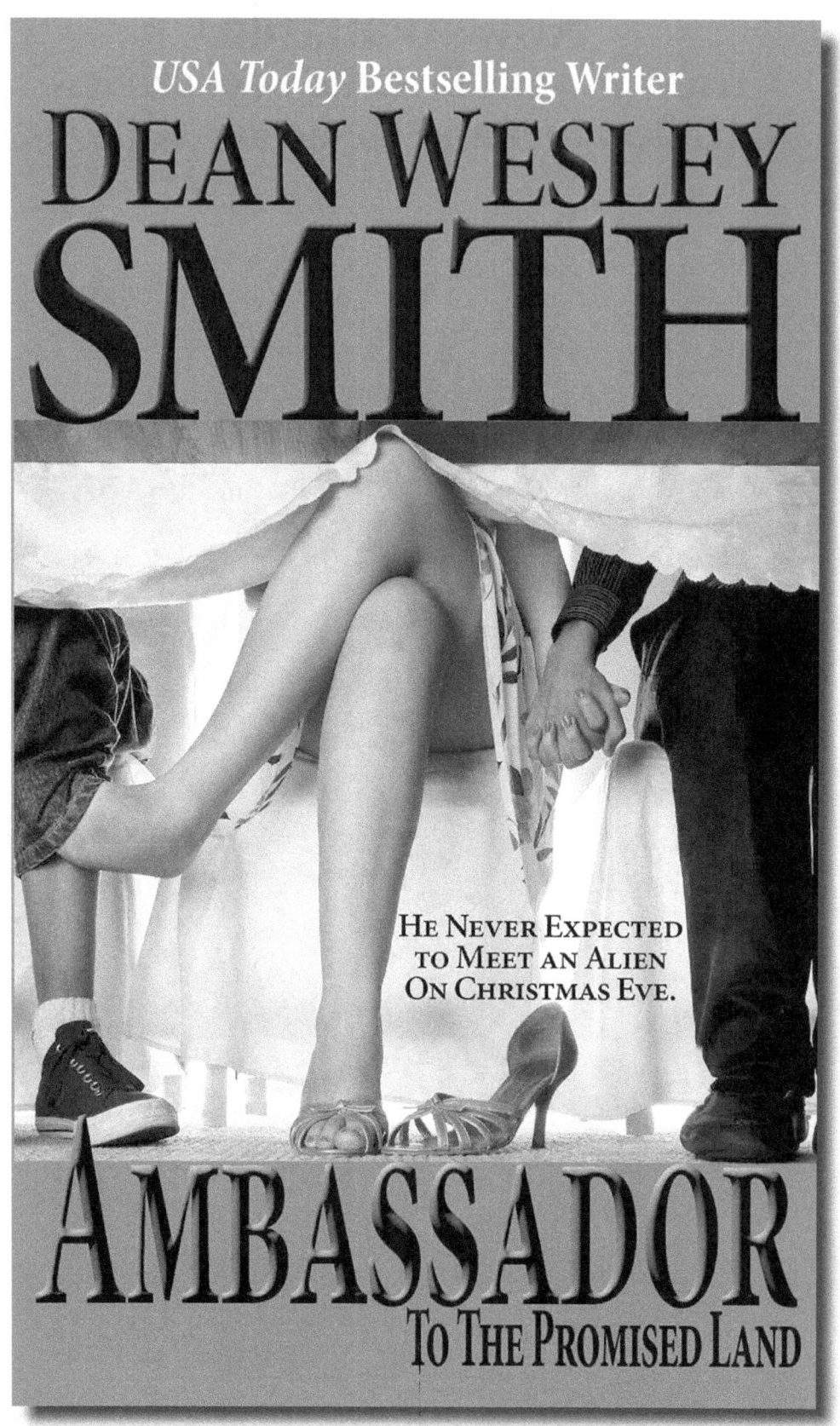

USA *Today* Bestselling Writer

DEAN WESLEY SMITH

He Never Expected
to Meet an Alien
On Christmas Eve.

AMBASSADOR
To The Promised Land

First contact with an alien race brings complications. And troubles.

Especially when the first contact occurs under a dining room table at a Christmas dinner. And especially in front of the promised land.

I wanted to bring this goofy little Christmas story back into the light since it was first published in the anthology First Contact *edited by Larry Segriff and Martin H. Greenberg from DAW Books in 1997. The anthology came out and vanished without a trace. I felt disappointed at that, since I really had a fond feeling for this light Christmas story.*

Now it's back, like that second piece of pie you knew you shouldn't have eaten.

AMBASSADOR TO THE PROMISED LAND

THIS CHRISTMAS EVE I met an alien, or maybe a ghost, and saw the Promised Land. Sort of like a bad Dickens nightmare, only it happened for real, right in the front formal dining room of my neighbors, Dotty and Harvey Jones.

My wife, Amelia, Amy for short, thinks the entire ghost/alien incident can be clearly explained. Now understand that Amy always says that, and more times than not, she's right. Her parents conceived her while on a vacation to the south Pacific, so they named her after Amelia Earhart, thinking that maybe she might be the reincarnation of the famous flyer. This start in life made Amy the most practical, down-to-earth woman I have ever met. She also hated to fly.

On the way back from the emergency room Amy said my alien/ghost incident was a combination of too much eggnog and the knock on the head I got when I looked up Dotty Jones's skirt while reaching for my napkin under the table at the annual Christmas Eve neighborhood dinner.

I didn't argue with her. But just for the record, it was before I hit my head, while I was reaching for my napkin and after looking up Dotty's skirt, that I had the ghost/alien incident.

However, Amy was right about the eggnog. I had drunk even more this year than the year before.

To my defense, I actually hadn't been trying to look up Dotty's skirt, even though her skirt was the shortest red thing I had ever seen, and ex-dancer Dotty most surely was worth looking at.

Granted I had been staring across the table at her all during dinner as her husband Harvey talked and talked and talked about his car dealership. Besides the eggnog, ham and sweet yams, she was the only interesting thing happening.

Pam and Howard McDonnell from two houses down hadn't said two words since dinner started, and Walter and Wendy Clark who had the house on the other side of mine looked as bored as I felt.

During most of dinner Dotty had been smiling back at me when Amy wasn't looking, laughing at any word I managed to get in edgewise in her husband's monologue. But I never once thought about dropping my napkin so I could look up her skirt.

To be honest, the idea just never crossed my mind.

No, I dropped my napkin like anyone might drop one at a Christmas Eve neighborhood dinner. I was reaching for a second helping of ham and the red cloth thing just slipped off my lap. It happens.

It has happened to me before. Even once in a really fancy restaurant I dropped one.

No big deal.

I did the normal thing required in good social settings such as Dotty and Harvey's formal dining room. I scooted my chair back slightly, and went under the festive holiday tablecloth to retrieve the napkin.

There, I came face to face, or make that face to legs, with Dotty's lower half.

She had legs that, from my perspective of head-under-the-tablecloth, clearly belonged in Playboy or Cosmopolitan. Now I'm a normal red-blooded American male, and any normal red-blooded American male would hesitate when faced with a vision as clear and pure as those legs.

And I did.

I hesitated.

And hesitated.

And hesitated.

There was no time passage for me under that table. I had left this plane of existence and gone on, drifting in a timeless place that existed only under that holiday dining table, in that close space between me and those legs.

I had no name, no reason, no pride.

It was like getting drunk back in high school.

Or the time Linda, my first girlfriend, let me slip my hand under her bra.

Or the time in college when I took mushrooms and ended up staring intently for hours at the design on a bathroom wallpaper.

This was like all those times, only more so.

Now, at age forty, I no longer did drugs. I had a great job in city hall, a wife of 14 years, two kids in junior high, and a three-bedroom house in a subdivision. I hadn't had a mind-altering experience in a long, long time.

Too damn long.

So I hesitated.

I forgot who I was, where I was, why I was even living.

I doubt I even took a breath.

I doubt I would have been able to take a breath.

But there was no doubt I had totally forgot about my napkin.

Then two things happened that changed the entire experience.

First, Dotty uncrossed her legs.

Now, from the perspective of my mind-altered state, this took about six wonderful and glorious years of slow motion.

It was a pure cinematic moment.

My camera-like gaze followed the line of her ankle.

The line of her calf.

The shape of her knee.

And then beyond.

Beyond to a place I should never have gone.

A place I had no intention of ever going. But I went because I was faced with the challenge.

And when challenged, any red-blooded American male will step up and face his challenger.

She uncrossed her legs, so I looked.

And I saw the promised land.

The gates of heaven stared me in the face.

I heard the Hallelujah Chorus.

Dotty wasn't wearing underwear.

Now, I swear, Dotty showing me the promised land broke the illusion. I came back to real time, the last bite of ham choking in my throat.

Seeing such a sight, under normal circumstances, would have sent me out from under the tablecloth, back into my chair with a red face and a giant desire to sprint for home.

But normal circumstances were not to be.

> *And when challenged, any red-blooded American male will step up and face his challenger.*

There was this second thing that happened.

At that moment an alien, or ghost, or whatever he was, decided to make a trip into my reality, or to my planet, right there under the table with me, while I faced the promised land and a new religion, all on Christmas Eve.

The alien/ghost guy stood about sixteen inches high, his bald head barely coming up to Dotty's right knee. He was naked as the day he was born, tinted pure white like any ghost on television, and I could see right through him like a clear plastic shower curtain.

Now again an event such as a short, naked, see-through white guy appearing under a table would have sent me back into my chair, and then maybe right down the street to a local bar to try to drown the memory.

But I couldn't move.

Not a muscle below my shoulders.

I fought and fought for all of ten seconds, but I just couldn't budge or even feel the rest of my body.

My mind screamed "Practical Joke!" as I panicked, fighting to move.

But after another long ten seconds of panic, a little voice in my head said, "Calm down. This is not normal."

Sometimes little voices can be so damn smart.

But I calmed down anyway, and without once looking at the little ghost/alien man, or the promised land, (avoidance is a good thing sometimes) I looked around under the table.

From what I could tell from my position (bent over double, head under the tablecloth) no one around me was moving either. Harvey's constant talking had suddenly stopped. In fact all sound had stopped from everywhere the moment the little guy appeared. I had never heard it this quiet in this neighborhood in the ten years Amy and I had lived next door. I could actually hear my own breathing.

Amy's legs beside me were not moving, still crossed. But that was nothing unusual. She could sit like that for hours and never uncross her legs. I swore she had no blood flow at times.

Harvey's right leg was frozen in mid tap. Wendy's legs were crossed and also frozen in position, her brown pant leg riding up above her sock enough to show me she hadn't shaved her legs in a few weeks, a piece of information I didn't really want to know.

And Dotty's legs were being held in the open position, leaving just about exactly nothing about the promised land to my imagination.

The short, white, naked, see-through guy did a full turn surveying his surroundings as I stared at him. He looked like a normal male, except for being very short, as pure white as a ghost, and transparent. Maybe he was a ghost. Maybe he was a

ghost Dotty and Harvey had been hiding. Knowing them, anything was possible.

Or maybe he was an angel who made a break from heaven when Dotty opened her legs and showed me the pearly gates. But if that was the case, why wasn't he making fast time away from her? I sure wanted to at that moment.

Maybe this was a bad movie and he was my conscious? Maybe he was here to punish me for looking up Dotty's skirt?

There was just no way of telling. Somehow I managed to keep the panic down to a dull roar in my head.

The little guy stopped looking around, then said something in a high, Mickey Mouse-like voice in a language that I might have guessed to be Latin, if Latin wasn't a dead language.

With that he got a little less glowing white, and a little more solid, as if he'd been fine-tuned a little. I could see through him still, but not as clearly.

He again said something in the strange language into the air, then made a nodding motion to himself. Then he turned to face me.

Surprise.

I managed not to panic completely again, but I swear my stomach had left my body. Up until that moment I wasn't sure he even realized that the head part of me wasn't as frozen in place as the rest of the body parts he could see. Obviously he did.

He looked me right in the eye and asked in a high, squeaky voice, in English. "Human?"

He actually wanted an answer.

Now I had never been asked a question before while in full-blown panic. It was just another first among many this Christmas Eve.

I took a deep breath, then managed to reply. "I think so. But at this moment I wouldn't put money on it." My voice sounded very weird in the complete silence of the world under the table.

He nodded, turned and said some more quick Latin-like mouse-words into the air, then faced me again. "Greetings. We are pleased."

"Hello to you, too," I said, sort of getting miffed. Panic had always turned almost immediately to anger for me, and this time was no exception.

"Now that we have that out of the way," I said, "would you mind telling me what's happening? And who you are? And what you're doing under Harvey and Dotty's formal dining room table?"

That got him confused, which was just damn fine with me. If I was confused, he was going to be confused right along with me.

He turned back to look into the air, said a few more quick words in his strange Latin, then faced me again. "Too fast," he said slowly. "Computers cannot translate."

Wonderful. The little white guy had computers. I should have expected as much. This had to be a prank by some computer nerd somewhere. Maybe the Wilson kid from down the block. He was always doing this sort of thing. I'd just play along until it ended. I nodded as best I could.

"Un-der-stand," I said.

The little guy listened for a moment to the thin air, then smiled, showing me a mouthful of sharp, pointed teeth. "Good."

"Who are you?" I asked. I'd have pointed at him, but my arms were no longer in use.

After he listened for a moment, he said, "I am friendly. Who are you?"

"I am confused," I said and with that the little white translucent guy smiled real big and nodded happily.

Now that we were formally introduced, I wanted some answers. "Where are you from?" I asked while he was still nodding.

After the customary pause to check the air beside him, he said, "Spattcha. I am from Spattcha."

Okay, that made sense to me. I could tell we were getting someplace now. I wasn't sure exactly where, but if it got me out from under this table, it would be a good place. I glanced at the promised land over the guy's shoulder, then asked, "Where is Spattcha?"

"Cannot see it from here," he said.

"To be honest," I said, "I'm seeing a lot more under this table than I ever expected to see, so you might be surprised."

Somewhere, no doubt, some computer nerd was laughing himself silly. But my little voice didn't believe what I was thinking about this being a joke. My little voice said I should be taking this translucent guy seriously, since he could freeze bodies and make all sound go away. But taking a sixteen inch white, translucent, naked man under a dining room table seriously was damn hard.

The short guy looked puzzled as he listened to thin air, then glanced around at his location. Now granted, his location must have looked damn strange to him. It looked damn strange to me, and I knew what I was looking at. Eight pairs of legs under the tablecloth, plus one head and a naked short guy. Weird by any measurement.

The short guy pointed at Amy's legs. "Human?"

"All but four days a month," I said.

That seemed to confuse the little guy even more, so he turned and pointed at Dotty's legs. Only he actually pointed at the promised land. "Human?"

"No," I said. "Fantasy, mixed with divorce, unemployment, and a drunken death."

Of course as I said all that I was looking at where he was pointing. What red-blooded American male wouldn't?

He listened to the thin air, then shook his head. "Our language computer is having problem."

"I can understand that," I said.

He listened, then frowned.

I was getting nowhere fast. And at that point I wanted to be moving anywhere that wasn't under Dotty's formal dining room table. "I have a simple question?" I said slowly.

After a moment he said, "I will answer question."

"Why is nothing moving around me?"

The short guy waited for a moment, then smiled like a contestant on a game show who could give the right answer to a question. "I am projection through space/time. Other humans still move, only very slowly. Time pass slowly here."

"And I can see and talk to you because...?"

The little guy consulted with the thin air for almost a full three seconds, then said, "you are inside my time/space influence. It was a good happening, to talk to a human. We only planned to look around."

He glanced at the air again, then turned to face me fully. "Little time left. I must do the event."

"Event?" I said, wishing like hell I could stand up straight and run. Or even feel my body enough to know that someday I might again stand up straight.

The little translucent guy nodded. "Event. I proud. I bring humans welcome."

He stepped forward and stared me right in the eye, smiling, his sharp teeth looking damn dangerous, even though I could see through them.

I didn't say anything, because, to be honest, I had no idea what to say. And again the panic had gotten my brain locked down tight.

After a moment he looked confused, looked off into thin air for a consult with his thin air friends, then turned back to face me. "Did you not understand?" he said slowly. "I bring welcome. My people. Your people."

Suddenly I understood. The little guy wanted me to represent my country and all the rest of the world and the entire damn human race, while bent over double, head under a holiday tablecloth, staring up my hostess's skirt.

It would be a challenge, but I was up for it.

"Welcome from all of us humans," I said.

He smiled real big as soon as his computer translated.

"Our people," he said. "We be friends some day."

"You will be returning?" I asked. Suddenly the thought of this little guy popping in and out all the time had me more frightened than I wanted to think about.

"Return," he said. "Need vast power. Right conditions. Your planet must circle your sun two hundred and eleven times first."

I hope I didn't show the relief I felt. "We will be waiting," I said.

The little guy flickered from pale white to bright white like an old television set going bad. "Must go now," he said. "Much information to study before next time."

"Don't stay up too late," I said.

The little guy frowned, then flickered and was gone.

Suddenly Harvey was talking again.

And Dotty was still moving those legs apart.

And I could feel my body again.

Then the worst thing possible happened. Amy, my wife in the real world above the table, tapped me on the back to see if I was all right.

Now I had just seen an alien, or a ghost, or whatever he was. And come face to face with the promised land. My panic was still way too close to the surface and I didn't need Amy tapping me on the back right at that moment.

But she did.

A simple, solid little tap.

But my reaction wasn't so simple. It was as if she had punched the "on" switch and every muscle in my body decided to move at once.

Now, even though I didn't, it must be remembered I was face to face with Dotty's legs at this point, bent over in my chair, tablecloth over my head.

So when Amy tapped me and every muscle in my body suddenly fired, I came up straight, the back of my head smashing into the underside of the formal dining table.

Dishes scattered, ham was tossed into the air, and people yelled.

But it wasn't over yet.

Intense pain made my entire body jerk, sending my chair smashing backwards into a glass corner table that held a big ugly plant.

I went down like a log, flat onto Harvey and Dotty's green shag.

Now granted, right at that moment I suppose I could have said I saw God, too. God would have been a nice addition to the evening I was having. But instead I'm fairly certain that all I saw was a bunch of swirling blue and purple and red lights clouding my vision. I doubt very much if those lights were God. More likely they were just revenge for me looking in on his promised land.

The next thing I remember I came to, still on the floor, but someone had dragged me out beside the table and turned me face up.

The light was beyond bright, and my head felt hollow and empty with someone ringing a loud bell inside it.

Amy was crouched beside me, holding a cloth to the back of my head and looking worried.

Harvey was swearing about how I broke his glass table, and Dotty stood over me, smiling, her long legs showing the way directly up into the dark, where I knew only trouble waited.

Luckily for me the emergency room was slow on Christmas Eve and we got out in just under two hours.

On the way home I tried to tell Amy about the alien without telling her about the promised land part. I even told her about the moment where I had represented the entire human race. After all, shouldn't she be proud of me? I had been the first human to ever talk to an alien. In two hundred and eleven years the world would know the truth when the aliens returned and I would be famous.

But being the down-to-earth Amelia Earhart namesake that I married, Amy just laughed, as if she was seeing right through me like I had seen through the little guy under the table.

After pulling into our driveway and parking, she patted me on the leg and suggested that I not tell anyone about my adventure with my alien friend.

Then she laughed again and told me that a bad headache and hallucinations were what I deserved for drinking too much eggnog and trying to look up Dotty's skirt.

Even though the lump on my head hurt something awful at that moment, I was smart enough to keep my mouth shut. Probably the only smart thing I had done all night.

~

The Third Seeders Universe Novel
now available from all your favorite booksellers in trade paper and electronic.

Dean Wesley Smith

*USA **Today** Bestselling Writer*

But Someone Keeps Eating the Cookies

SANTA'S SNACK

A mystery story about a grown man, an attorney, alone on Christmas Eve, who can't allow himself to believe in Santa Claus.

But someone keeps eating the cookies. Every year.

Just as it happened in his childhood. Maybe Santa Claus really does exist.

Or maybe, just maybe, this skeptic needs to understand where the jolly fat man lives.

SANTA'S SNACK

One

THE FAT OLD BASTARD ate the whole thing. Again.

I was twenty-seven years old, a lawyer in a big downtown firm, and lived alone in my parent's old Victorian house. I didn't believe in Santa Claus.

Yet again this Christmas morning, every crumb of the dozen sugar cookies I had left on one of Mom's best plates, every drop of the milk, was gone.

Just like every Christmas Eve for the last twenty years, the cookies and milk had disappeared at some time during the night.

"Got you this time," I said, staring at the empty plate.

For three years I'd been trying to catch the person eating the cookies, and for three years I had failed. But this Christmas this joke was going to end.

I turned and headed for the hidden cameras I had had installed around the room. Six of them, two on the shelves behind the couch, one on each side of the stone fireplace, one over the entrance, and one over the big bay window near where the Christmas tree sat. Nothing could have moved in the living room last night without me knowing about it.

Back when I was a kid I used to believe Santa actually ate the snack, but then when I learned that Santa didn't exist, I figured Dad did it.

And I had believed that for years.

One year, when I was home from law school for Christmas, before my parents were both killed by that damned drunk driver, I had asked Mom why she kept putting out the cookies and milk.

"Tradition," she had said, smiling at me as she slid the dozen sugar cookies onto the coffee table. It was always sugar cookies, with white frosting and some sprinkles. I loved the things, always had, still did. Every year as a kid I ate those cookies from two days before Christmas and a week after. Those cookies had been as much a part of Christmas for me as the presents and the tree.

My mom's answer of tradition had been enough of an answer for me that year. It sort of made sense in a Christmas fashion. My mom had been big into traditions, and I had to admit, I liked a few of them myself.

The next morning those cookies she had put out for tradition's sake were gone, just like always. I figured Dad must really enjoy his Christmas Eve midnight snack.

Then, on the Christmas Eve after I moved back in after their deaths, I found myself alone and remembering all the wonderful Christmases in the big old house. I really missed my parents, missed my mom's laugh, my dad's snoring from down the hall. And tomorrow I was going to miss waking up to the wonderful smells of my mom cooking a Christmas turkey. I knew this first Christmas was going to be rough, but I didn't expect it to be this hard.

Twice during the evening I put on my coat to leave and find a bar, and twice I stopped before going out the door. I think the problem was that I had made the house look a little too much like they were still here. I had put up a tree, in the same spot they always did, using the same decorations Mom used.

Traditions died hard in my family, of that there was no doubt.

I was sitting, staring at the tree when it suddenly dawned on me I had missed one tradition.

The cookies.

The coffee table looked empty without Mom's offering for Santa. Without the cookies there, it sort of made the room seem even emptier than it felt.

So being in a sentimental and sad mood, and wanting to not break any traditions of my parents so soon after their deaths, and wanting any excuse to get out of the house for even a few minutes, I went out and got some store-bought sugar cookies and some milk. Then on the same plate as she always used, I put out her offering.

It made me laugh at myself for going to such lengths to do such a silly thing, but for a while the room felt right, felt like a Christmas Eve like the old days.

I figured it was going to be sad in the morning when the cookies were still there and I finally got my answer as to who had eaten the cookies every year.

But the cookies and milk were gone the next morning.

I stood there in my bathrobe, the tree lights not even turned on, staring at the empty plate, totally freaked out. My stomach twisted in a combination of fear and excitement. More than likely some friend was pulling a trick on me, trying to cheer me up or something.

It spooked me, yet for an instant I believed in the magic of the moment, in the excitement of the holiday, in the tradition itself. Then the law school training took over and I started looking for how it had happened.

I checked the doors and windows. Nothing was open and nothing had been disturbed. And over the next few days I asked every one of my friends if they had eaten the cookies. They responded with varied looks of worry, followed by laughter.

Just like when I was a kid, the only logical explanation was that Santa ate the cookies and drank the milk, but there was no Santa.

And Dad was dead.

So there was no explanation.

Two

THE NEXT YEAR I put out the cookies and milk again, feeling damned silly again. I figured I had imagined the cookies gone last year, but just in case, this year I planned on sitting in the living room during the night. No one was going to pull some dumb stunt on me this year.

Somewhere along the way, more than likely during the sixth boring Christmas special, like a bad cliché, I fell asleep. When I woke up, the cookies and milk were again gone.

I ran like a mad man around the house checking every window, every door. No one had gotten in. I had even put on the security chains on both my doors.

Yet the damn cookies were gone again.

It couldn't have happened, yet it had.

That kind of puzzle will drive a logical-thinking lawyer nuts. Again I asked

my friends, and again got laughs and head shakes.

I spent the week between Christmas and New Years doing nothing but walking around inside and outside my house, looking for any way anyone might be getting in. I even went up on the roof and checked for an attic entrance. But I knew the big old house, had grown up in it, and there just wasn't a way inside that I didn't know about.

Those damned missing cookies ate at me the entire year.

The next year on Christmas Eve I made sure the glass was completely clean, and I used gloves to fill it and place it on the table with the cookies. And I did my best to again stay awake, without luck.

When the milk and cookies were gone again the next morning, and I got finished running around the house checking every window, every door for the tenth time, I went back to the empty plate and glass. I remember saying, "Got you now."

I carefully took the glass to a friend of mine who had some crime lab experience. Even though it was Christmas morning, as a favor for what must have seemed a very disturbed friend, he dusted the glass for fingerprints and found none.

Someone had drunk the milk without leaving a trace.

So now, finally, this year, I was going to know exactly how this trick was pulled off. This year I had the hidden cameras recording every inch of the living room and the offering of cookies and milk on the coffee table near the old stone fireplace.

And again the cookies and milk were gone in the morning, just like every year.

I played the recording back. The camera was focused clearly on the table and Santa's snack. I fast-forwarded to a point where suddenly the cookies were gone, then rewound to a minute before the moment and played the tape.

Nothing. One minute the cookies were there, the next instant they were gone.

It was exactly the same way on the other recordings from the other cameras. It took me a good half day of walking around my house, afraid to even touch the empty plate on the coffee table, before it dawned on me to check the time counter on the recordings.

No time was missing from any of the recordings. The cookies and milk had just vanished in what seemed like an instant.

That made no sense.

But nothing about the missing cookies made logical sense, and with no hard answers coming, all I could do was wait until the next Christmas and try something else.

But during that year my life changed.

I met Brin, a wonderful brunette woman with deep brown eyes and a swimmer's body. Brin was an attorney as well, working for the city, and had a six-year-old child named Zack from a previous marriage. We dated, going slow at first, then as we slowly fell in love everything changed.

We were married right after Thanksgiving, and by the time Christmas rolled around, she and Zack were living with me in my big old Victorian house. For the first time since my parents had died, it actually felt like a home again.

We did all the Christmas things, cutting down our own tree, putting presents under it, buying stuff for each other and Zack from Santa. And we even made sugar cookies together, although I swear more icing got on us than on the cookies.

Then, without me realizing it, it was Christmas Eve.

I had never told Brin about my crazy obsession of the last number of Christmas Eves. It just never came up. And I didn't see much point in telling her now. If the cookies disappeared again, we'd talk about it in the morning.

But for now it was Christmas Eve. The cameras were long gone, the tree was in a slightly different place closer to the window, and I hadn't even had the time to come up with a way to try to catch my cookie thief.

"My mom had a tradition," I said as I came out of the kitchen carrying a plate of the sugar cookies and a glass of milk. Brin was on the couch and Zack was on the floor, staring at the presents under the tree. I had built a small fire in the fireplace and it added a comfortable glow and warmth to the room.

"What's that?" Brin asked.

"We have to leave a snack for Santa."

Brin laughed and kissed me as Zack got excited, begging his mother to let him stay up and see Santa.

"Trust me," I told him, "Santa doesn't want to be seen. I know, I've tried."

"So did I," Brin said, kissing me on the cheek. "Three straight years."

"Then why can't I try?" Zack asked.

"Maybe next year," Brin said, laughing.

Three

After Zack had gone off to bed, Brin and I spent a few hours watching television, getting the last of the presents under the tree, and then we went off to bed.

Around four in the morning I awoke. For some reason I thought I had heard a noise down in the living room, so I went to investigate. The room was dark except for a few embers left from the fire, so I turned on the tree lights and looked around.

Nothing. And the cookies were still there, along with the milk. For some reason, that surprised me.

The lights of the tree were beautiful, the reds and oranges and greens casting wonderful shadows around the room. I dropped down on the couch and put my feet up beside the cookies, just letting myself stare at the tree and feel the wonderful calm and happiness that went along with the evening.

There was life in the big old house again. I just hoped my parents were watching from somewhere and smiling at the moment.

"Waiting for Santa?" Brin asked as she came into the room and joined me on the couch, her white bathrobe tucked under her for extra warmth.

"Just enjoying the moment," I said. "It's great having you and Zack here."

"It's great being here," she said, snuggling against me. "It feels like we're a family."

"We are," I said as she snuggled against me.

We sat there for the longest time, staring at the wonderful lights, enjoying the moment.

I wondered how many times my parents must have done the same thing. Maybe this was part of the tradition my mom had talked about.

Maybe it was the power of that tradition that had carried through the years, maybe bringing them back over the last

few Christmas Eves to eat the cookies I left out for them.

But now the cookies and the milk and playing Santa was our tradition, mine and Brin's.

I leaned forward and picked up the plate, offering a cookie to Brin. "Have a cookie, Santa?"

She laughed and took one.

"You know," she said, "I always knew my mom and dad were Santa. I just never expected to some day become one myself."

I took a cookie and put the plate back. "I know what you mean."

Over the next hour we talked, we laughed, we sat quietly staring at the lights of the tree. By the time we started out of the room to go back to bed, the cookie plate was almost empty, with only one cookie remaining.

Then, just before I reached to turn off the lights, I noticed the one last cookie was now gone.

"Ate Santa's last cookie, huh?" I asked Brin.

Brin turned, waiting for me in the doorway to the hall. "Not me. Five was my limit. See you in bed." She headed down the hallway.

I turned and stared at the empty plate again, just as I had done for the past four years.

Then suddenly Mom and Dad were standing beside the tree, smiling at me as if I were Zack's age, opening presents.

I wanted to call for Brin to turn around, see if she saw them too, but I didn't. This was just between me and my parents.

Mom smiled, Dad smiled, and then he held up the last cookie as if to say thanks.

I nodded a welcome and smiled as well.

Then as he bit into the cookie, they faded and were gone.

I stood there staring at the space where they had been, feeling content for the first time since they had died. I missed them, sure, but for some reason, for the first time I was at peace with losing them.

I flipped off the tree lights and headed for bed, just as I am sure Dad had done for years and years, his stomach full from the cookies and milk.

The next morning Zack stood staring wide-eyed at the empty cookie plate. I knew exactly what he was thinking, because at his age I had thought the same thing.

Santa hadn't forgotten him.

I had to wonder why, during the previous four years, I hadn't thought that same thing. Why hadn't I just accepted the fact that the cookies being gone proved I hadn't been forgotten. Alone, the idea hadn't seemed logical, but now, with a wonderful family around me on Christmas morning, it seemed perfectly right.

Santa always got a snack.

He hadn't forgotten to come to this house. It was a tradition.

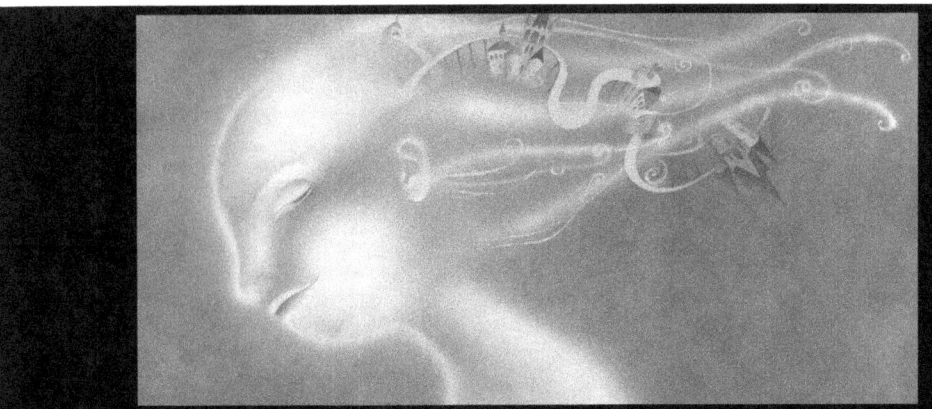

Poems by DEAN WESLEY SMITH

Existence

The guy that sat
in the third chair
of the fifth row
of my tenth grade
high school
math class
died
last night.

I can't remember what he looked like.

Dean Wesley **Smith**
USA Today Bestselling Writer

When Murder
Matters More
Than The Cookie

SPRINKLE ON A MEMORY

When murder matters more than the cookie.

Red sugar sparkles on white cookie icing. Blood drops on a snowdrift. Who would have thought that decorating Christmas cookies would remind him of a murder he may or may not have done.

Reality, dream, or memory: Only murder matters.

First published in Ellery Queen's Mystery Magazine *in 2005, I really wanted to give this story life yet again.*

SPRINKLE ON A MEMORY

One

Red sugar sparkles on white cookie icing.

Blood drops on a snowdrift.

Who would have thought that decorating Christmas cookies with my kid would remind me of a murder. A murder I had no real memory of doing, yet I had no doubt I had done.

I could bring back a few details. The feel of the cold of the night air, the white of the snow under the light from my car's headlights, and the smell of hot blood from the woman's throat. I have a memory of her blood spraying, just like all my victim's blood did. Her blood had left red dots all over the snow bank. Why hadn't I remembered her, or that night, or the blood on the snow before now?

Had I killed too many? Or maybe she was one I had yet to kill.

"You all right, Dad?" my daughter, Jennifer, asked.

My mind snapped out of the vision, or the memory, and came back to the kitchen table. The bright-lit room smelled of baking cookies and felt too warm by a few degrees.

I was sitting at our tablecloth-covered oak table, across from my daughter, Jennifer. My wife, Lisa, was taking another batch out of the oven. Decorating cookies had been a tradition in our family since before Jennifer was born. I always enjoyed it. It made it feel like the Christmas season.

I had my hand poised over a cookie, the few bits of red sprinkles still in my hand, the rest on the white icing.

Like blood drops on snow.

"Changed my mind," I said, smiling at Jennifer. "I think this one needs green."

"You're strange, Dad," Jennifer said, laughing and shaking her head before going back to work on getting the exact right color on an angel cookie.

My wife Lisa laughed also, but it was a fond laugh. For some reason she loved me and all my quirks. Why such a beautiful, brown-haired, brown-eyed smart woman would love me, I had no idea. But I was very glad she did.

Neither she nor Jennifer had any idea about my little hobby, as I thought of my killing. Everyone in the city, I was sure, had heard of me. I was what the newspapers and police called "The Foothills Killer." I got the nickname because I always dumped my victims up in the foothills above the city of Boise.

I picked up the bottle of green sugar sparkles and started to put them on the half-decorated cookie. But again the red

specks on the white frosting distracted me, brought back a memory I clearly had been holding back for a long time.

Blood splatters on the snow.

I remembered the woman now. It was my first kill, my first wife, actually, long before Lisa.

Her name was Stephanie, and we had met in college. She had been tall, blonde, with green eyes. Everything about her shouted sex, and I remember liking that the most about her.

For some reason Stephanie and I had been arguing the night I killed her. The police had never found her body, and never would. I had buried her up in the Boise National Forest, deep, very deep, and then killed our dog Harvey and buried him two feet above her, so anyone digging would find the dog bones and stop.

Since she had no parents or close family, I told friends she had taken Harvey and left me for New York City. She had always talked about going to New York to try to break into acting in the theater, and every friend we had knew that we fought all the time. So her leaving me was no surprise to anyone.

I acted upset, angry, then upset again.

Everyone bought my little hurt-husband play-acting.

And after some time had passed, I got a divorce and people stopped asking about her.

That was over twenty years and thirty-five other kills ago. And not once during that time had anyone even questioned me about any of the deaths. I was that good, and that careful. The Foothills Killer had the police stumped.

Now I was happily married, had a wonderful daughter, and taught school in a local high school. I even was an assistant coach on the football team. I only killed once or twice a year, always in my private storage building near the river that I had bought to store sports equipment.

Only Stephanie had been killed out in the open, where I couldn't control every detail. In the storage building, I controlled the details, controlled the mess, even had a shower to wash up in, along with a washer and dryer to clean my clothes. With gloves and hot water I washed down every woman I killed, then stood them up to dry. I always left them nude, never left any trace of myself on them, and dumped them by keeping my van on the pavement of a well-traveled road in the foothills.

I also changed vans every year.

So why now, sitting in my kitchen, did seeing red specks on a cookie take me back to the memory of that first murder? I hadn't thought of Stephanie for a decade.

Suddenly around the cookie I could feel the wonderful kitchen, the image of Lisa, slipping away. I tried to hold onto it, but I couldn't.

Two

THE FRESH SMELL of baking cookies was still around me, but now instead of a covered oak dining table, I was sitting at a Formica kitchen table. The room around me was smaller, clearly less expensive.

"Jason!" my wife demanded, glaring at me from across the room. "Are you all right?"

I glanced up into Stephanie's face, the face of the woman I had thought about killing for twenty-five years.

"Fine," I said. "Just day-dreaming."

Stephanie snorted and shook her head, clearly disgusted. "Wow, that's a surprise."

She always complained that I never seemed to be there, never talked to her, never wanted to touch her anymore. The truth was that she was right. I was always off daydreaming, imaging a life where I had killed her.

I glanced around, wondering what had happened to me? How I had become this weak person?

I had the memories of Lisa and Jennifer, yet I knew that in reality Stephanie and I had gotten married right out of college, had two children, one named Craig and one named Leslie. Both kids were now off at college and would be coming home in the next day or so.

Stephanie had wanted us to decorate cookies like we always did, so the kids would have some.

"Make it feel like Christmas," she had said.

I had agreed because it was just easier to agree with Stephanie than fight her. I had learned that long ago.

The cookie in front of me had white frosting with red sparkles, just like I imagined the snow would have after I cut Stephanie's neck. For twenty years I had imagined killing Stephanie, imagined doing my dream job of teaching high school.

I also imagined killing dozens of other women I had met in my corporate job, women like Stephanie who deserved to be killed and hung naked to dry.

But instead of acting, I simply did nothing.

That was the story of my life it seemed. I only dreamed of acting while doing nothing. And by doing nothing, I got nowhere. I agreed with my wife, worked my boring job, and came home to the same old bitching. Somehow I had lost the person I might have become.

All I had left was my daydreams.

I stared at the white icing on the cookie, letting the red specks become something besides sugar as I imagined killing Stephanie, slicing her throat, letting her blood spurt out over the snow.

Three

"JASON," LISA SAID, putting her hand on my shoulder as I stared at the cookie. "Can I get you something?"

"Yeah, Dad, take a break," Jennifer said. "You're acting even stranger than normal."

The memory of cutting Stephanie's neck, of killing all those other women was there again.

"I'm fine," I said. I glanced up at my beautiful Lisa. "Honest. I was just thinking how lucky I am to be here with you two."

"Oh, weird," Jennifer said.

Lisa laughed and kissed me. "I'm glad you're here too." She gave me a wonderful hug and went to get another batch out of the oven.

I looked around the kitchen, at my perfect family, at the wonderful, rich-textured room filled with the smell of fresh-baked sugar cookies. I had made a life for myself with Lisa. Not Stephanie. And it was in this life where I wanted to live.

I stared at the cookie with the red sprinkles, remembering how wonderful it had felt to cut Stephanie's neck and watch the blood spray.

Then I took another cookie, put white frosting on it, and again put the red sprinkles on it, just to remind myself how lucky I had it.

~

Now Available
from all your favorite booksellers
in trade paper and electronic editions.

DEAN WESLEY
SMITH

USA Today BESTSELLING AUTHOR

MORNING
SONG

A SEEDERS UNIVERSE NOVEL

DEAN WESLEY SMITH

HEAVEN PAINTED
as a Christmas Gift

A GHOST OF A CHANCE NOVEL

Poker Boy and his team have saved the world countless times. The Ghost of a Chance agency follows a similar charge. Superheroes and ghosts, all working for the greater good.

But as the holidays approach, both groups face a challenge with higher stakes than either can tackle alone.

The Ghost Agents, including newly dead recruits Belle and Nancy, team up with Poker Boy and his team to stop a deadly threat—and save Christmas.

HEAVEN PAINTED AS A CHRISTMAS GIFT
A Ghost of a Chance Novel

For Kris
Even more popcorn for the brain.

Section One
TRAINING NEW TEAM MEMBERS

One

NO ONE EXPECTS TO DIE. Belle Watson sure didn't. Not on a beautiful November day in downtown Boise, Idaho.

Of course dying wouldn't have been any better on a crappy, rainy day, but this Wednesday afternoon was far, far from crappy. Clear blue fall sky, the leaves on the trees lining the sidewalks bright orange and red, and the afternoon temperature a perfect sixty-five, with no wind. Boise in early November, with the threat of winter right around the corner, didn't get much better, and that made dying just flat seem impossible, especially at the young and healthy age of twenty-eight.

No one dies while taking a day off work to just spend time with her best friend and do some clothes shopping. Not a high-risk kind of activity.

Belle felt and looked good, better than she had felt and looked in years. She had dropped the thirty pounds she had gained from the eight-year horrid marriage to Brad Duncan, the high school quarterback who became the fat, sloppy, mean, self-proclaimed king of drunks.

He had seemed proud that he didn't work much and spent all his time in the Varsity Bar down off old Highway 99. He would see how proud he got when he didn't have her money so he could buy a drink.

She had only been in that bar once and had left in two minutes. It was dirty, smelled of piss and stale beer, and every surface she touched felt slimy. Yet her ex-husband had loved the place.

That alone showed how different they were.

The divorce had now been final for six months and Belle hadn't spoken with the slob in exactly six months.

And with luck, she never would again. To her friends and people at work she wouldn't even give him the title of her "ex-husband." To her he was just "the slug."

Now she had a brand new apartment in the beautiful, tree-lined streets of North End of town, with new furniture and a new red Mercedes convertible. She had also splurged on a brand new wardrobe that fit her thin, five-five frame perfectly and looked and was expensive. She didn't

need to worry about money since she didn't need to support the slug anymore and had saved her mother's inheritance.

Besides, her job paid real nice as well. She had managed to finish college and get a masters degree in forensic accounting, marrying the slug as she finished the last of her thesis. Wow, what a mistake that had been. He couldn't even manage finishing two years of college. That should have been her first clue, but in those early years, he still looked like the football jock he had been in high school and could sweet-talk her out of her panties without a problem.

That part of their relationship had ended not long after they got married and she hadn't missed it in the slightest.

Now, on this beautiful afternoon, Belle hoped to improve the already expensive wardrobe some by adding in some fashionable winter clothes.

Belle had her long blonde hair pulled back and felt great walking the wide sidewalk down two blocks from the capital building, her low heals clicking on the pavement. She had been born and raised in Boise and had grown to love the downtown area with all its small shops, older buildings, and tree-lined sidewalks.

Strolling beside Belle was her longtime friend from high school, Nancy Bend. Nancy was also freshly out of a divorce from a worthless idiot who she had supported for years by working at a high-level development job at a start-up computer firm.

Belle and Nancy had gone to college and done their master's work at the same time. Nancy had her degrees in computer technology and could make any computer just get up off the desk and dance. What Nancy did for a job looked like magic to Belle. Nancy said what Belle understood about corporation financing and network systems was flat out magic period.

Nancy had caught the bastard she had been married to sleeping with a waitress from Denny's where he spent most of his days drinking coffee and pretending to look for work.

Nancy hadn't talked to him either in five months, since the moment their divorce had been final. And Nancy had told Belle that sex with her husband had turned sour almost from the start and she didn't miss it either.

Belle and Nancy, after their divorces, had decided they needed to celebrate at least once a month, even though they spent a lot of time with each other normally, by taking a day off in the middle of the week, shopping, having a great dinner, going drinking, and otherwise just letting their hair down, so to speak.

Belle couldn't imagine the world without Nancy beside her. They spent most nights together having dinner and watching movies at one or the other's apartment.

Nancy was three inches taller than Belle, but just as thin. And Nancy also had money from the stock in the start-up firm she had been working at. Nancy had long brown hair that she usually kept up against the back of her head and large, green eyes that Belle loved.

And they made each other laugh. They had needed that laughter a lot over the last few years climbing out of those marriages. Luckily, for both of them, there were no kids involved. For Belle, the idea of having a kid with that slug of a human she had married made her just shudder.

Besides, she and the slug hadn't had sex in years and that had been just fine with her.

Belle and Nancy had been friends for so long, they basically did everything together. They had spent many a night drinking in the old Idanha Hotel luxury bar, laughing and holding each other while they cried and schemed during those years of first separation and then divorces.

And together, they had sworn off all men, which suited Belle just fine.

The November sky was clear, the weather warm, and they were shopping and laughing and enjoying life. Finally, for both of them, life was good again.

Dying was not in either of their plans for the day.

Two

DR. JEWEL KELLY sat across from her best friend, lover, and fellow Ghost of a Chance Agent, Tommy Ralston, eating breakfast in the cozy Golden Nugget Casino and Hotel buffet in downtown Las Vegas.

She had gone with scrambled eggs, a muffin, and some fruit, plus an orange juice. Tommy had skipped the fruit and gone for bacon.

As always, the food tasted wonderful, one of the real benefits of this new life Jewel found herself living. All food tasted better than she could have ever imagined food tasting.

She and Tommy were both dressed in their running clothes. They had just finished a two-mile run from their apartment in the University District to the Golden Nugget. Jewel would have never normally liked going out in public in her running t-shirt, sweat pants, and with her hair pulled back, but since not a person in the room could see them, she was getting used to being comfortable instead of fashionable.

She had been a general practice doctor in Buffalo Jump, Montana, working to pay off student loans when she met Deputy Tommy Ralston. They had been attracted to each other instantly, but on the way to a medical emergency just a short time after they met, they had crashed in his patrol car and both been killed instantly.

At that point, they had been recruited for an organization called "Ghost of a Chance." They basically worked as ghosts in the real world to help keep the future peaceful.

So they were both ghosts and now very much in love. And she had to admit, she was enjoying life a lot more now that she was dead than she had when alive. Sex was better, food tasted wonderful, and nothing except missions seemed that important.

While alive, she had been one of those people who didn't laugh much and thought everything critically important. She figured that medical school had made that worse. Tommy thought it had just been part of her normal personality.

It certainly wasn't now.

As Jewel was about to finish her eggs, K.J. Moore (their "handler" as he liked to call himself) appeared and pulled up a chair. Jewel was surprised, since they hadn't seen him in two weeks since they had solved a small crime with a casino employee taking a guest's money from the guest's room.

She and Tommy didn't ask why they were sent on some missions or why the missions were important. It seemed their main boss, whom they had yet to meet, knew which event would have lasting impact and which event to stop.

So now with K.J. here again, Jewel figured they had another mission.

K.J. was a short man with brown eyes who loved to dress in the wildest, but almost fashionable clothes. He at least thought them fashionable. But this morning he had on a fairly casual gray silk business suit, a bright pink tie, and pink loafers. Except for the first time they had met, that was as tame as K.J. got with his clothes.

"This looks serious," Tommy said, indicating K.J.'s outfit.

"Two new recruits coming on board," K.J. said. "And since I did such a good job with you two, my boss wants me to bring the new recruits to Las Vegas as well for a coming mission."

Both Jewel and Tommy laughed.

"What's so funny?" K.J. asked, pouting and looking hurt.

"You met us hours after we died, told us nothing," Jewel said, shaking her head, "and then told us to learn as we went and get to Las Vegas on our own."

"Worked, didn't it?" K.J. said, again pretending to look hurt and fluttering his big eyelashes at her.

She just laughed. Damn she loved the little guy even though at times he could be downright frustrating.

"So you want us to go with you and help with the two new people?" Tommy asked, picking up a piece of bacon and biting on it as he stared at K.J.

"Oh, would you?" K.J. asked. "That would be so helpful. It would mean a lot to me."

Jewel again just laughed. She and Tommy had only been dead since August, but clearly they knew now almost as much as K.J., who had been an agent for over a hundred years. And Jewel and Tommy were learning more about how to be a ghost every day. Surprisingly, there were lots and lots of tricks to it.

Tommy looked over at her and she shrugged. Then she said, "Better than letting these two new people try to learn this on their own."

"So we're in," Tommy said to K.J., nodding. "When are they dying and where?"

"About now," K.J. said, looking at his pink-banded watch under his gray silk suit sleeve. "In Boise, Idaho."

"It's going to take us half a day to get there," Tommy said. "Unless you want to teach us how to teleport."

"I'll jump all of us," K.J. said.

"Can we at least go home and change clothes?" Jewel asked.

K.J. looked at both of them, then waved his hand. "You two look fine. Typical American heterosexual couple."

The next moment the three of them were standing on a sidewalk in downtown Boise, Idaho.

The air was filled with sirens and ambulances were pulling up from all directions.

And the scene in front of them was far, far from pretty.

Jewel turned to K.J., feeling about as angry as she had in years. "If we knew this was going to happen, why didn't we stop it?"

K.J. just shook his head. "When a person is scheduled to depart the planet, we can't interfere with that unless The Brigade is interfering and we are trying to set things straight. You know that. But we can offer the newly dead a job if they want to stay and help out."

Jewel started to snap at K.J., but Tommy put a hand on her arm to calm her. As a medical doctor, her training had been to save lives, not let people just die.

So instead she turned back to the horrific crash site and the two well-dressed and very attractive women sitting on the sidewalk, shaking.

Three

BELLE WATSON heard the sirens coming from all the way up Capital Boulevard. It sounded like something awful was going on.

She and Nancy had just left a small boutique store tucked off to one side of Main Street and Capital, so they both stopped to look in the direction of the sirens.

To their left a few blocks was the big Idaho Capitol Building, built as an identical miniature of the big Capitol Building in Washington, D.C.

In the other direction to their right, three miles away over the Boise River and beyond the Boise State University campus, the old Union Pacific Depot with its tall spire dominated the hill. The sirens were coming from the direction of the depot and the noise was echoing between the big stone buildings.

"That doesn't sound good," Nancy said.

Belle had to agree. There must be at least six sirens going at once. It was all echoing and getting louder between the large downtown buildings.

"Maybe they are chasing one of our do-nothing husbands," Belle said.

"Oh, wouldn't that be funny?" Nancy said, laughing. "But not likely since neither of them could get their asses out of a chair to even give a chase to police."

"Real good point," Belle said, giving her friend a one-armed hug.

They moved back over against the stone wall of the old boutique building to watch the coming excitement as the sirens got louder and louder.

Belle found this sort of thing exciting. She had always found police and police work interesting, just never been around it much. And she always loved a good spy movie.

Suddenly, on their left, two other police cars screamed into the middle of Capital Boulevard and blocked it.

"Look!" Nancy said, pointing.

Belle saw what she was pointing at. Up the street toward where the sirens were coming from, another policeman ran out into the road and dropped a strip that looked to be full of spikes. Then he sprinted back for the sidewalk.

"They really want to stop whoever they are chasing," Belle shouted over the sirens to Nancy as two more police cars blocked the intersections of both sides of Main Street where it crossed Capital Boulevard. The police had effectively formed a box canyon for the fleeing vehicle and got all traffic off the road.

Nancy reached over and took Belle's hand, squeezing it, clearly as excited as Belle. It wasn't often you got to see the end of a police chase up close and personal like this.

And from the way the police were acting, there was no doubt in Belle's mind that it was going to end right here in front of them.

Suddenly, a large black pick-up truck shot into view with a couple lines of police cars in hot pursuit.

Belle was stunned at how fast it was going.

A man was leaning out the passenger window firing at the police chasing them with what looked like a shotgun.

Nancy squeezed Belle's hand, holding it tighter.

This looked just like something you would see in a movie. Belle couldn't believe it was actually happening in Boise and they were getting to watch it all.

The black truck hit the spike strip going at least a hundred by Belle's best guess. The driver instantly lost control of the truck and swerved hard left.

The man in the passenger window with the gun was tossed out, smashing headfirst into a parked car beside the road.

Belle wanted to turn away, but couldn't as the man bounced off the parked car and then smashed like a rag doll into the side of a red brick building. No chance he was going to survive that.

The driver of the truck managed to get it back under control slightly, but then lost it again because of his speed and flat tires.

Almost instantly Belle realized she and Nancy were in trouble.

The truck swerved left, then right, then came straight for them, faster than Belle thought possible.

She tried to push Nancy to one side, out of the way, but it did no good. The last thing she saw was the wide eyes of a guy in an orange prison jumpsuit.

Then the truck smashed her and Nancy against the stone wall.

Four

AS THE TRUCK cartwheeled down the wall and finally flipped over, Belle found herself sitting against the stone building on the sidewalk.

She was breathing hard and barely able to stop her body from shaking. Wow, that had been close.

Nancy was sitting beside her, eyes squeezed shut, her hands over her mouth.

"We made it," Belle said. "I don't know how, but we did. Are you all right?"

Nancy slowly opened her eyes and then looked at Belle with her large green eyes. She then took a deep shuddering breath and nodded. "I think so."

"Not sure how that truck missed us," Belle said, also forcing herself to take deep breaths. That had been far, far too close.

"It didn't miss those poor souls," Nancy said, indicating two mangled bodies on the sidewalk down from the truck.

Belle looked at them but couldn't focus her eyes on the ugliness, so she turned away and looked at Nancy.

"Are you sure you are all right?" Belle asked her best friend as two ambulance drivers ran past them headed for the bodies down the street.

"Not something I'm going to forget," Nancy said, taking another deep breath. "And I doubt I'm going to sleep real well for a time, but yes, I'm all right."

Nancy looked at Belle. "How about you? I felt you shove me at the last instant to try to get me out of the way."

"I think I'm fine," Belle said, moving her feet and arms.

Everything seemed to be working, but she had no idea how. The image of that man behind the wheel of the truck was etched in her mind. She started to look down the street toward the wrecked truck and the bodies along the sidewalk when three people appeared above them.

Two were wearing jogging clothes and the third, a short man, wore a gray silk suit and a pink tie and pink shoes. To Belle, the man looked like he belonged in San Francisco, not Boise.

The woman knelt down to look Belle and then Nancy directly in the eyes. "I'm Dr. Jewel Kelly. We need to get you up and away from here."

She offered her hand to Belle who decided the woman was more than likely right.

The doctor's grip was firm and helped her get to her feet.

The man in the jogging suit helped Nancy get up as well.

"Can't believe we managed to get out of that," Belle said.

"You didn't," the short man said, his face serious.

Both the doctor and the man in the jogging suit gave him a stern look and the guy in the silk suit shrugged. "I was told that complete honestly is always the best."

"Honesty, yes," the doctor said. "But timing could be better. You gave us time, remember?"

"Oh," the man said, looking down at the sidewalk.

Belle stared at the doctor in front of her. The doctor was tall, even in tennis shoes, and had long brown hair pulled back and tied. There was a lot of worry and compassion in her green, intense eyes.

"What did he mean we didn't?" Nancy asked.

The man in the jogging suit stepped back slightly, pulling the short man with him, and the doctor faced both Belle and Nancy.

"He is right, you did not make it out of the wreck."

Belle could feel the panic start to twist her stomach down into a knot. "Then how are we standing here?"

"We're dead," Nancy said softly.

The doctor just nodded. "Try to see the wreck if you can. Look for the clothes you are wearing."

Belle turned to stare the thirty paces up the street at the mess. A number of people were standing near the two bodies on the street, but not approaching them.

Belle couldn't seem to get the two bodies to focus. Then suddenly they did.

Nancy's body was the closest. She was only recognizable by her gray shoes and long gray dress slacks. The upper part of her body seemed to be mostly missing or twisted around in a way no body should ever be twisted.

Then Belle saw her own body, her own brown slacks and shoes, and she turned away.

Their blood was everywhere and the man in the orange jump suit had come through the front windshield and smashed against the wall as well. He was twisted on the sidewalk beside Nancy's body.

Blood flowed down the sidewalk and into the gutter.

Belle could feel the world starting to spin and she steadied herself against the stone building.

Then as if the light was getting shut off, everything went from dim to black.

Five

JEWEL SHOUTED, "HELP!" as the two women in front of her both fainted at the same time.

Jewel caught the blonde while Tommy caught the brown-haired one before she went to the sidewalk. K.J. just stood there, looking worried and upset.

Jewel turned to K.J, as she managed to hold the slumped woman upright. "Get us to a restaurant, quick."

The next moment the five of them appeared in a back corner of a Sizzler Restaurant. Through the windows it looked like the restaurant was off to one side of a large mall. Very few people were in the restaurant at the moment. A good choice of a place to go.

Tommy slid the one woman into a chair and held her in position by her shoulders while Jewel got the blonde into a chair beside her friend and did the same.

"Two wet napkins, two glasses of water," Jewel ordered K.J.

He nodded and vanished.

Neither woman showed any signs of coming around, so Jewel moved over in front of the blonde and checked her. Then she looked up at Tommy. "Just shock."

"Don't blame them," Tommy said. "If I remember right, I almost passed out as well when I realized the truth."

"The depression and shock will pass in a minute or two," K.J. said, appearing again with two glasses of water and two wet napkins. "It's standard and not fatal."

"We're dead," Tommy said, shaking his head at K.J. "Nothing is fatal. We just didn't need to put them through this."

"Sorry," K.J. said and handed one napkin to Tommy, the other to Jewel. He then set the water on the table in front of the two women and went around to the other side of the table and sat down like the world had ended.

"You all right?" Jewel asked K.J. as she put the wet napkin on the blonde's forehead.

"Never seen anything like that before," he said. "That's why I didn't go to your wreck site. Didn't ever want to see it."

Jewel understood completely. And in the last few months of working with K.J., she had come to understand he was a very delicate soul.

"So why did we arrive so soon after

the wreck?" Tommy asked as the woman he was holding upright started to moan.

"I was told I had to," K.J. said. "Boss's orders."

"Next time just send us," Tommy said. "We'll do it if you teach us how to teleport like that."

K.J. only nodded.

Jewel slowly let go of the woman's shoulders as she came to, also moaning. Jewel picked up the glass of water and helped the woman drink as Tommy did the same for the other one.

Then when it was clear they had both returned and were able to sit upright on their own, Jewel and Tommy moved to their own chairs.

"Just drink a little more water and keep the wet napkin on your neck and it will clear," Jewel said, watching both women as their eyes slowly focused. "Then we'll be glad to answer all your questions."

Both women nodded and did as instructed. Both of their hands were shaking.

After they set down their water glasses, Jewel decided she was going to take the lead for a few minutes to help out.

"My name is Dr. Jewel Kelly," she said, "as I told you on the street. This is my partner, Deputy Tommy Ralston, and this is K.J. Moore. Who are you?"

The blonde looked at her friend, then nodded and turned back to Jewel. "My name is Belle Watson."

"And I'm Nancy Bend," the brown-haired woman said.

"So what happened to us and why are we here?" Belle asked.

"Are we really dead?" Nancy asked.

"I'm afraid so," Jewel said. "But you haven't moved on to whatever follows death as most people do because an agency called Ghost of a Chance would like to recruit you both to help out."

Some Classic Dean Wesley Smith Stories
Available at your favorite booksellers.

"We are all agents," Tommy said. "Jewel and I died in a car accident in Montana a number of months back, so we know exactly what you are going through. K.J. here is our handler and reports up the chain of command and gives us our assignments."

"I don't feel dead," Belle said.

"Actually," Jewel said, smiling. "In a very short time you'll feel better than you ever felt while alive."

"One of the great perks about being dead," K.J. said.

"Are you sure you are up for seeing some proof on all this?" Jewel asked.

Both Belle and Nancy nodded.

"Tap the top of the table lightly," Jewel said, showing them what she meant.

They both did.

"Feels like a normal table, doesn't it, and it is," Jewel said. "But what you tapped is the ghost component of the table that basically exists for everything, including your clothes."

"Remember," Tommy said, "your bodies were still dressed, yet you are dressed in the same thing. You are now dressed in the ghost component of your clothes."

Both women looked at their clothes, then nodded.

Jewel wasn't sure if she should do this or not, but they needed to understand and understand quickly.

Jewel put her hand forward and stuck it through the table. Then she pulled it back out and tapped the table again.

Both women's eyes were wide.

"K.J.," Tommy said, "could you walk directly over to the buffet and back?"

K.J. nodded, stood, and headed for the buffet, walking through tables, a planter, a post and then finally part of the buffet itself before turning around and coming back.

"Now try putting your hand through the table," Jewel said as both women looked panicked.

Finally Belle did and her hand went right through the table.

She jerked back. "I didn't feel a thing."

"And you won't," Jewel said. "We're all ghosts."

"Can anyone see us?" Nancy said, glancing around.

"No," Jewel said, shaking her head. "Only other ghosts recruited can see you and there are very, very few of us. Everyone else passes on when they die."

K.J. came back over from the buffet area and looked at Jewel and Tommy. "I've got to get back. I need to get to my therapist and then spend the night in my hot tub with a good bottle of expensive wine to clear that wreck image out of my mind."

Jewel nodded and both of the women looked sort of puzzled.

"Are there any Brigade members close by?" Tommy asked.

Jewel nodded. A good question. The Brigade were other ghosts recruited to try to cause harm and change the future into a place of turmoil. She and Tommy and K.J. were the good guys, The Brigade the bad guys. It was the easiest way for Jewel to just think of it.

"None any closer than Seattle," K.J. said after a moment.

"Good," Tommy said. "What do you need us to do?"

"Get the new recruits up to speed as best you can and all four of you get to Vegas in a week or so at the latest."

"But…" Jewel stared to say, but K.J. was gone.

"Can we do that disappearing thing?" Belle asked, staring at where K.J. had gone.

"Not yet," Tommy said, clearly frustrated.

Jewel understood his frustration. She looked at the two women. "I'm afraid we're ghosts living in the real world. Which means we have some pretty major advantages and some pretty major disadvantages."

"What happens if we don't want to be part of this ghost agent thing?" Nancy asked.

"From what we understand," Jewel said, "that once you learn about all this, if you want to move on, the powers that be let you. But no one tells us what's on the other side. But this is all voluntary. You both were going to die today no matter what anyone did. It was your time. This agent thing is sort of a second chance to keep living."

"And honestly," Tommy said. "I think you'll both discover that living as a ghost is actually pretty amazing, once you get used to the idea."

"I'm far from that," Belle said and Nancy nodded.

"Don't blame you in the slightest," Jewel said. "And I remember the confusion I felt as if it was only a few months ago."

"It was only a few months ago," Tommy said, laughing.

"Oh, that's why it's so clear," Jewel said.

And for a moment she almost got a smile from the blonde.

Almost.

Six

BELLE SAT STARING at the two people in running clothes sitting across from her and Nancy in what looked to be the Sizzler Restaurant out by the mall off Franklin Boulevard.

She couldn't believe she was dead. Just flat couldn't believe it. Wouldn't believe it.

And Nancy was clearly having the same issue.

There was nothing these two could say to convince her. Seeing her own body must have been some sort of trick or something. Or she and Nancy had been drugged or something. She had just gotten her life completely in order. She couldn't be dead.

Yet she remembered the instant before the big black truck smashed into them.

She remembered the wide eyes of the driver.

That guy's face would haunt her nightmares for a long time, she had no doubt. But this had to be some sort of scam these two were trying to pull.

"Do either of you have family?" Jewel asked.

Belle had to admit, the couple sitting across from them seemed to care, but more than likely that was all part of the scam in some way or another.

"No," Belle said, not giving out any more information than that. Her father had been dead for a long time and her mother just died of cancer four months ago, after the divorce from the slob was final. No brothers or sisters. A couple of nieces, but no one else. But these two strangers didn't need to know that.

"Only a sister in California," Nancy said.

Belle knew that Nancy's parents had both died in a plane crash five years ago. Belle had helped Nancy with the estate and the grief, since Nancy's husband had been worthless for even that.

"Are you both feeling stronger?" Jewel asked.

Belle nodded. She was, and the feeling of complete lack of energy and caring was passing as well.

Jewel looked at Tommy, then back at the two women. "We honestly have no idea what to do next to help you get going with this new life."

"How about we just sit here for a short time," Tommy said, "let them gain strength, and we can tell them about how we ended up dying and then becoming Ghost Agents."

Belle watched as Jewel nodded.

"Honestly," Belle said. "I don't think there is much you can say that I'm going to believe. So how about Nancy and I just head home and you can give us that story later."

Jewel looked at Tommy and he just smiled. Then he said, "Sounds like the best idea to me."

Jewel just shook her head. "We'll stay close when you have questions."

"I think we'll be just fine," Belle said, standing. She was starting to get really angry at all this.

Nancy stood beside Belle and said to the two, "Thank you for your concern."

With that, the two of them turned and headed for the front door to the restaurant. Belle wasn't going to let some scam and a few magic tricks fool her. She wasn't dead.

Far, far from it. She felt great.

And she continued to feel great right up to the big front door to the restaurant. It was a large wood door with a brass handle and a big window filling the center of it.

Belle reached for the handle to push it open. What seemed to be an image of the door pushed open, but the door itself stayed in place and her hand went right through it.

She stopped and yanked her hand back, looking at it.

The image of the door she had opened closed normally, vanishing back into the big real door.

"Oh, no," Nancy said. "This is actually happening."

Jewel and Tommy had followed them.

"A trick we learned is to push open the ghost door and pretend the other door isn't there." Jewel eased by Nancy and Belle and pushed open the image of the door and walked through the other door.

She stood holding the ghost door open.

"Close your eyes if you have to," Tommy said.

At that moment, from behind them, a young kid and his girlfriend walked through Belle and Nancy, pushed the real door open, and went on out.

Belle got a clear image from the kid's mind about trying to convince his date to get high with him that night.

And from the girl that had walked through Belle, she felt disgust at herself for even agreeing to dinner with the guy because he was such a loser.

"What just happened there?" Nancy asked.

"A live person walked through you and you could read their thoughts and emotions," Tommy said. "It is one of the abilities you have as a Ghost Agent."

"There are many more," Jewel said as she held the ghost door open. The real door had swung closed again.

Belle just stood there, staring at the wooden and glass door in front of her, part of her mind saying this was all a nasty joke, part of her starting to believe this was actually happening.

Then she looked up at Jewel. "What do you think we should do?"

Jewel shrugged. "As we said, we don't know. We're brand new at this ourselves. So maybe learning how to move around and get home might be a good idea."

"It's what we did a while after we learned we were dead," Tommy said, nodding.

Again, a live person came up suddenly behind them and walked through both Nancy and Belle, pushing open the door and going out. The guy was overweight and smelled awful, as if he hadn't changed his clothes in weeks and lived on a cow farm.

"Oh, no!" Belle said as the thoughts of the man filled her mind. She could see that he had kidnapped two young girls from the Seattle area two days before and had them locked in soundproof rooms in his basement. He was looking forward to a night of playing with a young redhead before killing her.

"We've got to stop him," Nancy said.

"What?" Tommy asked.

"That man has two young girls in his basement," Nancy said.

Belle watched as both Tommy and Jewel instantly moved, both of them running after the man at full speed, both of them going through the walls of the restaurant.

Belle was stunned as Tommy reached the man first just as he was about to climb into a battered pick-up truck.

Tommy disappeared inside the guy and almost instantly the guy froze.

Jewel waved for Belle and Nancy to join them.

Belle took Nancy's hand and with their eyes closed they stepped through the door and into the warm afternoon air.

The man had dropped to the pavement and was shaking.

As Belle watched, Tommy stuck his head out of the guy's side and said

to Jewel, "Get the police headed here quickly. This guy is a real sicko. And we're going to have to help the police find the girls in his home. He has them well hidden."

Belle just stood there, stunned as Tommy went back inside the guy and vanished. Beside her, Nancy pulled out her cell phone.

"Don't I wish that would work," Jewel said to Nancy. "Come on, I'll show you how to call for real-world help."

Jewel took off at a fast walk toward the restaurant again.

Belle glanced at the scared look in Nancy's eyes and then took her hand and the two of them followed Jewel.

Belle was so glad Nancy was with her.

Seven

JEWEL WENT THROUGH the door and headed for the front ordering area of the Sizzler where a young woman with colored blue-and-red hair stood behind the counter, waiting for a customer near the register.

As Jewel went through the counter toward the young girl, she glanced back at the new recruits. They had both managed to come through the wall of the restaurant, eyes shut, and were now following her.

They were learning, but this clearly wasn't the best way to teach them. But there was no choice at the moment.

Jewel merged into the young girl behind the counter, learning instantly that her name was Francee spelled with two "e"s because it made her special and different. She was taking night classes at

Boise State University and had a boy-friend named Rob who didn't satisfy her in bed, but that she liked to game with.

Jewel quickly got Francee to look out the window and see the man sitting in the middle of the parking lot. Jewel made Francee feel extreme urgency as she grabbed the phone near the kitchen door and dialed 911.

Francee had already thought the guy creepy, so it didn't take much for Jewel, through Francee, to convince the police the guy was going crazy and was dangerous and that they needed to get here quickly.

Then Jewel left Francee's body after the police said they were on the way and faced Belle and Nancy. "That's how we have to call for real help."

"You can control a live person?" Nancy asked.

"We can," Jewel said, heading back out to where Tommy had the pervert sitting on the sidewalk. "That's what Tommy is doing with that guy to keep him from leaving."

"I would never want to spend time in that man's head," Belle said, clearly disgusted.

"None of us do," Jewel said. "But it's part of the job and, luckily, another person's memories flush out of our minds quickly."

Jewel went back through the wall of the restaurant just expecting the two new recruits to follow and not looking back.

She got close to the guy with the dirty clothes and bad farm smell on the parking lot and asked, "You all right, Tommy?"

"Just peachy," Tommy said, sticking his head out of the side of the guy. "Trying to remember what exactly I did to the senator. Figured this guy could use a lot of that as well. He's kidnapped and killed other girls before the two he has captive now. Want to help, Doc?"

"Not really," Jewel said as the two recruits joined her. "But I will, so scoot over."

Tommy's head disappeared back inside the dirty man and Jewel ducked down and joined Tommy inside the pervert.

Belle and Nancy and Tommy had been correct. Jewel saw instantly that this guy was truly evil in all ways. Tommy had him contained completely, but even with that she could see what he had done to other poor girls, where he had buried them, and what he planned on doing to the two in his basement.

"Meet me in this pervert's brain," she said to Tommy and the two of them moved into the man's brain, both shrinking down in size. Then, using her medical knowledge, she once again showed Tommy what to do to make this man scream in agony every time he thought of having sex, or even looked wrong at an underage girl or boy.

In fact, this guy was so disgusting, she helped Tommy make the pain feel worse. Even the slightest thought of sex and this guy would feel his entire penis burning like the worst urinary tract infection in history.

They had done the same thing to a senator who had been abusing young girls on their very first mission. They both figured it was the only way to protect young girls and kids from perverts like this guy and that senator.

"Police are arriving," Belle said from outside the guy.

"Get this guy to confess," Jewel said to Tommy, "and then let's go find the two girls he has trapped. I'll see what I can do to help the recruits understand what's happening."

"Not the kind of training I was expecting them to get," Tommy said.

"But the kind we got," Jewel said, remembering their first few hours as ghosts.

Jewel crawled out of the guy and stood, shaking herself and shuddering, trying to force the pervert's memories back and down and out of her mind. The late fall afternoon air felt wonderful around her and she let herself take a deep breath and look at the beauty of the changing colors of the trees before focusing back on the task at hand.

Two Boise Police were approaching the guy, hands on their guns, asking if the guy was all right.

Jewel had the two new recruits step back and said to them, "Now watch this. Tommy is going to get the guy to confess."

Suddenly the smelly pervert sitting on the sidewalk started shaking and sobbing.

"I don't want to hurt them. I don't want to kill them. I have killed too many already."

"Has he really?" Belle asked.

"I saw it when he went through me," Nancy said. "He has."

One cop immediately used a microphone on his shirt to call for backup and both of them drew their guns, standing their ground. Jewel could tell that they had parked their patrol car so that they were recording all of this.

The pervert was sobbing. "I have two girls in my basement, locked up. I don't want to kill them. I don't want to hurt them. Stop me, please stop me."

"You want to calm down now, mister?" one cop said, "and tell us what you are talking about.

"Read me my rights, I'll tell you everything. I'll tell you who I have killed, where I buried their bodies, everything. Just stop me from killing innocent girls again."

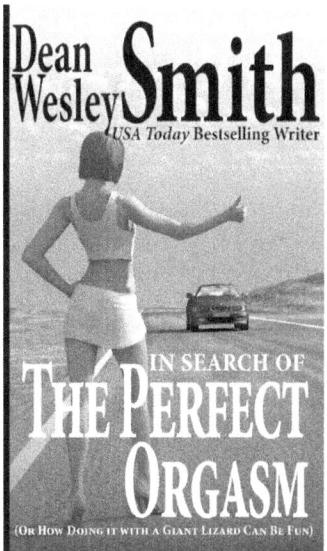

Jewel was impressed as one of the cops looked at the other and then started reading the pervert his rights.

Tommy just kept the pervert sobbing as he was read his rights and another patrol car pulled up.

"Do you understand these rights?"

Tommy had the pervert say, "I understand. Just stop me from killing the two girls in my basement."

"Where is your home?" one cop asked.

Tommy had the pervert give the cop the address. "Just a few blocks from here up Franklin."

Jewel and Belle and Nancy watched as for the next few minutes Tommy had the pervert recite names of who he had killed, where he had killed them, and where their bodies were buried.

Then Tommy made the pervert feel so much pain, he broke down crying and peed his own pants.

That's when Tommy left, climbing out of the pervert and shuddering while taking deep breaths of the afternoon air.

"You all right?" Jewel asked, stepping up to Tommy and taking his hand.

"Going to take a little time to forget that," Tommy said. "But right now we need to get to that guy's house."

"How are we going to do that?" Belle asked.

By now the guy was being handcuffed by two cops and being yanked to his feet. Jewel indicated that the two recruits follow Tommy as he strode to the cop clearly in charge, an older man, and merged with the guy's body.

"Take that pervert to lock-up," the older cop said. He then turned to another cop near him. "Get an emergency warrant for that residence. I'm headed there now."

Jewel turned and indicated that the two recruits follow Tommy. He climbed inside the patrol car and Jewel waited for the two recruits to get near the car. Then she simply shoved first Belle, then Nancy through the side of the car and into the back seat. Jewel then went around and climbed into the front seat while the two were getting untangled.

"Sorry," Jewel said as the two women got straightened out. "That's how we did it the first time as well."

With that, Tommy inside the cop clicked on his siren and headed out of the parking lot of the mall.

Jewel had seen the images of those two poor girls in that man's basement. She just hoped they would get there in time. The girls had very little air. They were supposed to die if the pervert didn't return within a certain time.

And that time was almost up.

Eight

BELLE FELT STUNNED riding in the back of the police car next to Nancy, speeding out Franklin Boulevard, sirens going on full. She wasn't sure if her mind could take much more in one day.

She was starting to become convinced she was a ghost after all, that she and Nancy really had been killed in that horrid accident downtown earlier. She had now walked through walls of restaurants, had a pervert walk through her, and been pushed through the wall of a police car. Yet she and Nancy seemed to be sitting fine on the back seat.

She had no idea how any of that worked.

Or if this was even real.

In the front seat the ghost named Jewel was watching the road ahead as her partner, Tommy, was inside the real cop who was driving.

"You all right?" Belle asked Nancy, turning to face her best friend in the world. Nancy looked stressed and worried, Belle could tell that much.

"In shock I think," Nancy said. "Too much information."

At that moment the cop slid the car onto a driveway and sped up a dirt road between trees.

Belle glanced back as two other police cars followed.

They came to a sliding stop in front of a single story ranch house that had needed paint for a decade or more. Belle couldn't even tell what color it had originally been. What had been a nice lawn at one point had now grown up into dried weeds and brush.

Jewel turned around to Belle and Nancy. "You'll have to climb out on your own. Just like going through a restaurant door, just pretend you are opening the door and climb out."

Then Jewel did just that as the cop in the front seat got out as well.

"Ready?" Belle asked Nancy.

"Don't see a choice unless we want to spend the rest of our lives riding in a cop car."

"Supposedly, we're dead," Belle said. "So I guess that would be the afterlife riding in a police car."

"Still not fun," Nancy said.

Belle watched as Nancy reached for the door handle, then in one motion opened the car ghost door and climbed out, going through the real door as if it were an illusion.

Belle took a deep breath and did the same thing on her side, her eyes closed.

A moment later she found herself standing outside the car.

Jewel and the officer Tommy was inside were headed for the front door over a worn front porch.

"We got the emergency warrant!" another cop shouted from another patrol car, then slammed the door.

The cop Tommy was inside kicked open the front door and went in, gun drawn.

Two other cops and Jewel followed.

Belle and Nancy followed all of them.

The inside was a trash dump and smelled like a backed-up sewer.

"Girls are in the basement," Jewel said as they entered the room.

Then Jewel turned and headed down the stairs. The three cops were clearly already headed down.

Belle glanced at Nancy, then shrugged. "I suppose it would be tough to hurt us," Belle said.

"Physically, yes," Nancy said.

Belle knew she had to see what she and Nancy had started. She had to see it through. So she quickly got out of the way of another young cop headed down the stairs and then followed him.

The basement smelled worse than the sewer smell of the house as she went down the wooden stairs.

Far, far, worse.

Mold and death and rot.

The smell choked her and she covered her nose and tried not to be sick.

The only light besides police flashlights was a single bulb hanging in the middle of the mostly empty room.

"They are hidden back here," the cop that Tommy was riding in said as he started to pull aside a shelf.

Behind the shelf was what looked like a metal wall with a combination dial on the side.

Belle knew that huge walk-in safe had to be more expensive than this entire dump of a house.

Tommy stepped away from the cop, looking panicked. "I don't remember getting the combination from the pervert."

"Damn," Jewel said, shaking her head. "I don't either."

"Damn, damn, damn," Tommy said. Then he turned and shouted to the ceiling. "K.J., need help at once! Emergency!"

Belle watched as K.J. appeared wearing only a light pink bathrobe. He instantly covered his nose.

"Take Jewel and get back to the pervert who lives here. We need a combination from him. Two women's lives are at stake. Hurry."

Then Tommy went back inside the cop who was ordering cutting equipment.

Jewel looked at Belle and Nancy. "Go in there. Comfort the two girls inside. Just touch them, give them calming thoughts. They need to conserve their oxygen. Tell them help is on the way."

Then Jewel and K.J. vanished.

Belle managed to avoid bumping into the four cops crowded down into the basement in front of the door.

She took Nancy's hand and without thinking the two of them went through the steel door, their eyes closed.

Inside, a faint light bulb was glowing, hanging from a cord in one corner. The inside of the safe wasn't much bigger than a small closet. Two young girls were tied up and on a filthy mattress covering the floor.

Both girls clearly had been crying, both were dirty, but both were still alive.

The girls had on jeans, stained dark blouses, and were barefoot. To Belle they looked young, far, far too young to be in this kind of situation.

"Now what do we do?" Nancy asked, moving quickly to the young girl on her right while Belle went to the one on her left.

"Help's coming," Belle said to the girl, but she didn't open her eyes.

Belle lightly touched her and instantly saw what the poor thing had been through since being taken in Seattle. It made Belle's stomach turn, but at least the pervert hadn't gotten around to sexually attacking them yet.

Belle knew the girl's name was Samantha and her only hope was to be home for Christmas. If Belle had anything to do with it, that would happen.

"This one is Samantha," Belle said. "Fourteen, from Seattle."

"This one's name is Connie," Nancy said. "Also from Seattle."

Belle focused on telling Samantha to just be calm, help was on the way, breathe lightly.

Belle could tell that Samantha was having trouble breathing, but by sending calming thoughts her breathing became less panicked, less forced.

Belle stood and went back out through the metal wall of the safe. "Tommy," she said to the cop Tommy was inside, "the two girls in here don't have long. Oxygen is running out."

Then Belle went back inside and sat beside Samantha, touching her, keeping her calm, learning about her love of horses and that she wanted to be a vet when she went to college.

"There has got to be something we can do," Nancy said. "I'm about to lose Connie."

"We get inside them," Belle said. "Like Tommy did with that pervert. Jewel said he was making the pervert feel things differently."

Nancy nodded. "Let's see if we can slow their breathing and their hearts and buy them some more time."

"Even a minute might be the difference between living and dying here," Belle said.

"These two sweet girls can't die in this stink hole," Nancy said. "I'm not going to allow it."

Nancy then lay down with Connie, vanishing inside her.

Belle did the same, finding herself completely inside Samantha. It felt really weird, but she also felt in control of Samantha.

Belle immediately willed Samantha to stay calm, to breath as shallow as she could, then she focused on slowing Samantha's heart and breathing.

Belle had Samantha think of good things, fun things, like last Christmas with her mother and father and brother. It had been a wonderful Christmas, especially when Grandma and Grandpa showed up Christmas morning.

Belle just kept Samantha's breathing very slow and shallow and her heart rate as low as she dared push it.

But still, she could feel Samantha starting to slip away.

There wasn't much time.

"Stay with me, Samantha," Belle said. "Help is coming. Stay with me."

Suddenly the big vault door swung open and medical personnel slipped an oxygen mask over Samantha's face.

Belle stayed with her, keeping her calm, taking deep breaths. She wanted to be sure the young girl would be all right.

Belle just kept Samantha's breathing very slow and shallow and her heart rate as low as she dared push it.

"Belle, Nancy, it's all right now," Jewel said.

With one more calming thought to Samantha, Belle moved sideways and up and out of the young girl.

A moment later, Nancy did the same thing.

"They are both going to make it," a paramedic said. "Let's get them to the hospital and fast."

Nancy quickly moved over to Belle.

Jewel had left the safe.

In all her life, Belle had never felt so relieved and so fulfilled in doing something.

"We saved their lives," Nancy said, softly.

"Maybe that's what this is all about," Belle said.

"I sure hope so," Nancy said.

So did Belle. She really, really hoped so.

Nancy took Belle's hand and the two of them stepped back out into the basement through the steel wall. Belle didn't even close her eyes.

Jewel and Tommy and K.J. were standing off to one side out of the way. All three were smiling.

"Great job," Jewel said.

"Fantastic," Tommy said.

"Can we get out of this smelly place now?" K.J. asked. "I'm going to have to throw this bathrobe away and scrub with my best French soaps to clear this off me."

"Take us back to the restaurant parking lot," Jewel said, laughing.

An instant later Belle found herself standing beside Nancy and facing Jewel and Tommy in the mall parking lot beside the Sizzler. The fresh air and cooling afternoon breeze felt wonderful.

"Be in Vegas and settled in by two weeks from tomorrow," K.J. said to Belle and Nancy.

Then he vanished.

Belle looked over at Tommy and Jewel, who were both smiling. "Is this what we do? We save people and put bad people away?"

"We do," Jewel said. "And more."

Belle looked at Nancy who was nodding as well.

"I think I want to learn more," Belle said.

"Great," Tommy said. "But how about showers, a change of clothes, and some dinner first."

Belle had no idea how she would do any of those things as a ghost, but they sure sounded good.

Section Two
A VERY STRANGE TRIP

Nine

BELLE AND NANCY sat in the back seat of a Mercedes SUV as Jewel had the driver, an elderly woman who owned the car, take them to Belle's apartment. The poor woman had just been coming out of the mall with packages and Jewel had merged with her and had her drive them.

Tommy assured Belle and Nancy that the woman would never remember a thing, but Belle wasn't sure if that was better or worse.

Tommy sat in the front seat mostly just taking deep breaths after what he had gone through inside that pervert's head. Belle didn't blame him at all. When she asked him why the deep breath, he had said it made the memories recede faster.

The woman stopped in front of Belle's apartment and all four got out.

Behind the wheel the poor woman suddenly looked puzzled, looked around, then shook her head and drove off.

"She doesn't live that far from here, so it will be fine," Jewel said. "She'll just think she got distracted."

The North End neighborhood of Boise around Belle's apartment was stunning this time of the year. The huge oak trees that formed canopies over the streets were all turning bright fall oranges and reds. And the air always smelled of cut grass and fall flowers.

It was the most beautiful place in all of Boise to live, and Nancy's apartment was only a few blocks down and one block over from Belle's. Belle had no idea what she was going to do next. But whatever it was, she was fairly certain she could no longer live here.

In fact, she wasn't certain how a ghost could live anywhere, for that matter. So many questions to be answered.

"I would suggest you pack some clothes and minor stuff and not stay here tonight," Jewel said.

"Agreed," Tommy said. "The police will be locking this up and posting guards at some point. Easier to get a good night's sleep if people aren't showing up at all hours of the day or night. Is there a great hotel with suites in town somewhere?"

"Homewood Suites by Hilton," Nancy said. "Out pretty close to where we were by the mall."

Belle nodded. "I hear it has great suites and water jet tubs in each room."

"I'd suggest we all go there then for the night," Jewel said.

Belle didn't much like the idea of not staying in her own apartment, but she understood. She didn't know how four ghosts could get rooms in a suite hotel, but she would learn that when the time was right.

"Belle," Nancy said as they started toward the front apartment door. "Look."

Belle looked where Nancy had pointed. Down the street a half block was a battered old blue van. Her ex-husband's van.

"What is the slug doing here?" Belle asked, shocked.

"Heard about what happened this morning to us," Nancy said. "I'll bet he's trying to rip you off before the police lock this up."

"Who's the slug?" Tommy asked, suddenly looking worried.

"My ex-husband," Belle said, turning and storming toward the front door. She might be dead, but she could still teach the idiot a thing or two.

She went through her own front door without closing her eyes and stopped in the middle of her living room. She had really, really enjoyed furnishing this place and had it exactly as she liked it, with brown cloth furniture, an oak dining room set, and a large screen television that she and Nancy had watched many a movie on.

"This is nice," Jewel said as they entered behind her.

"Thanks," Belle said. "I'm going to miss it."

"I can see why," Jewel said.

Nancy went past Belle and looked into the kitchen. "He's not in there."

Then Belle heard a scratching noise coming from her bedroom and she went that way, past the bathroom and into her bedroom.

Dressed in his normal baggy and stained jeans and an old work shirt, the slug was standing on one of her chairs trying to get something from a ceiling light over her bed.

As Belle got into the room, the slug said softly, "Got it."

Belle instantly knew what the bastard had. It was a miniature camera. He had been filming her.

As he stepped down off the chair, she went at him, thinking she was going to hit him and hit him hard, but instead she went inside him. And what she saw there in his mind made her sick to her stomach.

The creep had been filming her dressing and in the bathroom for years and selling it online to different porn sites.

And he had done the same thing to Nancy.

Belle wanted more than anything else to just stop the bastard's heart, but instead she backed out and sat down on the bed.

"You all right?" Nancy said, instantly at her side, holding her.

"You need to climb in there for a minute, see what that bastard has done."

"Are you sure?" Nancy asked.

Jewel nodded, so as the bastard worked to get a camera embedded in a headboard, Nancy merged with him.

Belle watched, expecting Nancy to kill the man, but she did as Belle had done and came out looking disgusted and angry.

"What's going on?" Jewel asked.

"The bastard recorded me in here and in the bathroom," Belle said, "and Nancy in her apartment as well. He did it for years and sold the recordings on the Internet."

Belle didn't know what to think. She couldn't let this bastard get away with this. But her ex-husband was just a pervert. Tame compared to the monster they had brought to justice earlier in the day. And Belle had a hunch that since she and Nancy were both dead now, not much would come of making anything official against him.

Nancy reached over and squeezed her hand.

Behind them, the bastard just kept working to get one camera out of the headboard. He had clearly spent some time hiding it there and now didn't want it discovered.

Belle looked up at Jewel who was looking worried, and Tommy who was looking angry.

"Can you do something to his mind for me?" Belle asked.

Jewel looked puzzled for a moment, then smiled. "What did you have in mind?"

"I'm thinking he needs to grieve for us some," Belle said, starting to smile at the idea that was forming in her mind. "How about at any mention of my name, of any picture of me, of any thought of me or Nancy, he just breaks down into sobbing tears and can't stop. Can you do that?"

"I can sure try," Jewel said, laughing.

Tommy was shaking his head and smiling.

Nancy just reached over and hugged her. "Perfect, just perfect."

"Let's wait until he gets done and outside," Belle said. "I don't want him here sobbing while I'm trying to pack."

At that, Jewel and Tommy both just applauded.

Ten

JEWEL WAS AMAZED at how strong Belle and Nancy were turning out to be. And they clearly cared for each other and knew each other from a lot of years of friendship.

Jewel had no doubt that the two of them would make a great Ghost Agent team.

Belle's ex-husband only took a few more minutes to get his cameras, then with one look around to make sure he hadn't disturbed anything too much, he went out the front door and locked it behind him.

Jewel followed him and merged with him as he went down the sidewalk toward the street.

The guy really was a low-level creep. And he loved his porn. Jewel could see that he hadn't actually loved Belle for a lot of years, but had been using her to support him and make some money selling candid pictures and film of her and Nancy.

He really, really deserved to be taught a lesson and Jewel was going to be glad to do it.

She quickly planted the thoughts in his mind about how much he was going to miss Belle and Nancy.

And then she used feelings and memories from the death of his dog at a young age to make the grief real and uncontrollable when he thought of the two women.

Then Jewel took off all restraints on holding back the grief. He would not be able to, ever. No matter the situation.

She then made sure at the slightest thought of Belle or Nancy, he would break down and cry uncontrollably. And she added that women on porn videos would all remind him of Belle and Nancy, no matter what they looked like.

Jewel made sure all of it was in place in the creep's mind. Not even intensive counseling would be able to fix this problem for him.

Then, as she left his mind, she gave him a suggestion about looking at the most recent images of Belle he had gotten off the camera feed.

She walked away as he collapsed on the sidewalk, sobbing and wailing and crying.

It was not a pretty sight.

Belle and Nancy were both beaming and applauding the show.

Tommy was laughing. As Jewel came up to him he said, "Remind me to never get you mad at me."

She kissed him and said, "I can't ever imagine being mad at you."

"Good," he said.

At that, all four of them turned their backs on the sobbing man on the sidewalk and went back inside.

Eleven

BELLE PULLED her favorite summer dress out of her closet to pack. But even though the dress was in her hand, and she could feel the light silk texture, it still remained on the hanger in the closet.

She turned to show Nancy who was standing by the door. Nancy just shook her head.

Jewel was sitting on the bed trying to explain the ghost element of everything to both of them. Tommy was in the living room taking a nap.

"So you are saying that we can get as many free clothes as we want?" Belle asked. "And it won't be stealing?"

"That's right," Jewel said. "You take the ghost element and it replaces itself after three or four hours in the original. So you can go back and take it again and again."

"How long will the ghost clothes remain in our closet or drawers?" Nancy asked.

"So far I haven't lost a one," Jewel said. "But until this trip, I ran my hand over all of them every day. They might all be gone when I get back from this trip and I might need to go shopping again. I never asked K.J. that question, to be honest."

"Unlimited shopping," Nancy said, shaking her head. "This is sounding better and better."

"Wait until you taste the food," Jewel said. "It's why Tommy and I are dressed like this in our running attire. We had just finished running when K.J. came to get us. We have to exercise every day so we can eat what we want. Everything tastes so fantastic."

"So food is the same way as clothes?" Belle asked, putting the dress on the bed and turning back to pull out more.

"It is," Jewel said. "Say you take an apple from a buffet. The original apple remains, but you have an apple in your hands as well. K.J. thinks food tastes better because we are eating the essence of it. I would tend to agree with him."

"Looks like we're back to running," Nancy said, laughing. "As Belle will tell you, I love to eat."

"Doesn't show," Jewel said.

"Thank you," Nancy said, indicating her thin body. "This is from time in the corporate gym every day."

"Well, on this job we have lots of time," Jewel said.

Belle suddenly realized she was going to miss her job. It had been challenging. Not as rewarding by a long ways as saving those two girls' lives, but still a good job.

"You don't need to take too much tonight," Jewel said. "We can come back tomorrow and get what you want to take to Vegas."

Belle shook her head. "I loved this place. I had made it a home, but I feel it's now part of something else, something I can't touch or have any more. So I don't want to come back."

"I felt the same way about my little house," Jewel said, nodding.

"We'll make a new home," Nancy said, nodding.

"And since everything is free," Belle said, "I'm looking forward to that."

Belle figured out what she wanted and packed the clothes into the ghost equivalent of one of her rolling luggage bags that she usually carried on planes. She made sure she had a couple pair of shoes, then changed into Levis, a silk blouse, and tennis shoes.

Since no one could see her, there was no reason to dress up for traveling as she normally did.

Finally, after taking the ghost elements of some of her favorite jewelry, she said, "I'm ready."

Nancy led the way out of the bedroom, followed by Jewel. Belle looked back one more time at her bedroom. It was just a bedroom. No real memories in it and honestly, she was glad to be leaving it after what her creep of an ex-husband had done recording her in it.

She stopped in the bathroom and packed a few personal items, then left her suitcase in the small dining area and went to the kitchen. There, on a top shelf she pulled down a white sauce dish about the size of a child's shoe. It had been her grandmother's.

The real one stayed on the shelf. She only held the ghost one.

After a moment she put it back and the ghost one vanished back into the real one.

"Guess there are some things that are better to just leave."

She headed to the living room where Jewel had got Tommy moving. He really looked groggy.

Nancy was looking at Belle, worried.

She came over real close and asked, "Are you going to be all right?"

Belle looked up into the wonderful concerned green eyes of her best friend and nodded. "I think I will be. Let's go get you packed."

Nancy nodded and hugged her, and to Belle that felt wonderful.

And comforting and right.

Jewel and Tommy went out the door first, followed by Nancy.

With one last look around, Belle said, "It was nice while it lasted."

Then she turned and headed out of her apartment without a look back.

The slug of her ex-husband had managed to make it another twenty steps toward his car and was lying on his back sobbing.

Belle just broke out laughing as a cop car showed up.

She wondered how the idiot was going to be able to explain the secret surveillance cameras in his pocket. She knew that every time he tried, he would break into uncontrollable sobbing.

Jewel and Tommy, arm-in-arm, went past the slug. Then Belle, arm-in-arm with Nancy, walked by the creep.

She couldn't think of a better way to leave that jerk.

Then Belle shouted ahead to Jewel. "Thanks. And I hope you teach me how to do that at some point."

"Be glad to," Jewel said over her shoulder, laughing.

They walked down the sidewalk toward Nancy's apartment as the sobbing of Belle's ex-husband echoed through the otherwise quiet neighborhood.

Twelve

JEWEL AND BELLE helped Nancy get packed, then the four of them walked three blocks over to a stoplight on a major street. To Jewel the late afternoon was starting to feel cool. After three months in Vegas, she had forgotten what being chilled felt like. And she was only wearing her jogging clothes, which were fine when exercising, but didn't provide a lot of protection when just moving normally.

When a large white SUV with a man driving stopped to wait for the signal on the big intersection with mansions and large trees on four sides, Tommy moved out and slid in the driver's door and took over the guy.

Then Tommy instantly jumped back out. "He's headed in the opposite direction we need, and the guy is in a hurry to catch a family dinner."

Jewel nodded. They didn't mind hopping rides with people, as long as it didn't cause them trouble.

They waited for two more lights before a man in a large white van stopped at the light and Tommy tried again.

After a moment, the man gave them a thumb's up.

"Now that's still going to take me time to get used to," Nancy said, indicating that Tommy was now controlling the man behind the wheel.

Jewel understood that. It had taken her months to get used to some of this, and she wasn't sure if she still was yet.

Jewel quickly helped both Belle and Nancy get into the car with their bags, tossing the bags through the sidewall of the van.

After she was sure the two women were in place in the back seat, she slid into the passenger seat just as the light turned green.

"So someone's going to have to give me directions," the man said, his voice sexy and his smile wonderful. The guy was dressed in a three-piece gray suit and wore a blue silk tie

"Wow, who is this guy?" Jewel asked Tommy.

"Local news anchor headed for a boring gathering of charity fundraisers out near the airport. He doesn't know where this hotel is."

"Glad to help on that," Belle said from the back seat. "Just stay on this street and get through town to start with."

Ten minutes later they were jumping out of the van at an intersection near the hotel. Tommy didn't want the guy to be seen in the parking lot of a hotel since so many people would recognize him. So Tommy had him pull over and pretend to be talking on his cell phone until all three women were out with their bags.

Then he climbed out.

The poor guy looked at his dead cell phone, shrugged, put it away, and started back into traffic.

As the four of them turned and started toward the hotel, Jewel finally realized that she and Tommy not only were still in their jogging clothes, but they had no supplies at all. No bathroom stuff, no change of clothes or underwear or anything.

"You know," Jewel said to her partner as they walked ahead of the two women down the wide, tree-lined sidewalk, "You and I need to do some shopping and get a few things to make it through the night and to wear tomorrow."

Tommy laughed, glancing down at his blue sweat pants and tan t-shirt. "Good point."

Jewel turned to the two women. "How far is that mall from here?"

Belle pointed to Jewel's right. "About four blocks. Easy walk. But not sure when it closes."

"Easier shopping after closing," Jewel said. "No people to dodge that way."

"Oh," was all Belle said.

Nancy just laughed. "I'm starting to like this new life, or death, or whatever, even more."

"Let's get rooms first, then food, then clothes," Tommy said.

"A perfect plan," Jewel said, looking back over her shoulder. "Sound good to you two?"

"We're just following and learning," Belle said.

"But I am getting hungry," Nancy said. "And I think I need to pee. Is that normal? Do ghosts pee?"

Tommy laughed and said nothing.

Jewel remembered wondering that same thing.

"I'm afraid most everything stays the same in this state," Jewel said.

"And what happens if the lid is down?" Belle asked.

Jewel laughed. "You pee in the sink."

"Oh, great," Belle said.

"It's ghost pee," Tommy said, laughing but not turning around. "No one will notice."

"What about periods?" Nancy asked.

Jewel laughed. "So far, that hasn't been part of this new state of being."

"Oh, thank you for small miracles," Nancy said.

"Small!" Belle said. "Hell, that's a major plus to being dead in my mind."

"I'll second that," Jewel said.

"Amen to that," Tommy said.

Thirteen

BELLE WATCHED as Jewel went through the counter at the front desk of the suites hotel and into the woman working behind the counter. The woman looked to be about sixty, with a haircut right out of the nineteen-sixties. She had on slightly too much make-up, especially red lipstick. A moment later the woman was typing on her screen, clearly looking up reservations.

The big lobby around them was comfortable, decorated in brown tones, with high ceilings, a wide staircase leading up to a mezzanine level, and a number of seating areas with cloth couches and chairs. A huge stone fireplace dominated one side of the big room and the light brown carpet looked thick and comfortable.

After a moment, Jewel stuck her head out of the desk clerk and looked at Belle and Nancy. The woman suddenly looked like she had two heads, since Jewel's head came right out of the woman's shoulder. That was creepy-looking, actually.

"You two want to share a big suite?"

"Sounds great to me," Nancy said.

"I'd love it as well," Belle said. After the day, she really didn't want to find herself alone in a hotel room. Having Nancy beside her would be perfect.

Jewel nodded and her head disappeared completely back into the woman's shoulder.

In another thirty seconds or so, Jewel appeared completely, leaving the woman standing to one side of the computer doing what she had been doing before.

As Jewel walked back through the counter to them, she said, "I've blocked two suites for the night for maintenance scheduled for tomorrow afternoon."

"Perfect," Tommy said.

"We're not going to keep the hotel from renting those, are we?" Belle said, if they run out of room.

"They are far, far from full," Jewel said. "In fact, over two-thirds of the hotel is sitting empty right now. So won't cost them anything."

Belle wasn't sure why she had suddenly worried about that. More than likely her job of corporate accounting had her mind working that way.

As they headed up the stairs, Nancy asked Jewel and Tommy a question that had been starting to bother Belle as well.

"Is it normal to not feel grief about dying?"

Jewel just shrugged as she and Tommy reached the first landing and kept going.

"We were bothered by that as well," Tommy said. "It felt as if we should have been angry about being killed, but neither of us were. We think it's because this feels so real. We haven't really left the world, just been given a new job to do."

"In fact," Jewel said. "When I asked K.J. about that, he said simply 'What's to mourn? You're still here eating great, living free, doing an important job, and having great sex.' I think he was exactly right. We are still alive, just in a different state is all."

Belle could understand that. All of this was feeling very, very real, even though she could go through things and make other people do things and who knew what else. One moment she had been alive in the other state, then a truck had hit her and she hadn't felt anything, just ended up in this state.

"So other people just move on to the next world?" Nancy asked as they reached the first floor landing and turned to go up another flight of stairs.

"Almost everyone," Jewel said. "From what we understand and have been told."

"White tunnel and all?" Belle asked. She wasn't much of a religious person, but afterlife had always interested her.

"That's what K.J. said," Tommy said. "But you would have to ask him to get more information."

They reached the second floor and Jewel led them down the hall to the right, all the way to the end. "You two can take that one, we'll take this one."

Jewel pointed to two doors.

"I need a shower," Tommy said. "So can we meet in thirty minutes back here?"

"Take showers, get changed into comfortable clothes," Jewel said. "And we'll go get dinner and then do some shopping."

"Perfect," Belle said and Nancy nodded.

Jewel and Tommy turned and vanished through the door to their room, leaving the two standing in the hallway.

"Guess we don't need keys to anything anymore," Nancy said, laughing.

"Guess not," Belle said, smiling at her best friend.

She turned and with her eyes only slightly opened walked through the door and into the huge suite.

Tall windows ran along one wall looking out over the trees, the neighborhood, and the mall beyond. The sky was colored with a beautiful sunset since it was just about seven in the evening.

The room was furnished in comfortable-looking cloth couches and chairs in varied brown tones. The carpet was a soft brown and a number of lamps were turned on around the area.

Through an open door to the left Belle could see a huge king bed and she headed that way, pulling her suitcase.

"Wow, this is something," Nancy said. "It's bigger than my apartment."

Inside the bedroom, Belle spotted a huge walk-in closet. She pointed at it. "Guess people who stay here travel with a ton of clothes."

Nancy laughed and dropped her suitcase by the closet, then went to look at the bathroom.

"I take it back," Nancy said. "The bathroom is bigger than my apartment."

Belle followed her into the gigantic tile and mirrored bathroom. The glass shower could hold ten people and the big jet tub next to it could hold another ten.

There were three sinks in the long vanity counter, something Belle had never seen or could see a use for.

"And look," Belle said. "They left the toilet seat lid up."

"Oh, thank heavens," Nancy said, laughing.

Nancy went back into the bedroom and started to undress, putting her blouse on the bed, then her slacks. Then she peeled off the matching blue underwear and bra she had been wearing, finally standing there in the nude.

All Belle could do was stare. Nancy was the most attractive person she had ever seen, and Belle loved it every time Nancy undressed in front of her.

Nancy glanced at Belle. "Come on, we only have thirty minutes. I'll wash your back if you wash mine. I want to rinse as much of this day away as I can."

"I can't agree more," Belle said, finally kicking herself into gear.

Nancy had just gotten the water temperature set in the huge shower and was stepping in through the glass when Belle got into the bathroom. Belle quickly unwrapped the ghost version of the hotel soap from a basket on the vanity and joined Nancy in the huge shower.

Nancy looked at her and smiled, blushing slightly. "Anyone ever tell you that you have a wonderful body?"

"Only you," Belle said, staring in to the green eyes of her best friend. "But so do you, you know. Anyone ever tell you that?"

"Not a soul but you," Nancy said.

The next thing Belle knew, Nancy was holding her tight against her wonderful-feeling skin.

Belle hugged her back and the two of them stood there like that under the warm water for a very long time.

Belle loved the hug and everything about it.

Finally Nancy pushed back slightly, keeping her body against Belle's. "Thank you for trying to save my life this morning."

Belle didn't know what to say, but before she could say anything, Nancy smiled. "I'm damn glad you didn't succeed. Otherwise, I wouldn't be here with you like this, and I would have been totally heartbroken you were gone."

Then Nancy hugged her again, long and hard.

The sensation of Nancy being against her naked skin felt fantastic, and she could feel herself becoming aroused.

Belle kept hugging her, hoping the moment would never end.

Finally, Nancy pushed back slightly, her wonderful face flushed from either the heat or the moment. Belle had an idea her face was the same way.

"Wash my back," Nancy said. "We keep this up much longer and we won't make dinner."

"And that's a bad thing how?" Belle asked, surprised but excited at the hint that Nancy had just given her. Did they really have the courage to take their friendship to the next level?

It seemed Nancy did.

And Belle had wanted to, secretly, for years.

Nancy smiled as big as any smile that Belle had ever seen. Then she turned around and braced herself against the tile of the shower wall, the water flowing over her head and down her back.

Belle spent the next wonderful five minutes exploring every inch of Nancy's back, butt, legs.

Then Nancy did the same to her.

And never in all her life had Belle been so turned on.

Fourteen

JEWEL AND TOMMY managed to get showered and get their running clothes back on and into the hallway about the time that the two new recruits appeared from their suite. The shower felt wonderful after the long day and Jewel had almost decided to stay in and help Tommy with his shower, but knew if they did that, they would be late for dinner.

Both women had wet hair (just as she and Tommy did) and they were wearing the same comfortable clothes they had changed into in their apartments.

"Anywhere close to eat at 7 p.m. that won't be too crowded?" Tommy asked.

"Sizzler is about it," Nancy said. "In the parking lot of the big mall. There are restaurants on the other side of the mall, but they would be jammed this time of night."

Jewel looked at them. "Can you handle going back there?"

"Oh, sure," Belle said. "I like the place and it's big enough we can find a table out of the way."

"Always a good plan," Jewel said, impressed that they were already thinking like that.

"I think it would be fine as well," Nancy said.

"Lead the way," Jewel said.

Belle smiled at Nancy and they turned and headed for the stairs.

It was a nice walk as the sun was setting. Belle and Nancy led them along the tree-lined sidewalk in front of now-closed office buildings. Jewel enjoyed the walk, but the evening air was chilling right down and Jewel wished she had something heavier to wear. She would shortly.

About ten steps in front of her and Tommy, Belle and Nancy walked side-by-side, at times laughing at something one of them said.

"They are going to make a great team," Tommy said softly so the two women in front couldn't hear. "We got to get their auras contained, though. They are simply radiating."

Jewel laughed. "That's because dying has given them the freedom they both needed to be with each other. See how the colors of their auras are merging in places. They are in love."

"Seriously?" Tommy asked.

"If we opened up our auras," Jewel said, "ours would match like that as well."

Tommy nodded. "Let's get theirs contained and if we can't do it, let's call K.J. and have him teach them. Those things could be seen from space."

"After dinner," Jewel said, laughing. She smiled at the man she loved more than anything in the world. He was always thinking and caring about others.

"You are right," he said. "First we need to show them how to get dinner in a buffet and restaurant."

Jewel smiled at her partner. "That and answer about a thousand questions I'm sure they both have."

"Yeah, good point," Tommy said, smiling back.

Jewel was glad the air-conditioning in the restaurant wasn't on. The restaurant was so big that the ninety-plus people in the place didn't make the restaurant feel crowded.

Tommy found a table in the back that looked to be in a closed section and then Jewel and Tommy led both women toward the salad bar.

"This will feel just like normal," Jewel said. "Once you get used to it. Everything has a ghost component, so you just serve yourself like normal."

Jewel grabbed a plate from the stack, then started fixing herself a salad.

Both women watched. Finally Belle said, "That just flat looks strange. You are picking things up and filling your plate, but nothing is really moving."

"We function on what seems to be a slightly altered plane of existence," Tommy said.

"Too much," Nancy said, holding up her hands. "For the moment let's just say I grab a ghost salad and go sit down."

Jewel laughed. "That's how I think of it as well."

"Perfect," Belle said. She reached over and grabbed a cherry tomato and popped it in her mouth.

Jewel watched as Belle's eyes got large. "My god, that's the best tomato I have ever tasted."

"Everything tastes wonderful," Jewel said.

At that moment, a young waitress appeared from the kitchen carrying a large tray of food on her shoulder.

"Hold off for a minute on the salad," Jewel said, handing her plate to Tommy. "Let's go see what's on the menu for the main course."

Jewel led the two women over to where the waitress set down the huge tray on a stand. From what Jewel could tell, the tray was filled with plates of steaks and baked potatoes. There was also a couple baskets of fries and a basket of fried shrimp.

"See anything you like?" Jewel asked the two.

"What do you mean?" Nancy asked.

Jewel reached over and grabbed a plate with a steak marked medium rare and a baked potato with everything on it.

The real plate stayed in place, but Jewel could feel the heat of the plate in her hand.

"Found what I wanted," Jewel said. "If there's nothing on this tray that appeals to you, there will be more coming out of the kitchen regularly from the looks of this crowd."

"This won't affect the taste of the food for the person eating that meal?" Belle asked, pointing at the real plate still left on the tray.

"K.J. told me it didn't when I asked that same question," Jewel said.

She turned and threaded her way to the table in the back and put the steak on the table in a place facing the restaurant.

Then she went over and grabbed a full glass of water off another tray and some silverware and put those beside the steak. Then she headed back to the salad bar to get a small salad.

Belle and Nancy had gone back to the salad bar and were standing out of the way of an elderly couple working to get salads. Tommy already had a plate full and was headed back to the table.

"Leave my steak alone," Jewel said to him, smiling.

"No promises," Tommy said, giving her an air-kiss as he went past.

A couple minutes later, Jewel had a salad and was back at the table.

It took the two new recruits a little longer, but they made it, talking about what had happened when Belle accidently brushed one of the waitresses.

"The waitress was having the same problems I had in college," Belle said as she and Nancy joined Tommy and Jewel. "Not enough money, a shitty boyfriend she doesn't really like but who wants to get married, and pressure from trying to keep grades up to get into grad school."

"It's amazing what you will see in people's lives," Tommy said. "For the most part, they are good people."

"The waitress was a good person," Belle said. "Just hit home to feel her struggles."

"You made it," Nancy said. "She has a chance if she's as smart as you are."

"I married the perverted slug, remember?" Belle said, smiling at her friend.

"Everyone makes mistakes," Nancy said, and the two laughed.

Jewel was so happy to see them laughing. Especially so soon after being killed.

"Great job saving those two girls' lives this morning," Tommy said. "You two had an amazing first day and it's not even done yet."

Both nodded thanks and blushed slightly as they went back to eating their salads, commenting on how everything tasted better and clearer.

Jewel worked on her salad for a moment, then couldn't take it any longer and pulled the steak plate over and dug into the steak and potato. She was hungry and she didn't care what they thought, she was going to eat.

Fifteen

BELLE COULDN'T BELIEVE how amazing all the food tasted. She loved Sizzler when alive, but didn't remember being that much in love with their food. But now it all tasted amazing, as if she had suddenly had her taste buds turned on.

She ate until she was far too full, almost unable to stop even then.

After dinner, they walked over to the mall. The streets were well-lit and clean, but very few people were out. The air was chilly, but not cold.

It was nine in the evening and the mall had just closed, but as Jewel had said, that didn't matter at all. And Belle felt she was getting pretty good at walking through walls and closed doors. She could now even keep her eyes mostly open.

The mall had been remodeled a few years back and looked fairly new, in bright blues and browns, even though Belle knew it had been here for thirty plus years. The ceilings were high and everything was well lit. Employees were the

SMITH'S Monthly

only ones still around, working on nightly closing routines.

Christmas decorations were in most stores and windows, and it suddenly dawned on Belle that this coming Christmas was going to be very, very different. She had never really had much of a Christmas routine. Last year she and Nancy had given each other gifts, and had gone with each other to their company Christmas parties. And on Christmas Eve they had watched movies at Belle's house and drank eggnog and decorated a small tree.

The next day Nancy had cooked them both a wonderful ham dinner and they made Christmas cookies with icing that they ate on for a week.

Neither of them had any family, and now, even more, this Christmas was going to be just the two of them.

Tommy and Jewel seemed to be old hats at finding what they wanted in stores, plus small suitcases to take it to Vegas with them. Since both Nancy and Belle both had full suitcases, they just walked along, testing what they could pick up.

Belle stayed close to Nancy, and Nancy seemed to want to stay close to Belle as well. With every hour that passed, Belle felt better and better. It was as if the weight of the live world was lifting from her shoulders.

She didn't need to worry about money ever again, although she had no idea yet how she would find a home or apartment to live in. Food tasted wonderful, clothes were free for the taking, and she and Nancy seemed to have decided to test more limits on their friendship, which Belle had dreamed about for years.

After that wonderful shower, all she wanted to do was touch Nancy's wonderful smooth skin and silky brown hair.

At one point, as Tommy finished up getting some Levis, Nancy turned to Jewel and Tommy. "Does feeling better and better happen with everyone who dies?"

Tommy shrugged and Jewel laughed. "If I remember right, it happened to us over the first few days. But does it happen to everyone, we have no clue. Except for K.J., we've never met any other Ghost Agents before you two."

"So there aren't very many of us?" Belle asked, still trying to get a grip on that fact. "Everyone else just moves on to the next world?"

"K.J. says there are very, very few Ghost Agents that can stay behind. Maybe a thousand at most scattered all over the world."

Belle just shook her head as Jewel and Tommy packed their clothes into their ghost suitcases and headed back out into the mall area.

The fact that there were only a thousand Ghost Agents just seemed impossible to Belle. She understood the part about it being her time to leave, to die, but to be handed this opportunity to stay around and keep enjoying life and feeling better and better seemed completely unbelievable.

And what was very, very strange to her was that she wasn't angry or upset or even sad in the slightest about dying. She kept thinking she should feel something more than happiness, but she didn't.

She was dead and she liked it a lot more than being alive so far, and it was only the first day. What did that say about her life?

Nancy asked the next question Belle was thinking.

"Why us?" Nancy asked.

"Guessing," Tommy said, "It's because of your skills and who you are as people. I was a cop, Jewel a doctor."

"I know business and finance and networks," Belle said, shrugging. "What good will that do?"

"Honestly," Jewel said. "We don't know. But in this modern world, I'll bet your knowledge is going to come in handy on more than one mission. Plus look what you two did this morning. You had just come through your own death and immediately jumped in to save two young girls. I have a hunch that kind of ability to act is a large part of why you two were picked."

"So what is your real world skill set?" Tommy asked Nancy as they headed back down the silent mall toward the door they had come through.

"Computers," Nancy said. "Again something I'm not sure will be valuable or not."

Both Jewel and Tommy laughed at that. "Oh, trust me, you are going to be of immense value. Both of you."

"But I can't touch a computer," Nancy said.

"But that young woman sure can," Jewel said, indicating a young blonde who was pulling down a garage door-like grate over a small store entrance to close it for the night. "And you can control her, be inside of her, and through her fingers make a computer dance the tango. Just as I did with the reservations clerk at the hotel."

Belle suddenly started to understand. She could do the same thing when it came to corporations. And in this modern world where big corporations were treated as people, Belle could navigate that world easily, especially if she was in control of the right person.

"Come to think of it," Jewel said after a few more steps, looking at Belle and Nancy and then at Tommy, "the four of us form a very, very powerful team."

At that, all Belle could do was agree.

Sixteen

JEWEL AND TOMMY led the way back along the sidewalk in the crisp evening air toward the hotel, both dragging small suitcases full of clothes and a few bathroom supplies to get them through the night and back to Las Vegas.

Belle and Nancy followed them about ten paces back.

At one dark area between streetlights, Jewel turned around and was almost blinded by the auras radiating off the two women. Belle and Nancy were completely glowing with bright oranges and reds and blues and other major colors dancing off their skin. It was stunningly beautiful.

And where the two auras met, Jewel felt like she was looking into the sun.

She turned back to Tommy. "Take a look behind us."

Tommy did and said, "Wow, that's bright. We got to do something about that."

Tommy stopped and said clearly into the air, "K.J., need a little help here for a few minutes."

Belle and Nancy stopped, looking puzzled.

"With clothing or without?" K.J.'s voice asked from the air around them.

"With, please," Tommy said, shaking his head.

Belle and Nancy both laughed.

Jewel really liked K.J. The Ghost Agent could really be funny.

A few minutes later K.J. appeared in a bright blue bathrobe and pink bunny slippers. He was almost steaming, which made Jewel think he had just gotten out of a hot tub.

"Wow," K.J. glancing at Belle and Nancy, "we have a light show to rival the 4th of July over the Bay."

Both Nancy and Belle looked around, then looked back at K.J. clearly puzzled.

"That's why we called you here," Tommy said. "Figured we needed to get that wrapped up a little."

K.J. nodded. "And I got a little more on the coming mission as well. It's going to be interesting, to say the least."

Jewel was feeling both excitement and dread about another mission. And if K.J. thought it interesting, who knows what it might be.

K.J. pulled his bathrobe tight around his waist, making sure the tie was secure. Then he slicked back his wet hair and stepped toward the girls. "Let's get this done before we all go blind, and not in the fun sexual way we all love so much."

Jewel and Tommy both chuckled, but both recruits just looked puzzled.

"Can you see anything around Jewel and Tommy?" K.J. asked the two new recruits. "Colors, auras?"

Both Belle and Nancy looked at Jewel and Tommy and shook their heads.

"Release the Kraken, or whatever you call your auras," K.J. said.

Jewel easily released the skin-tight containment around her aura at the same moment Tommy did.

"I should have brought my sunglasses," K.J. said, shielding his eyes.

"Wow!" both Belle and Nancy said at the same time.

Jewel had to admit that her aura and Tommy's had gotten even brighter and more powerful and much larger over the last few months. They had just kept them contained, so she hadn't noticed. And she was amazed how in certain areas her aura just flowed together with Tommy and joined his and his joined hers to be even brighter, just as Belle and Nancy's did.

"Enough," K.J. said, covering his eyes and waving his arm.

Jewel contained her aura down to her skin at the same moment Tommy did.

"Now look at each other's auras," K.J. said to the new recruits. "See all the bright colors? See the areas where the two of you merge, where you are in love. Given enough time, you'll be able to read some things from auras."

Both Belle and Nancy just stared at each other, their auras moving faster and brighter as they got more excited.

"Now, think of your aura only at your skin," K.J. said, "like you have a tight shield around you."

Nancy's aura vanished down against her skin a fraction of a second before Belle's.

Belle looked at K.J. "We can see auras because we are dead?"

"Yes, one of the many, many skills you have that will come in handy," K.J. said. "But Tommy and Jewel were right to have me get your auras contained as soon as possible."

"Why is that?" Nancy asked.

Jewel and Tommy both smiled.

"They will tell you tomorrow," K.J. said.

"Can we let out our auras again?" Belle asked.

Jewel remembered asking K.J. that exact same question.

K.J. nodded. "Just think of the shield holding them against your body open."

This time Belle slightly beat Nancy and both of them stood there staring at the colors flowing around them.

"It is so beautiful," Belle said.

"As beautiful as you," Nancy said to Belle.

"And that's my clue to depart," K.J. said, shaking his head. "Close up those auras and leave them closed for now. At least until you understand them all better."

Both women nodded and the auras around them sucked in tight against their skins.

K.J. turned to Jewel and Tommy. "Get to Vegas and get these two new recruits trained by Thanksgiving. From what I have been told, our mission starts the day after and it's going to need all four of you and me at full power. But it might turn out to be sooner, much sooner."

"That bad?" Tommy asked.

Jewel felt suddenly very worried.

K.J. shrugged. "Not sure how bad. I'm just repeating what my boss told me."

"So you know anything about the mission at all?"

"Something about the fact that we have to protect Santa Claus," K.J. said, shaking his head. "I met that old elf once and he's going to be a job."

"Santa Claus is real?" Tommy asked.

Jewel felt too shocked to even try to speak.

"Real and really damned annoying if you ask me," K.J. said, shaking his head. "Just get these two new agents up to speed on all the tricks you two know and in Vegas by Thanksgiving. I'll be having meetings and learning more tomorrow, I hope."

With that he vanished.

Jewel looked at Tommy and then the two women.

The silence on the Boise sidewalk was stunning. Even the cool breeze seemed to have stopped for fear of disturbing that moment.

"Maybe he's kidding," Tommy said after a moment.

"I'm not kidding," K.J.'s voice said in the air around them. "Wish the hell I was."

Section Three
BASIC GHOST TRAINING

Seventeen

It was only a little after ten in the evening by the time Belle and Nancy got back into their suite. They were to meet Jewel and Tommy at 9 a.m. in a nearby breakfast restaurant.

Belle felt stunned at the entire day and she could tell that Nancy did as well. She also knew she was tired, but far too wound up to sleep.

And both of them had promised to not talk about or even think about the craziness about Santa Claus. That was just about fifty billion times too much to think about at the moment.

But K.J.'s words about her and Nancy being in love echoed in Belle's mind. She knew she was in love with Nancy at a hundred different levels, but to have someone see it so clearly in their matching auras was really something.

Yet, Belle had seen the same thing clearly when Jewel and Tommy opened up their auras. It was clear to her that in a vast area, and a very bright area, Jewel and Tommy were completely joined.

"Are you believing any of this?" Nancy asked as they sat down on the comfortable cloth furniture in the living room area of the suite, facing each other.

"Some, yes, some no, other parts I'm just confused."

"My feelings exactly," Nancy said. "I know I need sleep, but I don't want to yet."

Suddenly Belle had an idea. "How about we take another walk through the hotel."

Nancy looked puzzled. "Why?"

"To prove some of this stuff to ourselves," Belle said, "without the others around."

"Not sure what you mean," Nancy said, smiling, "but I'm game."

Belle stood and took Nancy's hand, which felt wonderful in hers. "Follow me."

Belle turned and walked toward the wall where there was no door.

"Let's be careful to not walk into an elevator's shaft or out a side wall," Nancy said. "We might be dead, but I have a hunch we can't fly yet."

"Good point," Belle said, laughing.

So instead she steered Nancy through their big main door and out into the hallway. She looked down the hallway. For about ten rooms it was nothing but one room next to another.

Belle pulled Nancy through the door of the neighboring suite. It was dark, with just one light in the entry turned on. No bags, nothing.

"No one home," Belle said.

She headed toward and through the wall into the next suite. It felt very weird to just be walking through walls like this, but she had a hunch given time she would get very used to it.

It was about ten in the evening and a middle-aged woman was in the next suite. She was clearly alone and working at a table on some business papers. She was thin and still dressed in a gray business pantsuit, but had kicked off her high-heels. She had no wedding ring on at all.

"That's kind of sad," Nancy whispered. "She looks very stark and alone."

Belle laughed. "No need to whisper. We're ghosts, remember. She can't hear us."

"Right," Nancy said, shaking her head. Then in a normal voice she said, "Look at her aura."

After Nancy said that, Belle realized that she could hardly see the woman's aura. The flickering light was pale and small and not full of a lot of life or color. Mostly just all the intensity and excitement had been washed out of it.

Belle walked over and put her hand through the woman's arm. She could instantly see the woman's thoughts and memories and desires and hopes. Sadly, the woman had very few hopes. She wanted to be promoted, she loved her job in computer sales, she had no pets, no family, and most of the people at her home office in Denver didn't much like her and she knew it and didn't really care.

The woman liked working and being alone and that was it.

Belle pulled away from the woman and looked at Nancy. "Her aura represents her life. Basically nothing but her work."

Nancy just shook her head and Belle took Nancy's firm hand and the two of them went through the wall into the next suite. It also was vacant and dark.

"Guess we don't need to worry about bumping into anything," Nancy said, laughing as they walked through the edge of a dresser.

Belle also laughed. "I'm not going to miss those bruises on my legs from my desk at work. Not going to miss work, for that matter."

"But the people there are going to miss you," Nancy said as they went through the wall and into the next suite.

"Maybe," Belle said, not really wanting to think about that. "Let's think about that sort of stuff tomorrow."

"Agreed," Nancy said, squeezing Belle's hand.

In the next suite a guy sat on the bed in his underwear watching something on television. His back was propped up against pillows and he looked to be about Belle and Nancy's age, clearly in good shape physically.

His wife sat at a desk working at a laptop computer in a blue bathrobe. Both had larger auras than the single business-woman two rooms back, but there didn't seem to be any area where the auras overlapped.

This time Nancy walked over to the woman and touched her shoulder through the bathrobe. Belle watched as Nancy's eyes went sort of vacant for a moment, then Nancy returned to her eyes and stepped away.

"Wow, that's really something to see someone's full life just by touching them."

"What's her story?" Belle asked.

"Her name is Candice and she's having an affair with a co-worker back in Denver." Nancy indicated the woman at the desk and the man on the bed. "The two of them are married and haven't made love in a long time. She's disappointed because she really still loves him, but just doesn't know how to connect with him again."

Belle nodded and went over to the guy and touched his bare shoulder. Actually, she put her hand slightly inside his skin.

Belle could instantly see that he was madly in love with his wife and hoped that she would come to bed and make love with him. But since they had drifted

apart in the last year, he knew he was going to be disappointed, so he was trying not to think about it so they wouldn't fight.

Belle pulled back and looked at Nancy. "His name is Evan and he's in love with Candice, but is waiting for her to make the move to get things back on track. He's afraid they'll fight if he suggests anything."

"Now that's sad," Nancy said, shaking her head.

"It really is," Belle said.

Nancy smiled at her. "You want me to give it a try, see if I can help them? See if I can get Candice here moving. Jewel said we could do that sort of thing, remember?"

Belle didn't know what to think. She did want Nancy to try, but was afraid of what might happen if they weren't trained.

"You stay here and if I get into some sort of trouble, get Jewel and Tommy," Nancy said.

Belle nodded.

Nancy took a deep breath and then turned and sort of vanished inside the woman.

Watching her do that scared Belle. The idea of losing Nancy was just more than she could handle at this moment.

After a few seconds, Nancy appeared again, smiling at Belle. "This is no problem and I think this idea might work. I'm planting suggestions about what she needs to do to her husband and how horny she is. I think there's room for both of us in there like Jewel and Tommy did in that killer. Come on."

Belle moved over beside Nancy and Candice as Nancy disappeared inside Candice again.

Belle touched Candice, but couldn't put her hand into her skin.

"You're going to have to shrink up some," Belle said to Nancy, assuming she could hear her.

Candice nodded and Belle touched her skin again and this time her hand went in. She just moved inside of Candice and could feel Nancy there as well, as if they were both in a small car together, only Candice's body was the car.

"Wow," Belle said, "this is strange. I can see the room and hear the television and everything. And I know you are here and can sense and feel you and I can read Candice's thoughts."

"Neat, huh?"

"How can I hear you in here?"

"Darned if I know," Nancy said, laughing. "We'll ask Jewel and Tommy tomorrow."

Belle could see that what Candice's Denver lover did that Candice enjoyed was let her take complete control in the lovemaking. But Candice was afraid to do that with her own husband. But Belle knew that Evan would love that.

"How about we get Candice out of this robe and get her ordering her husband around a little," Nancy said, laughing.

"A perfect idea to me," Belle said.

She could feel that she was getting aroused as well as she and Nancy both kept giving Candice suggestions.

Finally Candice closed down the laptop, slipped out of her blue robe and stood in front of the mirror looking at herself.

"Wow, this is a good-looking woman," Nancy said.

"Got to agree there," Belle said feeling even more aroused. All Belle wanted to do was see Nancy naked again. And soon.

Very soon.

Belle and Nancy got Candice to turn to Evan on the bed, who was staring at her naked body with wide eyes.

"Get that television shut off," Candice said, her tone strict.

Evan scrambled to do that.

"You like what you see?" Candice asked. She stood in front of Evan, her legs spread, her hands on her hips, giving him a full look of her wonderful charms.

Just by doing that, Belle could sense how aroused Candice had become.

"I love what I see," Evan said.

"He would have to be a rock to not like what he's seeing," Belle said and Nancy laughed.

"Good," Candice said. "Now get out of those shorts and lay back. I'm doing the driving."

Evan just nodded like a puppy and hurriedly slipped off the shorts.

"I think we might want to get out of here and let them enjoy their evening," Nancy said, her voice sounding like she was almost panting.

"I agree," Belle said, feeling more aroused than she had felt in years and years. "How about we go enjoy our private evening together?"

"Now you are talking," Nancy said.

They both left Candice as Candice climbed on the bed and started to play with the already aroused Evan.

By the time Belle and Nancy had turned and headed for the door into the hallway, Candice had straddled Evan's crotch and let out a deep sigh.

"Now try to buck me off," Candice ordered her husband as Belle and Nancy went through the door.

All the way down the hallway to their suite Belle and Nancy laughed.

And held hands.

When they got back inside their suite, they headed right for the large bed, both taking off clothes as fast as they could.

And for Belle, that wasn't fast enough.

Eighteen

JEWEL AND TOMMY already had breakfast in the I-Hop and were sitting waiting by the time Belle and Nancy showed up, walking across the parking lot from the hotel hand-in-hand.

Jewel and Tommy had gotten up early and had already been in the restaurant for an hour. They had been planning how to teach the two new Ghost Agents and what was the next step. Jewel was happy that they had both agreed to give Belle and Nancy time here in Boise if they wanted to take it to settle affairs, say goodbye to some people, and so on.

Jewel knew that she and Tommy hadn't done that, but that didn't mean Belle and Nancy wouldn't want to.

Also, they had decided that for the moment, they wouldn't talk about the crazy mission that K.J. had mentioned about Santa Claus. That just seemed to not be worth the discussion until they knew more. And Jewel had a real hard time believing it as it was.

"Are we late?" Belle asked as she and Nancy came up to the table and sat down across from Jewel and Tommy.

"Nope, we were just up early and figured we'd just get some breakfast," Jewel said. "And make some plan for the next few weeks."

Both Belle and Nancy nodded.

"Wow, I'm hungry," Belle said, glancing around. "This place smells wonderful."

Jewel had to agree with that. From the smell of fresh coffee to cooking waffles and warm cinnamon rolls, she was almost ready for a second breakfast. And she had just finished eating fifteen minutes before.

"How are you keeping live people from sitting at this table?" Nancy asked glancing around at the half-full restaurant.

Jewel pointed at the hostess. "She has the table reserved for a special party, she thinks on orders from her boss."

"Perfect," Nancy said, nodding.

"I'm famished," Belle said, standing. "I'm going in search of some food, since no ghost waiters are around at the moment."

Jewel and Nancy both headed off to look at a tray of food a waitress had just brought out from the kitchen.

"They seem to be doing fine and catching on quickly," Jewel said.

Tommy nodded. "There is just something about being in this new ghost-place, which feels like we are actually alive. And as happened with us, they got to help someone yesterday on their first day to show the value of doing this."

Jewel could only nod agreement as both women brought back plates of food. Belle had an omelet and bacon and toast. Nancy had a waffle, eggs over easy, and toast.

Both plates smelled wonderful and Jewel couldn't believe she was getting hungry again. Food tasted so good in this ghost state, it was everything she could do to stay trim.

Belle and Nancy dropped their plates off in front of their chairs, laughing about something, and then went back to get orange juice and water.

After a moment they finally settled in.

Jewel and Tommy let them eat for a minute, talking about the incredible taste of their food before asking them the first question.

"What we do next is up to you," Jewel said. "We don't know if you want to stick around Boise and say goodbye to old friends and family or not."

"We talked about that in the shower this morning," Belle said. "We don't think so, unless you both think it would be a good idea."

Tommy shook his head and Jewel felt relieved.

"We didn't," Tommy said, "and we haven't missed that yet."

"I figure there is no real need for closure," Jewel said, "since this still feels alive and we aren't leaving this world."

"We came to the same conclusion," Belle said between bites. "We can always come back at any point, right?"

"You can," Jewel said. "And there is a lot of time between missions."

"So what do we do next?" Belle asked, "If we don't stick around?"

"I would say that after breakfast we get our baggage and head for the airport and jump a flight to Vegas," Jewel said. "Get you two settled into a place and practicing some of the new skills you have."

"Wonderful," Nancy said. "I love Vegas."

"We did a little practicing last night," Belle said.

"We went for a walk into other people's rooms," Nancy said, smiling. "We helped a couple having marriage trouble get their sex lives up and running again."

"Yeah, we were both inside the woman at one point, trying to get her to go seduce her husband," Belle said. "How come we could hear each other talk while inside the same person?"

Jewel just sat there, stunned. She honestly didn't know what to say.

She glanced at Tommy, who was also looking stunned. It had taken K.J. telling them they could both be inside the same person a week after they died before they figured that out. Yet Belle and Nancy had done it on their own last night.

"Did we do something wrong?" Belle asked, suddenly looking very worried.

"Oh, heavens, no," Jewel said. "It just took us a lot longer to figure out we could both be inside the same person at the same time is all. And how to do it."

"Actually," Tommy said, "we didn't figure it out. K.J. told us."

"We watched you two do it with that killer, remember?" Belle said.

Jewel nodded, remembering that was the case. But she was still surprised these two picked it up so quickly.

"So it was all right to help that couple?" Nancy asked.

"Oh, sure," Jewel said, still surprised at how far Belle and Nancy were in accepting their new world.

"Jewel saved a woman's life from cancer our first days in Vegas," Tommy said. "We got inside her and made her go to the hospital and demand to be screened."

"That must have felt great," Belle said, smiling at Jewel.

"It did, to be honest," Jewel said, remembering just how wonderful that felt.

"So I have one more question for the moment," Nancy said, finishing her plate of food and pushing the empty plate to the center of the table. "What happens to the dirty ghost dishes?"

"If we don't touch them after six hours or so," Tommy said, "they just vanish."

"So other people are going to be eating here with our dirty ghost dishes on the table?" Belle said, looking sort of disgusted.

"That's why we usually clean up our tables," Jewel said, laughing. "Dumping the dirty ghost dishes in with other dirty dishes. It just feels wrong to leave them unless we have no choice."

Nancy laughed and touched Belle's arm and both of them smiled.

There was no doubt to Jewel that Belle and Nancy had become a couple and were getting closer by the minute, which was wonderful to see.

Nineteen

BELLE FELT FULL, especially after going back for a cinnamon roll and splitting it with Nancy. The roll had tasted fantastic, better and more intense than any cinnamon roll Belle had eaten before, and she had eaten her share when married. Part of the thirty-five pounds she had gained while being so unhappy with the slug of a husband.

Now, as Jewel and Tommy did, Belle planned on doing a lot of exercising because she really didn't want to know if a ghost could gain weight or not.

She was really starting to like Jewel and Tommy more and more and the conversation over breakfast went from different things they could do to how Jewel and Tommy had met.

Then, just as they were about to stand and head for the hotel to get their things before going to the airport, K.J. appeared, looking fairly dapper in a blue three-piece suit, blue leather shoes and a white-gold earring in one ear.

Beside him stood a woman who took Belle's breath away, not because of the woman's beauty, but because the woman just radiated power.

She was a good ten inches taller than K.J., seeming to tower over the little man. The woman had on a stark gray business suit that fit her perfectly. She had her brown hair pulled back perfectly and no jewelry of any kind. Her face was angular, like a model's face, and her dark eyes seemed to see everything.

K.J., standing to one side and behind the woman, without saying anything, indicated with his hands that they should all stand up. Belle had only met K.J. a few times, but she had been around corporations enough to know when one person thought another person very powerful.

K.J. clearly thought this woman was powerful, of that there was no doubt.

All four of them quickly stood.

The woman smiled and reached out her hand to Jewel first. "I'm Laverne. I just wanted to meet the four of you before we all face what's coming up defending Nick."

"I'm Jewel," Jewel said.

The woman smiled and nodded. "I know. And you are Jewel's partner, Tommy."

Tommy shook the woman's hand. "Nice to meet you."

From what Belle could tell, neither Jewel nor Tommy knew who this woman was, but they clearly caught the same sense from K.J. that the woman was important.

Then the woman turned to look at Belle and Nancy.

To Belle, it was as if her entire life was suddenly known under this woman's intense gaze.

"I'm very sorry about the accident yesterday," Laverne said. "But the world's misfortune in losing both of you is our good fortune in this case. Welcome."

Belle shook Laverne's firm hand and managed to say, "Thank you."

"Yes, thank you," Nancy said, also shaking Laverne's hand.

Then Laverne turned back to K.J. "I'm hoping you can get this great team

up to speed quickly. We are going to need them."

"Is your team on this as well?" K.J. asked.

"Many teams are," Laverne said, "from many different branches of the gods. It's that important. I'm coordinating it all. And yes, Poker Boy and his team will also be trying to help out where possible."

"Wonderful," K.J. said, nodding. "We'll be ready for whatever you need us to do."

"Thank you," Laverne said. Then she turned to the four of them and said, "Nice meeting you all."

And then she vanished.

K.J. seemed to deflate like a kid's balloon with a hole in it. He barely managed to sit down in Tommy's chair at the table.

Belle and Nancy and Jewel sat back down and Tommy pulled over another chair.

Belle stared at the man who was supposed to be their boss. He was sweating and his hands were shaking. She couldn't imagine him having that reaction at all. From what Jewel and Tommy had said, K.J had been killed almost a hundred years ago and had been a Ghost Agent for all that time.

Jewel handed K.J. a glass of water and he managed with two hands to get it to his lips and not spill much on his blue suit.

"So who was that?" Tommy asked. "Never seen you have a reaction like this."

"That's the first time I have had the opportunity to meet Laverne," K.J. said, taking another drink of water and then finally putting the glass down.

"So Laverne's a powerful Ghost Agent?" Nancy asked.

K.J. shook his head. "Oh, no, she's very much alive, and has been that way for a hundred thousand years or more."

Now that rocked Belle back on her chair and she glanced at Nancy who looked just as shocked.

"Laverne is one of the most powerful gods there is," K.J. said. "She tends to run most everything these days and even more powerful gods often do as she asks."

"G o d s ?" Jewel asked.

Belle flat didn't know what to think.

"I told you my boss was a god, remember? And that building floating over Las Vegas you saw the first time we got down there is Poker Boy's office. He's just a superhero working for the gods, but a powerful one."

Both Jewel and Tommy nodded, but Belle had no idea what he was talking about. She was totally lost.

K.J. took another sip, then he said simply, "Laverne is Lady Luck herself."

"Lady Luck exists?" Nancy asked, clearly as stunned as Belle was feeling.

"You just met her," K.J. said, nodding. "Laverne is Lady Luck. I met her about thirty minutes before now for the first time. There are all sorts of meetings going on to try to figure out how to stop this problem with Santa Claus, or Nick as she calls him."

"What exactly is the problem?" Tommy asked. "Or do they not know yet."

"Oh, they know," K.J. said.

"Brigade behind this?" Jewel asked.

Belle glanced at Nancy who only shrugged. There was no doubt the two of them had a ton to learn.

K.J. laughed. "The Brigade could never pull this off. This is way, way bigger and more important. We don't even need to worry about the Brigade while this problem is going on."

Jewel turned to Belle and Nancy. "We'll explain the Brigade later."

Belle just nodded. There was a lot more than just that last few sentences to explain, starting off with meeting Lady Luck. And gods, and so much more.

"So what do people think is going to happen?" Tommy asked, "That we need to help stop?"

"Whoever is doing this isn't just going after old Nick," K.J. said. "If we or one of the other teams can't figure out what's happening and stop all this, Christmas, as we know it today in this country in this time period, will basically be erased from all the world's consciousness in all of history, as if it never existed."

"Oh," Tommy said, sitting back.

Belle looked at Nancy, who looked stunned and distant. Belle knew that Christmas had been very important to Nancy when she had been young, so this threat was hitting her close to home. Belle had liked Christmas as a kid, but found it annoying mostly as an adult without family.

"That's right," K.J. said. "If we don't stop this, not only won't there be a Santa Claus, but there won't even be a Christmas."

"And what's going to take its place?" Jewel asked.

"Nothing," K.J. said. "You see, Poker Boy and his team have saved the entire

> *K.J. took another sip, then he said simply, "Laverne is Lady Luck herself."*

planet at least a half-dozen times over the last five years."

"Seriously?" Tommy asked. "How?"

K.J. waved his question away. "Long stories for later. But let me just say that without Christmas, Poker Boy would not have come into the superhero world and thus, without Christmas, this world will cease to exist, destroyed because Poker Boy and his team weren't around to save it over and over and over."

"Oh," Jewel said.

And now, for the first time since she died yesterday, Belle actually felt afraid.

She reached over and took Nancy's hand.

Touching Nancy, Belle could feel herself calming a little.

But not much.

Twenty

BELLE AND NANCY quickly packed their things from their room.

They had walked from the restaurant back over to the hotel deciding they wouldn't talk about the coming problem until K.J. could explain a lot more about the world to them.

In fact, he was going to need to explain just about everything.

"Let's come back to this hotel when in Boise," Nancy said as they were leaving the room.

"I agree," Belle said. "That shower was wonderful."

"Bed wasn't bad," Nancy said, smiling and kissing Belle.

Belle kissed her back, and after a moment Nancy broke them apart. "We start that again and we'll never meet Jewel and Tommy to catch a flight to Vegas."

Belle had to agree, but didn't want to. She couldn't believe how much she loved kissing Nancy. And exploring that wonderful body of hers. Every touch felt wonderful, every kiss felt electrifying.

Belle never imagined she could feel like that with another person, let alone another woman. But it felt perfect and now she couldn't imagine not being intimate with Nancy.

And Belle had a hunch that had nothing to do with what had happened to them yesterday. They had been headed in this direction before, and more than likely it was only a matter of time and a few glasses of wine one night before it happened even if they had remained alive.

Now they didn't need wine. Belle could barely keep her hands off of Nancy and Nancy seemed to be the same way with her.

It was wonderful.

In front of the hotel the four of them managed to pile into the back of a hotel shuttle van heading for the airport. Belle and Nancy got into the very back seat while Jewel and Tommy into the center seat. The live person going to the airport was a gray-haired businessman who sat in the front seat and talked with the driver all the way about the weather and how he was going to miss summer.

Belle loved how much easier it was as a ghost to climb into a van like this. She didn't have to worry about bumping her head or hips or anything.

On the way to the airport, Jewel turned around in the seat so she could see them and gave them some pointers around navigating crowded areas.

"We do it two ways," Jewel said. "We either climb inside someone and have them take us."

"So everyone is our own personal cab?" Nancy asked and Belle laughed.

Both Jewel and Tommy both laughed while nodding.

"Pretty much," Jewel said. "Watch auras when climbing into someone, though. Black in an aura is a color you want to avoid. Stay with the brighter ones."

Belle nodded. That made sense. For a more enjoyable ride, it would be better to be inside a happy and active person where possible.

"We also just move along the walls," Jewel said. "Very few live people walk right beside a wall unless forced. And when we run into someone like that, we can always duck through the wall to avoid them."

Belle realized that Jewel was right. In crowded places such as airports, people stayed right to the center of the big areas.

"So problems with walking through people?" Nancy asked.

"None," Jewel said. "But every person you walk through or brush, you get their thoughts and memories. Granted, those thoughts and memories fade fast, but walking through the middle of a crowd could really get disconcerting."

"You ever tried that?" Belle asked.

Both Tommy and Jewel shook their heads.

"Better to ride inside just one person in that case," Jewel said.

At the airport, they bailed out of the van and moved quickly off the sidewalk and through the wall of the airport into the ticket area.

Boise had a very modern, but fairly small airport. A lot of flights out of this airport were private jets, but the airport itself had a good thirty gates.

Belle was pulling her ghost luggage, as was Nancy, and they moved to a place where they were out of traffic, but could see the departure schedule.

"Nothing heading directly for Vegas in the next seven hours," Tommy said, sounding disgusted.

"You know, this is silly," Jewel said, shaking her head. "And it's going to take us two planes and two airports to get to Vegas."

"Or waiting seven hours," Tommy said.

Belle had no idea what Jewel and Tommy were annoyed about. Boise was a small airport and it just didn't have that many direct flights to most places. As someone in her office had said about flying from Boise to another city: "You can't get there from here."

So Belle had been expecting this. She glanced at Nancy who just shrugged.

"K.J.," Jewel said into the air. "Little help."

After breakfast and meeting Lady Luck, K.J. had excused himself and vanished. He was clearly still shaken. Belle was starting to understand that K.J. might be their connection to the powers above them, but he was a very gentle soul who got upset easily.

K.J. appeared a moment later, still in his blue suit. He looked like he had a little more color to his face than he had an hour before.

"No direct flight to Vegas in the next seven hours," Jewel said. "We're going to waste an entire day just getting home."

"Now that's just stupid," K.J. said. "What airport doesn't have a direct flight to Vegas?"

"This one," Tommy said.

Belle and Nancy both laughed.

"So how about a ride back to the Golden Nugget where you got us from?"

"You want to leave these two to make their own way there?" K.J. asked, pointing to Belle and Nancy. Then he smiled and winked at them.

A moment later the five of them were standing out of the way in what looked like a moderate-sized buffet.

Belle felt instantly comfortable here. The colors were oak and browns and gold. There were lots of empty tables and numbers of booths overlooking through huge windows what appeared to be a large pool a story below. And the smell of ham and bacon and fresh bread was wonderful.

How could she be hungry? They had only finished that large breakfast just over an hour or so ago.

"Thank you," Jewel said, smiling at K.J.

"Back to meetings," K.J. said. "Who knew being dead had so many meetings?"

"Keep us informed," Tommy said.

"Oh, trust me," K.J. said, "you're going to see a lot of me, just to try to explain the person that you met this morning, let alone try to stop the end of the world."

Tommy and Jewel nodded.

"Get these two settled into a suite here and started on their training," K.J. said. "I'll check back in tomorrow over breakfast, right here at nine. I'll try to explain some of what I know is happening."

With that he was gone.

"Welcome to Las Vegas," Jewel said, smiling at Belle and Nancy.

"Best flight I ever had," Nancy said.

"Are we going to learn how to do that?" Belle asked. She had no doubt it would be wonderful if she and Nancy could just teleport all over the place when needed.

"K.J. says we will," Tommy said. "But he hasn't taught us how yet."

"Maybe we're supposed to learn to do it on our own," Belle said.

Jewel and Tommy just sort of stared at her with that.

Twenty-one

THEY GOT to the big, oak front desk of the Golden Nugget by mostly staying to the edge of the hallways against the walls as they moved through the casino. Jewel managed to only brush a couple people in an area crowded with slot machines. And none of the people she brushed were anything but normal people with normal problems enjoying a few days in Las Vegas.

Belle brushed two or three people as well and each time had to stop and shake her head. Nancy seemed to be handling the other people's memories better than Belle, but Jewel could tell that Nancy was still bothered a few times.

They stood off to one side out of any traffic pattern near one end of the big check-in desk. The desk ran for a good fifty feet filling one wall and at the moment had a good ten employees working terminals behind the counter.

A line of patrons snaked back and forth in the big lobby between two huge pillars, controlled by thick ropes.

"I think she's the supervisor," Tommy said, pointing to a woman at a terminal at one end of the counter helping a woman with a wide flower-hat and shorts.

"So what are we going to do?" Belle asked.

"Big casinos like this one," Tommy said, "have beautiful suites that are held back in case a large gambler shows up. The suites are never rented out, only comp'd."

"The stated price on some of the suites is a thousand dollars a night or more," Jewel said. "Makes the hotshot gamblers dropping money feel pampered."

"Wow," Belle said. "Who knew?"

"So I'm going to climb inside that supervisor," Jewel said, "and get her to hold a comp suite for a few days that you two can use until we find you something better. And I need to hold the suite so no one can ever trace that this supervisor did it because we don't want to get her in trouble."

"Can I watch?" Nancy asked.

"Sure," Jewel said. "It would be great learning for you."

And since Nancy was so good at computers, this is exactly the kind of thing she needed to be learning.

"Think the woman can hold three of us?" Belle asked.

Jewel looked at both Nancy and Belle and shrugged. Since it had only been her and Tommy before, it never occurred to her that three Ghost Agents could occupy one person's body.

"Might as well try to find out," Jewel said, laughing.

She turned to Tommy. "Want to try to join us as well?"

Tommy just shook his head and smiled that smile that Jewel loved so much. "No thanks. Three women inside another woman seems a tad beyond my range of kinky."

Belle and Nancy laughed and Jewel kissed him. Then she said to him, "Watch the luggage."

Jewel turned to Belle and Nancy. "Come on, girls, let's go see how many people we can pack into a poor desk supervisor."

"What am I watching the luggage for?" Tommy said. "Ghost crooks?"

Jewel glanced back over her shoulder at Tommy as she and Belle and Nancy headed for the front desk of the hotel.

"No, dear," Jewel said, giving him a wink. "Just trying to make you feel useful."

Tommy stuck his tongue out at her as all three of them laughed and kept walking.

The three of them went through the front desk and stood off to one side until the moment the supervisor was done with the woman with the big hat. Then Jewel stepped inside the supervisor and made herself smaller.

The supervisor was named Carrie and was originally from St. Louis, but had moved out here with her boyfriend, who then dropped her and went home. She had decided to stay and really loved her job and the nightlife of Vegas.

Carrie's goal was to work her way up in the hotel business and in a year she had made great progress.

A moment later Nancy joined Jewel inside the supervisor.

"Make yourself smaller," Jewel said.

"Got it," Nancy said.

A moment later Belle joined them. "This the right place for the party?"

Nancy and Jewel laughed.

"How can I hear you both in here?" Belle asked.

"K.J. explained to me," Jewel said, "that we exist on a slightly different plane of existence. So what happens on the other plane, the real world plane, doesn't bother us. When inside another person, we can interact with the real plane because people have ghost elements as well as everything, but that's about all."

"So we could be standing inside a stone wall," Belle said, "and be able to hear each other and sense each other like this."

"Exactly," Jewel said.

Jewel showed Belle and Nancy how to take over the woman's movements.

"Is she going to remember any of this?" Nancy asked.

"Not a bit of it," Jewel said. She then had the supervisor bring up on her computer the available suites. As Jewel had expected, there were at least ten open, all waiting for major customers to arrive. None of the suites were reserved or even shown to regular guests or the reservations department.

Jewel knew from the woman's mind how to reserve those suites and how most reservations for those suites came down from either corporate or the casino floor or the sales departments.

"Can I try driving?" Nancy asked.

Jewel knew that both Nancy and Belle could read the same knowledge from the supervisor's mind, and since both of them were much better at computers and corporations, this was again a great training exercise.

"I'll release control of the supervisor's body," Jewel said. "Just feel what you want and you should be able to control her."

Jewel eased back and Nancy took control as if she had been doing it for a very long time.

"Perfect," Jewel said.

The next thing Jewel knew, the supervisor's fingers were flying over the keyboard and screens were flashing up and then vanishing.

"There," Belle said.

Nancy stopped. "Perfect."

Then again the supervisor's fingers were flying over the keyboard, and a moment later Nancy said, "Done. Printing keys to hold back in the reserve drawer."

Jewel wasn't sure what Nancy had done, it had all happened so fast. As a doctor, Jewel had been sort of experienced with computers, but only enough to get by with modern medical treatments and getting e-mail and other web activities.

"So what just happened?" Jewel asked as the supervisor got the two keys, slipped them into an envelope, printed the room number on the envelope and dropped it in a back drawer, tucked in where it would not be noticed easily.

"I went into corporate," Nancy said, "untraceable, of course."

"Good," Jewel said.

"And she found the perfect person to have a room reserved," Belle said.

"Actually," Nancy said, "you spotted it. This casino, as most major corporations, has a sales and banking branch not located in Las Vegas. I had one of the major vice presidents in the corporate division send in this request to hold the room for five days."

"The request came from his personal computer," Belle said, laughing.

"He's in Japan at the moment and won't be back for a week," Nancy said, "so I made it look like a prank hack just got through is all."

Jewel just felt stunned. Together, these two were going to be unstoppable.

Nancy cleared all evidence from the computer and all trails other than the request coming from corporate. Carrie, the supervisor looked like she had done exactly as she should have done.

"Perfect," Jewel said. "You two are amazing."

"Thanks," Nancy said.

"That's nothing for her," Belle said. "She's that good."

"And from the sounds of it," Jewel said, "we may need that good."

"Thanks," Nancy said. "Can I give Carrie our host here a few suggestions on how to move up this corporate ladder a little faster?"

"By all means," Jewel said. She showed both Belle and Nancy how to influence future actions of a person and Nancy gave their supervisor host a few suggestions on some information. And Belle gave their host a couple of ways to act in meetings to gain power in corporation settings.

Jewel just shook her head. None of this stuff was anything she had ever guessed went on. She had been really, really sheltered in her medical education, that was for sure.

"So let's go rescue Tommy from all the luggage," Jewel said, laughing as the two women finished with the supervisor.

"He had a tough job," Belle said.

"But someone had to do it," Jewel said, laughing as she emerged from the supervisor's body and smiled at the wonderful man she loved more than anything in any world.

Twenty-two

BELLE AND NANCY made their way to their suite in the Rush Tower of the Golden Nugget Hotel pulling their suitcases while Jewel and Tommy headed to their home in the University area about two miles away. Belle had no idea how they had managed to get a home that didn't always have people coming and going from it, but she would ask them later.

All four of them were to meet for a late lunch back at the buffet in two hours. So much had happened this morning already, Belle couldn't believe it was only a little after noon Las Vegas time.

And she really couldn't believe that she and Nancy had only been dead for about a day. Belle hadn't felt bad at all about dying and was enjoying the new freedom of this new existence more than she wanted to admit.

For some reason, not being upset about her own death bothered her. But not enough to ruin her growing good mood.

And she was really enjoying being with Nancy. Belle was so glad the two of them had decided to take their friendship to the next level. It felt so right in so many ways.

"Wow!" Nancy said as they walked through the door into their suite.

And Belle had to agree. This suite was amazing and very, very comfortable. The suite was decorated in oak and brown tones, with soft couches and chairs in a huge living room area near an oak wet bar. The floor was covered in plush carpet and the room had tall ceilings and windows that seemed to just go on and on.

Right now the natural desert light gave the room a warm glow.

"I might never leave this room," Belle said.

"Wait until you see what's in here," Nancy said, indicating a door to the left. Beyond the door was a huge bedroom, with two closets and a bed that seemed far bigger than any king-sized bed that Belle had ever seen.

Nancy put her suitcase against one closet door, then headed for the bathroom with Belle following her.

"Now that's going to be fun," Nancy said, pointing to a huge jet tub that filled a corner of the room under a huge window that looked out over Las Vegas.

"That it will," Belle said, smiling at her.

A glass-walled shower filled the other corner that was larger than some bedrooms Belle had seen.

"The toilet seat is down, thankfully," Nancy said, laughing and pointing.

"Well, that makes it perfect," Belle said.

And it was perfect as far as she was concerned.

She moved over and took Nancy into her arms. Nancy put her arms around Belle's neck and just melted against her.

"You sure feel wonderful for a dead woman," Belle said.

Nancy laughed. "I'm feeling a little guilty about being in such a good mood after dying so recently."

"Yeah, me too," Belle said. "Should we be mourning or something?"

"Can't see much reason for that," Nancy said, "since it sure feels like we are still alive."

"Actually," Belle said, "it feels better."

And she pulled Nancy tighter and kissed her.

After a moment Nancy pulled back slightly and smiled. "We have over an hour until we have to be back down to the buffet. You want to break in the tub, the shower, or the bed?"

Belle laughed and then kissed the woman she was falling even deeper in love with.

Finally she pulled away enough to say, "How about the shower and the bed."

"Perfect," Nancy said, kissing her back as hard as Belle could remember ever being kissed.

The kiss was wonderful.

And an hour and a half later, they were only five minutes late to lunch, which Belle considered a minor miracle.

Twenty-three

JEWEL WAS IMPRESSED at how fast Belle and Nancy picked up being

Ghost Agents. They seemed to need to only be guided once and then they would run with the idea from there.

They met for lunch, then the four of them spent the afternoon moving all over Las Vegas, working on controlling people, hiding inside people, and just learning all the basics.

As they moved around, Jewel and Tommy explained what they knew about the overall world, which they admitted, wasn't much at all.

And at one point Jewel pointed out the floating office that was Poker Boy's office. "It's invisible to everyone but us, I guess," Jewel said.

Belle was stunned at the square, glass-encased room just floating way up there.

"The view from there must be stunning," Nancy said.

Jewel was also impressed at how Belle and Nancy just loved to laugh and loved being ghosts. And they clearly loved each other as well. They seemed to always be touching in one form or another, which made Jewel realize that she and Tommy were the same way. They also always touched and laughed a lot.

They all decided that instead of trying to find a restaurant, they would just go back for comfort food at the Golden Nugget buffet and talk about all they had done during the day. They were to meet K.J. in the same place in the morning with more information. Jewel was fairly convinced he would be happy at the progress Belle and Nancy had made.

They worked their way back to the Golden Nugget buffet and by seven in the evening were talking and eating.

Then Jewel noticed Nancy looking at the entrance beyond the cash register to the buffet. There was a small lobby out there beyond a planter wall with low green plants that divided the entrance area at the top of an escalator from the restaurant. There were three empty booths along the planter wall and no one in the lobby area that Jewel could see.

"Something out there?" Jewel finally asked, glancing over her shoulder.

"No, nothing," Nancy said, laughing. "I just keep thinking that K.J. expects us to learn all this on our own, for the most part, right?"

Jewel nodded. "Drove us crazy at first."

"And Tommy keeps asking him to teach you how to teleport, right?"

Jewel looked at Tommy and he nodded.

Jewel had no idea where this was going.

"So I'm going to go out to the lobby," Nancy said, squeezing Belle's hand. "Be right back."

And then she just vanished.

"Oh, shit!" Belle said.

Then Belle waved and smiled.

Jewel and Tommy spun around.

Jewel flat couldn't believe it.

Nancy was standing in the lobby.

Then she vanished.

And she was again sitting next to Belle, who hugged her long and hard as Jewel and Tommy turned back around.

Jewel just stared at Nancy. She could think of nothing to say.

Flat nothing.

"My turn," Belle said, laughing.

She stared at the lobby behind Jewel and an instant later she vanished.

Nancy laughed and waved "hi" and then before Jewel could turn back around, Belle was back in her seat.

"Damn this is fun," Nancy said, the smile on her face so big it looked to Jewel like it might hurt.

Jewel just glanced at Tommy, who looked completely shocked. Finally, Jewel leaned forward. "How did you do that?"

"We're dead, right?" Nancy asked.

Jewel and Tommy nodded. Jewel had no idea what had just happened, but she really, really wanted to know, so she said nothing.

"So all day we've been walking through walls and doors and sides of cars and climbing in and out of people, right?" Nancy asked.

Again Jewel and Tommy just nodded.

"So we're not really restricted by physical laws that much if we don't want to be," Nancy said. "So I just believed I was standing in the lobby and I was."

"That's all I did as well," Belle said. "I just knew I was standing in the lobby."

Jewel opened her mouth to say something and flat couldn't think of anything to say yet again.

Tommy nodded and turned around and glanced at the lobby. Then he vanished.

He waved from the lobby and then reappeared.

"Give it a try," Tommy said, touching her. "It's as easy as they say it is."

Jewel nodded, doing her best to not think about anything. She felt the same as she had felt right after they had died. Scared and puzzled at the same time.

She glanced back at the lobby and then just knew she was standing there.

And suddenly she was standing there, right in front of a group of overweight tourists in far too tight shorts coming at her like a herd of cattle. She was between them and their food.

She knew she was sitting at the table again and she was.

Belle and Nancy applauded and Tommy gave her a long kiss.

"That's going to take some practice," Jewel said, laughing.

"Tomorrow," Tommy said.

"And there's one more thing Nancy and I were talking about before lunch that we wondered about," Belle said.

"What's that?" Tommy asked.

"After that I'm almost afraid to ask," Jewel said, shaking her head. And she was. These two women were clearly two of the smartest and quickest thinkers she had ever met. And they didn't seem to think they had any restrictions at all.

Which it seemed they didn't.

"We have been wondering why we can't do this?" Nancy asked.

Slowly, as Jewel and Tommy watched, both Belle and Nancy, hand-in-hand, just floated up off their chairs about five feet and then drifted back down.

Jewel had her mouth open.

And for the third time in just a few minutes, there was not a damn thing she could say.

Finally Tommy said, "K.J., some help here."

"We didn't do anything wrong, did we?" Belle asked, suddenly very worried.

"Oh, heavens, no," Tommy said, shaking his head. "I just need some explaining from K.J."

Jewel was still doing her best to just catch her breath. She had just watched the two new recruits teleport and then fly.

"Thirty seconds," K.J.s voice came out of thin air.

"Do me a favor," Tommy said, smiling. "Float up there near the ceiling until K.J. gets here."

Both Belle and Nancy laughed and a moment later Jewel watched the two women float up to the ceiling.

"Smells wonderful up here," Belle said to Jewel and Tommy.

"Yeah," Nancy said, "We going for seconds shortly."

At that both of them giggled as K.J. arrived and glanced around. "I thought you had the two new agents with you."

"We do," Tommy said. "And that's what we want to talk with you about."

Jewel just smiled at K.J. and pointed upward.

K.J. glanced up as Belle and Nancy waved and then came floating back down to their chairs.

"Oh, shit," K.J. said, softly. "How did you two do that?"

"I'm betting it is sort of the same way they showed us how to do this," Tommy said.

An instant later all five of them were standing in the middle of the lobby.

Then they were back at the table.

K.J. barely managed to pull up a chair and sit down before his knees gave out and he fell down.

"What's wrong?" Jewel asked.

"It took me over thirty years to learn how to teleport," K.J. said, "and I never knew Ghost Agents could fly."

"That's all right," Jewel said and patted K.J.'s hand. She winked at Belle and Nancy. "That's what you get for recruiting two really smart women."

Twenty-four

BELLE MOSTLY JUST LISTENED, sitting, holding Nancy's hand, as K.J. gave them some tips on how to teleport to places they couldn't really visualize.

"You sort of slow down time right as you arrive," he said. "Saves you landing inside something you don't want to be inside of."

He pointed to a woman walking at a normal pace and then suddenly she was frozen where she stood and all the sound and everything vanished.

Then she moved and the sounds of the restaurant and people talking and background music came smashing back in.

Belle just sort of shook her head. It hadn't felt that noisy in here until all noise was taken away.

"This isn't actually stopping time," K.J. said, "No one can do that, but you can move between instants of time. When you teleport long distances to a place you can't visualize, do it between instants of time and that way if you land in a wrong spot, you can adjust before coming back into time."

"And we can all do that?" Nancy asked.

K.J. nodded. "Since you learned how to fly and it never dawned on me to try that, I'm sure you can. Just imagine stepping between instants of time. Nancy, you first and take us all with you by imagining a bubble around this table."

Nancy nodded and a moment later the sounds vanished and the few people in the buffet froze.

"Wow, this is nifty," she said, squeezing Belle's hand.

Then the sounds came back and K.J. pointed to Belle.

She took a deep breath and just imagined a bubble around the table and that bubble slipping between a flow of time, like a rock in a river.

Again the sounds vanished and everyone else in the buffet froze.

"Wonderful," Nancy said and kissed her.

Belle had never imagined feeling this powerful. She was suddenly like a superhero. She could teleport, slip between moments of time, fly, walk through walls, and control people inside their minds. All that while being dead.

K.J. spent the next half hour training them and giving all of them pointers on teleporting. Then he finally just looked at Belle and Nancy. "You got everything I know, how about teaching me how to fly like that."

Belle looked at Nancy who just shrugged. "Same principle," Belle said.

Nancy nodded. "Exactly. Which was what gave us the idea it was possible. We are not restricted by physical world limitations that much. So why should gravity restrict us."

"So we just imagined ourselves floating," Belle said, "and we were, just as with the teleporting and the going between instants of time."

K.J. nodded and a moment later floated up off his chair, drifted around the room for a few moments and then came back to the table, never once moving his legs or touching the ground.

Tommy and Jewel did the same thing next, both smiling like they had been given the perfect gift.

K.J. nodded as Tommy and Jewel returned to their chairs. "I have another meeting tomorrow and I'll report to the powers-that-be that you four are ready for action and can do all this now."

"So any leads on the big problem with Christmas?" Tommy asked just an instant before Belle could. She was loving this new state of existence. She didn't want it to end anytime soon, let alone have the entire world end as well. She couldn't even begin to imagine how that could happen.

"Nothing," K.J. said, his voice low and worried. "I'll meet you back here for breakfast after my meeting."

At that he vanished.

After a moment Belle looked at Nancy. "Ready for seconds?"

"I am famished," Nancy said.

"Should we fly, walk, or teleport to the buffet?" Belle asked, laughing.

Both Jewel and Tommy just shook their heads as Nancy said, "Teleport."

And an instant later they were standing in front of some of best-smelling prime rib Belle could imagine.

Twenty-five

THE NEXT MORNING, Jewel and Tommy had jumped from their home to the buffet and were both loading up plates when K.J. arrived and started doing the same. A moment later Belle and Nancy appeared, both with wet hair. Jewel was amazed at how both looked so radiant and happy.

While Jewel and Tommy wore jeans and cotton shirts with light jackets, Belle and Nancy both had on white shorts that showed off their long legs and trim figures. They both wore fluffy silk blouses and matching-colored tennis shoes. Belle's blouse was blue, Nancy's a light green. They had clearly done some shopping after leaving the restaurant last night.

Jewel had never seen such enjoyment in two people before. Not a word about being killed a few days before, not a sour word about the mission. They just always seemed to be smiling and laughing and figuring out new stuff, which was wonderful.

In college and medical school, she had never really been around people like them before. All her friends and other students were always taking everything in life very seriously. Being around Belle and Nancy was like a wonderful breath of fresh air and they made her smile even more.

K.J. today was dressed in a robin's-egg-blue three-piece silk suit with a bright red tie and bright red sneakers. The bright red handkerchief sticking out of his breast pocket seemed to pull it all together somehow.

Belle complimented him on his look as she got a waffle and he bowed and smiled in appreciation.

Jewel took her standard scrambled eggs, a slice of ham, and toast with strawberry jelly, then jumped to a table near the back and off to one side that she doubted anyone would sit at. The buffet wasn't that busy this morning even though it was a Saturday. There were only about forty people scattered around the huge space.

After everyone had food and were eating, Tommy asked K.J. if there was any progress.

"Nothing," K.J. said. "But we do have some sort of timeline."

"The timeline done by the people who can look out ahead in time some?" Jewel asked.

K.J. nodded. "The world will come to an end on the first day of December if we don't stop this."

"What day is it now?" Belle asked as Jewel tried to remember the date.

"November 15th," K.J. said. "We have fifteen days."

Jewel sort of stared at her eggs and no one said a word. Only fifteen days and not even the most powerful of powerful had a clue what was going to happen. What could she do to help? She felt helpless.

As she finally forced herself to take another bite of eggs, all sounds in the restaurant cut off and all the live people froze.

Laverne, Lady Luck herself, appeared near K.J. and he stood so quickly he almost went over backwards.

Laverne was again wearing a gray silk business suit that fit her perfectly and her hair was pulled back giving her face a stern appearance.

Jewel stood almost as fast, as did Tommy and the two women.

"Sorry to bother your breakfast," Laverne said, "but I need you five to come with me to listen to a meeting. Nothing may come of it, but meetings at this point with Poker Boy and his team tend to bring up questions that lead to answers."

"Will they be able to see us?" Tommy asked.

"I doubt it," Laverne said. "Just listen and give me any ideas you might have."

A moment later all six of them were standing in a large room with what looked to be a fifties diner booth filling the middle of the room. The floor was a black and white checkered tile and the seats of the booth were bright red vinyl.

All four walls of the room were floor to ceiling windows. The entire room appeared to be floating a thousand feet above the center of the Las Vegas strip. Jewel could see planes on approach to the airport directly even with the room.

To Jewel the view was stunning, but if not for the wood railing along the inside of the glass, she would have felt as if she would fall out of the room at any moment.

There was nothing else in the room but the booth and some chairs.

"Poker Boy's office," K.J. said as Laverne nodded to them and stepped toward the table, leaving them standing about three steps away to listen.

There were six people already at the table.

"Poker Boy is the one in the fedora-like hat and leather jacket," K.J. said. "The woman with the long brown hair sitting beside him is his girlfriend, Patty Ledgerwood, aka Front Desk Girl."

At that moment Patty turned and looked back at them, frowning slightly before turning back to face the table. Jewel wondered if Patty had somehow sensed them.

Poker Boy looked to be in his mid-thirties and had an expressionless face and a square jaw. Patty was just stunning in her beauty, almost a classic Greek look.

Everyone at the table seemed to be working on a number of huge milkshakes. Poker Boy and Patty were sharing a vanilla one.

"The man with the rolled-up sleeves on the other side of Poker Boy is called Screamer," K.J. said. "And the woman next to him is Sherrie, one of Laverne's daughters and Screamer's wife. All four of them are superheroes. Poker Boy works for the gambling side of things. Patty works for the gods of hospitality, Sherrie works for the gods of food and beverage, and Screamer works for the gods of law enforcement."

"Wow, there are a lot of gods," Belle said, the same thing Jewel was thinking.

"You have no idea," K.J. said. "The man in the tan button-down sweater across from Patty is Stan, the God of Poker and the elderly looking man beside him is Lamplighter Ben, a god in the knowledge and books area. He used to be the God of Lamplighters when that profession existed."

Jewel watched as Lady Luck pulled up a chair to the end of the big booth and asked, "Any ideas at all?"

"We have The Bookkeeper running the numbers as fast as he can," Poker Boy said. "So far nothing."

Jewel had no idea who The Bookkeeper was and didn't want to ask K.J. at the moment. She imagined he was another superhero or god of accounting or something.

"And nothing from any other angle either," Screamer said.

"There doesn't seem to be a motive here at all that we can find," Patty said. "Nick has some enemies, sure, but even his known enemies are worried and trying to help on this one."

Jewel glanced at Tommy who seemed to just be listening intently.

Beside him both Belle and Nancy were doing the same thing. K.J. was shifting from foot to foot nervously.

"I don't think this is aimed at Nick," Poker Boy said. He turned to Laverne. "What would be left after this world was destroyed if we hadn't saved it that first time from being chewed up by the cross-dimensional insect things?"

Laverne shook her head. "Nothing, really. The gods that could would have escaped to other dimensions at the last moment to live in exile. The Earth of this dimension would have been a barren wasteland. Nothing at all to gain for anyone wanting that to happen."

"So no one gains," Stan said, shaking his head. "So we're back to square one."

"Not really," Poker Boy said. "We know that no one would gain, and I am convinced that destroying the world has nothing to do with attacking Nick. So what we have left is an accident."

"It's not intentional?" Patty asked.

Poker Boy just nodded. "That's what I would bet."

"Great," Screamer said, "someone is going to destroy the world by accident."

Jewel watched as Poker Boy turned and directly faced Laverne. "When you said that all of Christmas will be erased from all memories and all of time, how is that possible?"

"Sort of the same way we can see this coming," Laverne said. "All of life is connected in one fashion or another. There is a vast network of energy that connects us all in many different ways and on many different levels. Some of us see the connections and can use them, as all of you do in your own ways with your own powers."

"So it is along these life connections that Christmas will be erased?" Patty asked.

Laverne nodded.

Beside Jewel, Nancy and Belle both laughed.

She glanced at them.

"Life is a giant computer," Nancy said. "Who knew?"

"More like a giant internet among all life forms," Belle said.

"And the life computer has a virus, or more than likely a worm," Nancy said, shaking her head.

"A worm set to erase Christmas," Belle said.

Laverne turned away from the table and looked at them. "A worm?"

All six live people at the table with Laverne looked stunned and surprised to have Laverne talk to someone they couldn't see.

Jewel knew what a worm or computer virus was. Sort of. But she sure would never have thought of it.

Tommy was nodding slightly and K.J. just looked puzzled.

"We can explain it," Belle said.

"I'm about 99% sure that's what is going on," Nancy said.

"Trust them on that," Jewel said to Laverne. "I've seen them work on a computer and it's magic in the best way."

The First Four Seeders Universe Novels
Available at your favorite booksellers.

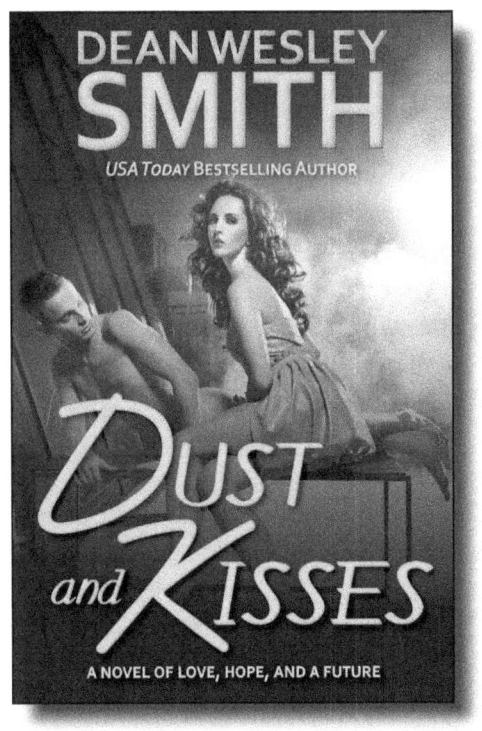

"Now you just need to figure out who can work on the big computer of life," Belle said.

Laverne started to open her mouth, then shut it and just stared at them.

Jewel wasn't sure if that was a good thing or a bad thing.

Section Four
CAN ANYONE SAVE CHRISTMAS?

Twenty-six

BELLE FELT OVERJOYED to figure out what the problem was they were all facing. She had no idea how all of life could be hooked together, but it sort of made sense when she thought of it.

And it really made sense considering what they were learning since she and Nancy had died.

From everything people had been saying about the problem, wiping a memory from everyone, wiping out an entire history, sure felt like wiping a hard drive of a computer. Or corrupting data in a cloud storage.

And Nancy knew computers better than anyone alive or dead and she saw the same thing clearly. Something had gotten into life's connections and was going to eat at the memory of Christmas, deleting it.

Belle had no idea how that was possible, but she also didn't know how she could be here after being killed and how an invisible office could float above

Las Vegas. So something that seemed impossible before might be very likely, considering everything.

Laverne turned back to the table of live superheroes and gods and said, "I invited some guests to this meeting. Have you ever heard of the Ghost of a Chance Agency?"

Only the older god named Ben nodded.

"Wow, we are super secret, aren't we?" Jewel said to K.J. and he just shrugged.

"We recruit for the Ghost of a Chance Agency some very special people right after they die," Laverne said. "There are less than one thousand agents in the entire world helping solve problems in a similar manner that you all do. Five of the best Ghost Agents are standing with us right now. And two of them have come up with an idea that might be the solution."

"And we can't see them because they are ghosts?" Poker Boy asked.

"I could sense them," Patty said, nodding.

"That's correct," Laverne said. "They do the same job we all do, only just outside of the living world. But they exist and work in the living world."

Laverne waved her hand and Belle couldn't feel anything different, but suddenly all six at the table sort of sat back.

Laverne motioned that the five Ghost Agents should come a little closer. "This is Jewel, Tommy, K.J., Belle, and Nancy."

Each of them raised their hand slightly as Laverne introduced them. Belle felt a little like she was in school being introduced for the first time.

Then Laverne looked at Belle and Nancy with her penetrating dark eyes. "Explain again what you just said to me."

Belle shrugged. "If life, all life, at all levels, is hooked together in some fashion, that would mimic the connections in both a corporation and a computer or internet system."

"Somehow, someone," Nancy said, "either by accident, or with another purpose, infected the life connections with a virus or a worm that would travel along those connections and remove Christmas from all consciousness."

"More than likely not realizing the consequences of the action," Belle said.

All six at the table were nodding and clearly thinking. Belle was impressed. It was no wonder this team had saved the world four or five times already. Even having five ghosts appear in front of them didn't faze them from the task at hand.

Poker Boy looked at Laverne. "Who would have access to this life computer in any fashion at all?"

"You all do with your powers," Laverne said. "But in limited ways, which is why powers are limited."

"So let's start with a logical place first," Poker Boy said. "Who hates Nick enough who has the capability to try to erase his name from the life connections?"

"Krampus," Ben said. "The horned devil of Christmas."

Laverne shook her head. "Kramp and Nick play chess three times per week now and Kramp helps Nick and the rest of the elves with the last minute preparations each year. They are best friends and have been for centuries now."

Ben nodded.

"But didn't Christmas sort of overshadow the Krampus Day celebrations in the past?" K.J. asked, surprising Belle. "I seemed to remember that from my history somewhere and some great Krampus parties a few years back."

"They did," Ben said, nodding. "But that was far, far before the modern Christmas traditions came about."

Poker Boy glanced at K.J. and then back to Laverne. "Does Krampus have a son or daughter?"

"Flick," Laverne said, nodding slowly, clearly thinking. "He's a god in the entertainment and party world and through his father's connections might have enough access to understand the larger scale of things."

Laverne stood. "Thank you one and all. I'm going to go talk with Nick and Kramp and get their take on this, and then see if we can find Flick."

"Don't forget to turn us back invisible, please," K.J. said.

She smiled. "I didn't change your status. I just allowed them to see you is all."

With that she returned the five of them to their table in the buffet, where the wonderful smell of eggs and bacon hit Belle and she realized she just hadn't had much breakfast before all that started.

"Anyone have any idea who exactly Krampus is or was?" Jewel asked.

All five of them shook their heads.

"They were some great parties, though," K.J. said as he sank into the same chair he had earlier, almost shaking.

Belle glanced around at the live people in the room. One good-looking woman with long silver hair was sitting at a table munching on a light breakfast and working on her laptop computer.

She pointed the woman out to Nancy, who nodded.

Belle watched as Nancy transported over to her, melded with her, and a minute later, after the woman's fingers were done flying over the computer, emerged.

"I'll explain who Krampus is after we all get more food," Nancy said, appearing back at their table. "I have a hunch we're going to need it very shortly."

Belle could only agree to that and hand-in-hand, she and Nancy walked to the food area of the buffet.

Twenty-seven

JEWEL WAS GLAD that Nancy let them get something more to eat before explaining Krampus. They were all almost finished eating when Nancy finally told them what she had found out about Krampus, how his holiday had been taken over by Christmas, mostly in Europe hundreds of years before.

"He looks like what many modern pictures of the devil would look like," Nancy said, "with long horns and no red suit or pitchfork."

"Wonderful," K.J. said, shaking his head. "I wore a costume to a party that looked like that, only the horns were detachable sex toys."

All four of them laughed and Jewel could feel the mood lifting again.

"Laverne says they are friends now," Jewel said after Nancy explained about the good kids and bad kids. Good kids were rewarded by Santa, the bad kids were taken by the horned Krampus.

"Wouldn't surprise me," Nancy said, shrugging. "But what has me puzzled is how anyone gets access to the life connections, or even can see them."

Jewel pointed to the woman with the laptop. "You can't see the internet and the connections, but you used it and got into it through an access portal."

"Maybe life has access portals?" Tommy said, glancing at K.J.

K.J waved his hands in defense. "Don't look at me. I died a hundred years ago, remember. I'm not even sure what the Internet is."

Again all four of them laughed and Jewel patted K.J.'s arm.

"I got a thought," Nancy said. "Jewel, Tommy, would you release your auras?"

Jewel glanced at Tommy who only shrugged. She imagined her aura free from being held against her body.

Tommy did the same thing.

"Holy crap," K.J. said, covering his eyes.

"Might want to move back about fifteen feet," Nancy said, laughing.

Belle nodded. "This is like looking into a spotlight."

So Jewel and Tommy stood and moved back so they were standing just near one of the main aisles to get into the food area. Jewel had no idea why, but at this point she was really starting to trust Nancy and Belle and their ideas.

Both Nancy and Belle just stared at them. Finally Belle said, "There!"

And she pointed to something above Jewel and Tommy.

Jewel looked up, but could see nothing but the bright colors around her.

A moment later Nancy and Belle were floating over them.

"Stay as you are until we return, would you?" Belle asked.

"We're here," Tommy said.

Jewel watched as both of them looked at something for a moment and then turned upward, clearly following something Jewel could not see.

They hovered about twenty feet in the air over the large room and looked around. Both of them were pointing and indicating different things.

Jewel didn't want to break their concentration, so she just stood there watching without saying anything.

Tommy did the same.

Then Belle and Nancy vanished out through the roof of the room, clearly following something.

Jewel just stayed where she was. So did Tommy beside her.

"Anyone have any idea what they are doing?" K.J. asked, staring up at the ceiling from his position at the table with all the dirty dishes.

"My guess," Jewel said, "is that they are like electricians following a wire."

"What wire?" K.J. asked.

"They saw something in our auras that seemed to connect out," Tommy said.

"Remember how Laverne said that we are all connected to this big life computer?" Jewel asked.

K.J. nodded. Then he sighed. "I think I had better get Laverne here. We may have just gone in over our head again."

Jewel agreed, not moving.

K.J. looked up at the ceiling. "Laverne, if you have a moment, we might need a little help here."

A moment later, Lady Luck herself appeared next to K.J. who stood quickly.

Laverne glanced at Jewel and Tommy, then asked, "Where are Belle and Nancy?"

"They were looking for an access to the life connections and saw something coming off the top of our auras," Jewel said. "And they are following that."

Laverne frowned, staring at the auras around Jewel and Tommy for a moment. Then suddenly she frowned, clearly seeing whatever it was that Belle and Nancy had seen.

"Oh, damn," Laverne said, softly and then vanished.

K.J. turned white and sat back down.

Jewel wasn't sure if it was a bad thing when Lady Luck swore, but she had a hunch it was.

She just hoped that didn't mean that Belle and Nancy had gotten into bad trouble.

But since there was nothing she could do, she and Tommy just stood there, their auras open to the world.

Twenty-eight

BELLE AND NANCY held hands as they floated up through the roof of the buffet and then through the floors above until finally coming out onto the roof.

They stopped there.

In both Jewel and Tommy's auras, there had been a very clear golden stream flowing up and out of the room.

As Belle and Nancy had floated up to the ceiling, they could see golden streams flowing from everyone in the room. Some were faint, others bright.

They were all very clear once they knew what they were looking for.

Now, as they stood on the roof of the hotel, they could see millions of golden streams of bright light flowing upwards from the buildings and around the building from the entire area of Las Vegas.

And it all formed a stunningly beautiful golden tower stretching up into the sky like a moving golden stream.

If Belle looked close enough, most streams were moving only outward, but others had light flowing in both directions, passing like streams of traffic on a busy freeway.

Clearly every stream had an ability to both send and receive some sort of connection.

The entire column just kept flowing and moving and shifting. It was so beautiful, Belle felt stunned to the very core of her being.

"How come we couldn't see this before?" Nancy asked, her voice almost breathless.

"I don't know," Belle said. "But if looks like a river of gold is flowing out of the city and into the sky."

"Not all of it gold," Nancy said, pointing out what looked like a faint black line among some of the closest gold streams.

Belle had a hunch that was a truly evil person at the end of that line.

"Let's see what happens if we touch an aura stream," Belle said, reaching over a few feet and putting her hand through a thin golden ray of light coming up through the roof near them.

She instantly knew the woman this stream was coming from was sitting at a slot machine near the pool area and losing. Her name was Callie and she was seventy. She had lost her husband a few years back and loved to play slot machines and she kept herself to a tight budget. Playing slots gave the woman a reason to get up in the morning and it wasn't costing her much at all. In fact, so far this year, she was up slightly which gave her a sense of pride.

Belle pulled her hand back and the memory of Callie faded almost instantly. "Just like touching a person."

Nancy nodded. "So this is everyone's connection to the interconnected structure of life," Nancy said.

"And this is how erasing Christmas will be done in each person," Belle said. "Along these channels of connection."

"You seemed to have solved that problem," Laverne said, appearing beside the two of them.

Belle had been expecting Laverne, but her sudden appearance still startled.

"You knew all this was here, didn't you?" Nancy asked.

"Actually, I did," Laverne said, nodding. "But as with all auras and such, I had tuned it out centuries ago. Very few can ever see the beauty of all this."

Laverne indicated the shimmering and glowing streams of light moving off the city floor and forming the giant column in the air.

To Belle, it was the most beautiful scene she had ever had the luck to witness.

"So where do they go?" Belle finally asked after a moment.

"Let me show you," Laverne said.

She reached out and offered a hand to both Nancy and Belle.

Belle took her firm hand and nodded.

A moment later they were following the river of beautiful golden threads up into the sky. At first the threads stayed close together in the massive column, sometimes being joined by other groups of threads, but then after the city of Las Vegas was only a large spot below them, the threads started to spread out again like the top of a flower.

And eventually the stream from Las Vegas merged into what looked like a golden lake surface.

Only Belle and Nancy and Laverne were under the surface.

They were above the height airlines flew, Belle knew that, yet she felt warm and could breathe just fine. Laverne must have the three of them inside an invisible bubble for some reason.

And even stranger, Belle felt no fear of falling at all. Maybe that came from being dead already and knowing she could both fly and teleport.

"This flows and covers the entire planet," Laverne said.

She pointed to a nearby thread. "See how that thread touches and sometimes joins many other threads as it moves off?"

"That person influences a lot of other people, don't they?" Belle asked.

"They do," Laverne said, nodding.

"And from the looks of it," Nancy said, staring at the incredible ceiling above them of flowing golden threads. "The six degrees of Kevin Bacon actually has some real meaning."

Laverne looked puzzled.

"There is a theory," Belle said, laughing, "that every person in the world is only six connections or less from Kevin Bacon, the actor. It's a party game, but pretty accurate."

Laverne nodded and then said, "Very accurate."

"So this destructive instruction for people to forget Christmas will somehow be introduced into this and flow to everyone," Belle said.

"That seems like exactly the way it is to be done," Laverne said.

"I wonder if it has been introduced into this network yet?" Nancy said.

"I'm afraid it has," Laverne said.

And with that all Belle could do was stare at Lady Luck as they hung many thousands of feet in the air just under the golden cloud of the life force of everyone in existence.

Twenty-nine

LAVERNE AND BELLE and Nancy appeared back at the table near K.J. and again K.J. damn hear hurt himself standing quickly.

"Thanks," Belle said to Jewel and Tommy. "We're done."

Jewel tightened her aura back against her skin. Then she and Tommy moved back over to the table.

"Anything?" Jewel asked.

"Actually a lot," Nancy said, nodding, but saying nothing more.

To Jewel, both of them looked a little haunted and not laughing at all anymore. She had no idea what they had seen, but it was clearly something very important.

"Poker Boy and his team are having another meeting in a few minutes," Laverne said. "I would like all of you there again. You two discovered the delivery method, they may have found who did it. Or at least that's the message I just got."

Jewel nodded, starting to feel slightly excited that this might get solved. And she was dying to hear what Belle and Nancy had found. But that could wait.

A moment later the five of them were again standing next to Laverne in Poker Boy's office. This time, besides milkshakes on the table, there were baskets of fries that smelled wonderful.

Clearly all of Poker Boy's team could still see them and nodded hello to them, as if seeing five ghosts was a normal occurrence to all of them.

The same group as before sat in the same positions. From what Jewel remembered of names, it was Poker Boy, Patty, Screamer, Sherrie, Ben, and Stan around the big booth from left to right.

At that moment, a large busty woman in a far-too-small waitress uniform from the 1950s appeared carrying two more baskets of the wonderful-smelling fries. Jewel had no idea how that uniform managed to hold in all of that woman, but it did.

The waitress smiled and nodded at the Ghost Agents, so she could see them as well. The waitress put the fries on the table. "Dig in."

Laverne went over and sat down at the end of the table, taking a fry.

The five of them moved a little closer so they were standing to one side of the booth so they could see Laverne from the side.

The waitress glanced at K.J. and winked. "Been a while there, K.J.," she said. "Still got that fantastic hot tub?"

Jewel glanced at K.J. who was blushing and nodding.

The waitress again winked and then turned and vanished back into what seemed to be an invisible doorway.

Jewel started to ask K.J. who that was and he waived her question away with a whispered, "Later."

"Belle and Nancy have found the life connections surface that connects everyone in the world," Laverne said. "Something I had forgotten was there, to be honest."

Poker Boy started to ask a question and Laverne stopped him. "Not important now other than we know how the memory erase will be transported to everyone. I understand you might have found out who planted this destructive problem in our life connections network?"

Poker Boy nodded and then said, "The Awgwas."

Jewel had no idea who that was and from the looks on the faces of Belle and Nancy and Tommy, they didn't either. K.J was just looking puzzled.

"They were destroyed by The Huntsmen and others over a hundred years ago," Laverne said, clearly looking puzzled as well.

Poker Boy nodded to Ben and Laverne turned her attention to the older-looking god.

"Some history first to make this understandable," Ben said.

Laverne nodded that that would be a good idea.

"The modern Santa Claus, as we know it now, wasn't so much invented, but documented by L. Frank Baum," Ben said. "In his book 'The Life and Adventures of Santa Claus.' It was that book that set most of the modern beliefs about Nick."

"Is Baum still writing?" Sherrie asked.

"I loved those stories when they came out," Patty said.

Poker Boy looked at Patty, clearly shocked.

Jewel was surprised as well. From her understanding, L. Frank Baum wrote way back in the late 1800s and into the early 1900s. So that meant that Poker Boy's girlfriend was at least a hundred years old.

"He's writing under other names now," Ben said. "Never really stopped."

"But we had to force him to write fiction under his new names," Laverne said. "No more documenting real world stuff. Between him and the Grimm brothers, more problems have been caused by their books over the centuries."

Jewel was just stunned. She really only knew Baum from the movie "The Wizard of Oz." Was Oz a real place? How could that be possible?

Then she reminded herself she was in a floating office over Las Vegas and she had been dead for a while. And Lady Luck was sitting at the table in front of her. Of course it was possible.

Finally Screamer seemed to get it back together before anyone else. "What does this have to do with our current problem and who are the Awgwas?"

"The Awgwas were a band of trolls that hated Nick," Ben said. "They hated that he helped kids stay good during a year with presents, because if the children weren't good, the children could be turned to the dark side by the Awgwas."

"The Awgwas caused a lot of the traditions that you hear Nick doing," Laverne said. "Going on his rounds at night because they couldn't see him, and going down chimneys because they would guard doors. And so on. It got so bad, and Nick was doing such great things with his presents for children, that finally The Huntsmen got a small army together and wiped out the Awgwas. No one shed a tear."

Jewel was stunned at that cold-blooded statement from Lady Luck.

"So how did they cause this problem?" Laverne asked.

"When we went to find Flick, the son of Krampus," Poker Boy said, "it was clear he didn't do it. In fact, he and two of his people have been helping Krampus and Nick try to discover what is going on."

"They are the ones that found the reference back to the Awgwas," Ben said. "Nick went almost completely pale at even the mention of them."

"And we traced it from there to some dark magic the Awgwas used right before they were destroyed," Poker Boy said.

"How did they get it into the conscious stream?" Laverne asked.

"They planted it in the subconscious of normal townspeople around them," Poker Boy said. "It was passed from parent to child, completely hidden, and would not trigger until the number of people infected with the dark magic reached a certain number. A number large enough for the black magic to have enough power and begin to spread."

"That number was reached a week ago," Ben said, "and the dark magic spell started spreading to make people forget Christmas."

Jewel was almost afraid to take a breath, the silence in the floating office was so intense.

"Got any idea how to stop it?" Laverne asked.

Poker Boy and the rest of his team just stared at the table in front of them and shook their heads.

"Belle and I can stop it," Nancy said from beside Jewel.

Every head in the room snapped to look at the two new Ghost Agents. Both were nodding.

"It's a virus, or a form of worm in a system," Nancy said.

"I know systems," Belle said.

"And I know how to navigate networks," Nancy said. "If there is access to that system and a way to kill that problem once we face it, we can stop it from spreading and kill the problem."

And once again the silence in the floating office seemed almost too intense for Jewel to bear, but she said nothing.

Thirty

BELLE AND NANCY both stood there in the intense silence, waiting for someone to speak. Belle was confident that she and Nancy could kill this spreading problem if they could get some way to access all those golden streams that represented every person on the planet.

She didn't know how they would get access, or how they would track what they were searching, or how they would kill it when they found it, but she was sure they could do it. Convinced.

Finally, Laverne stood and came to face both women. "What exactly do you need?"

"A way to access the consciousness network," Nancy said.

"A way to map the network as it exists," Belle said, "so someone with fantastic math and computer skills."

"Bookkeeper," Poker Boy said from the booth.

Laverne nodded.

Belle had no idea who that was, but clearly someone they all thought brilliant at computers.

"And a way to kill the virus when we find it," Nancy said.

"Or someone with us who has the power to kill it," Belle said.

Nancy nodded.

Laverne never once moved as they spoke. She just stared at the two of them with her intense dark eyes. Belle refused to let those eyes rattle her.

"Those three things. Nothing more?" Laverne asked.

"Not that we know of at the moment," Belle said.

"But it is critical to move quickly," Nancy said. "The more a virus like this one spreads into a system, the more powerful it will become and the harder it will be to fight."

Laverne nodded and turned to Poker Boy. "In a minute, I will show you and Patty and the Bookkeeper the consciousness net that these two reminded me existed. It will be up to you to get the Bookkeeper what he needs to map what I will show you."

Poker Boy nodded and said nothing.

Laverne turned to Ben. "Access to the consciousness net? Has that been done before to your knowledge?"

Ben shook his head. "Nothing like this. It would take a containment field of immense proportions to protect anyone going into that. It would be like being bombarded with the thoughts of a million people at once. Unprotected, that would cause instant insanity."

Belle felt her stomach cramp up at the thought of that.

"We don't need to go inside all the information flow," Nancy said. "We just need to be able to skim through it in some fashion. Or even over the top of it."

"And see the patterns of it," Belle said, instantly understanding what Nancy meant. "When searching for problems in computer systems, or corporation systems, you didn't need to get lost in the details, in the data. You just need to be able to see the infection and how it infects the data."

Nancy nodded.

Laverne again did not move. "You saw the vast surface of consciousness. Would you be able to find the problems skimming along the surface without dropping inside?"

"If we knew the connections," Nancy said. "So the mathematical mapping would be critical. And how we would connect as well."

"We are connected," Belle said, smiling at the woman she was falling in love with more and more by the minute. "We would just need to have our minds opened up to see our own connections and how they connect to the surface."

Laverne nodded. "That is possible. But I feel you will need a full crew with you for this fight, both on the inside and the outside."

Belle looked puzzled.

"I will gather some of the strongest of us to destroy the black magic when you find it," Laverne said.

"I understand black magic," Patty said.

Again Poker Boy looked at her with a puzzled expression on his face.

"I know," Laverne said. "Which is why I would ask you to host Belle and Nancy and Jewel inside your mind for this fight. And let them track along your connections."

"I would be honored," Patty said, nodding. "I will be able to protect them from the black magic as well."

Laverne nodded.

"So we have the connection into the network," Nancy said.

"And you will put a team together to fight the black magic when we find it," Belle said. "So we just need the map of the structure and where the problem was planted."

"Get rested," Laverne said to the five of them. "I will let you know how long this will take to get ready. And K.J. and Tommy, you will both be needed as well for a different task."

With that the five of them were back in the warm sounds and wonderful smells of the Golden Nugget buffet.

K.J. slumped into a chair again at a table full of their dirty breakfast dishes. None of them had cleaned them off yet and they hadn't yet vanished either.

Belle had no idea what to think, other than she was again feeling hungry.

She took Nancy's hand and they walked toward the food once again. It had been a long day and it wasn't even noon yet. And Belle had a hunch the day was going to get much longer very quickly.

As they walked, Nancy pointed at all the golden threads streaming from the forty or so people around the buffet. The threads left their auras and swirled up through the ceiling.

"Who knew we were all so connected," Nancy said.

"I'm just glad we are," Belle said, squeezing Nancy's hand.

Thirty-one

JEWEL WORKED at clearing off some of their old dishes and tossing them in a bus tub nearby as Belle and Nancy walked toward the food. Jewel planned on getting something more to eat as well, but after that meeting, she felt she just needed to do something to not think much.

K.J. had slumped into one of the chairs at the table and looked washed out. He clearly, in all his time as an agent, had never worked around Laverne before.

Tommy sat down as well. "Got any idea why Laverne wanted you to go with them on this?"

"Not a clue," Jewel said. "When we were all three inside that woman at the front desk, we seemed to mesh well. Maybe that's it. Or maybe it's something medical because of my background."

Tommy nodded. "More than likely medical. That makes sense, since you are good at controlling emotions and such in people."

Jewel nodded and finished with the dishes. She wasn't afraid, just confused.

She sat down as well and faced K.J. "So who was the waitress?"

"Name is Madge," K.J. said. "She's been around forever, knows everyone and everything that is going on. She's a super-hero in the food and beverage area."

"So she's been to your famous hot tub?" Tommy asked.

K.J. smiled and seemed to come back into his eyes a little as he remembered something. "She has been there a few times."

"So these parties you throw are co-ed parties?" Jewel asked.

"Sometimes," K.J. said, smiling.

"So why did you blush when you saw Madge?" Jewel asked.

K.J. laughed and looked up as Belle and Nancy were approaching with plates of food. "Just say," he whispered, smiling at Jewel and Tommy, "that Madge can hold her breath under water longer than anyone I have ever met."

Jewel was convinced she blushed and Tommy just about went over backwards laughing.

Both Belle and Nancy looked puzzled and Jewel waived them off. "Just men being crude. So any ideas why Laverne wants me going along with you two?"

"We were talking about that at the buffet," Belle said. "I think it's your medical training."

"I agree," Tommy said. "From the sounds of this, the black magic has gotten into brains like a bad tumor."

"A very bad tumor," K.J. said, shaking his head. "Magic is something that is avoided at all costs in our worlds."

"What is it that we do then?" Jewel asked, now clearly puzzled.

"We are using our own talents, our own skills," K.J. said. "Superheroes and gods do the same. The use of magic has been forbidden for more centuries than I would ever want to think about it. Mostly because it almost always turns dark and consumes those who use it."

"So there is no magic in holding that office in the sky?" Belle asked.

"None," K.J. said. "That is all the natural power of Poker Boy doing that."

"So the black magic is going to show up clearly in those infected?" Jewel asked.

"I honestly don't know," K.J. said. "But my guess is the same as everyone's, that your medical knowledge and understanding of human brains and bodies is why you are going along inside Patty on this ride."

"But what does she want you and me to do?" Tommy asked, looking at K.J.

"No idea," K.J. said, taking a deep breath and shuddering. "And that scares me more than I want to admit."

Jewel patted his hand. "I'm sure it's going to be fine. Come on, let's get some lunch."

K.J. nodded. "A last meal is always a good idea."

Jewel just shook her head. "We're dead, remember. You had your last meal a hundred plus years ago."

"Oh, party-pooper," K.J. said. "A guy can whine, can't he?"

Everyone laughed and Jewel and Tommy and K.J. left Belle and Nancy eating.

Thirty-two

K.J. WENT HOME after lunch to San Francisco, Jewel and Tommy jumped to their home, and Belle and Nancy jumped back to their suite in the hotel.

The day was bright and the suite felt warm and comforting to Belle in all the brown tones and tall windows. And right now, after this morning, she really needed warm and comforting.

She really loved it here and in Las Vegas. And she knew Nancy did as well. If they survived this, or if the world survived this, there was no doubt to Belle that the two of them would settle here in

Las Vegas. They hadn't talked about it, but neither of them had anything left in Boise, and neither of them had connections to anywhere else. They could make Las Vegas a wonderful home.

The two of them walked into the bedroom and both changed into casual and comfortable clothes, including tennis shoes. Then they went to the big bed and just lay there, fully dressed, holding hands and staring at the bright high ceiling.

The bedspread felt soft under Belle and she had used one pillow to prop up her head just enough to be comfortable.

Doing this felt wonderful and natural to Belle. She could feel her energy slowly coming back. She hadn't realized that the morning had worn her out so much.

"You need to nap?" Nancy asked.

"No," Belle said. "I just need to lay here for another minute or two."

"Perfect," Nancy said.

Silence filled the room for the next few minutes. Not uncomfortable silence, but the silence of rest and the silence of two people who didn't always need to talk to be close.

Belle closed her eyes a few times, but decided she would rather just rest looking at the high ceiling and all the warm light. Her mind was just moving far too fast to actually fall asleep even for a few minutes.

"How long do you think it's going to take to map that network?" Belle asked, finally breaking the silence.

"It seems like a large network," Nancy said, "but considering what you and I are used to, it's fairly small. Only the number of billions of humans on the planet for each main connection. So someone good with programming computers could set that program up and have it mapping in an hour at most. Another hour for the program to run. It's been almost two hours, so any moment now."

Belle knew Nancy was right. In the computer world, the business world, seven billion was a small amount of bits of data. They had both dealt with systems far, far larger.

"The mapping in a way that we can use it will be the problem," Nancy said.

Again Belle nodded, agreeing and squeezing Nancy's hand. "Like a bad disease. We have to find the infected cluster and then make sure we track every connection."

"I just hope we can save the carriers," Nancy said.

"We will," Belle said, shuddering slightly at that thought. "We have to."

"Yes," Laverne said from the foot of the bed. "We have to."

Belle and Nancy both sat up and smiled at Lady Luck herself.

"Time to get going on this?" Belle asked as they both moved off the bed and stood.

"First," Laverne said, turning and walking out into the living room area of the suite, "explain to me how this network works. I am not very familiar, I am afraid, with computer systems."

Belle nodded as Laverne stopped and faced them.

"In this hotel there is an electrical system," Belle said, indicating the lights. That is a network similar to what we are talking about."

Nancy nodded. "The power comes in at one spot and spreads out until it ends up in that light, that outlet, and so on."

Laverne nodded and said nothing.

"That outlet is connected to a light fixture in the casino by the network," Belle said. "It might not be a direct connection in any fashion, but following that connection, we can eventually get to a light fixture in the casino."

"And as with the electrical in this building," Nancy said, "or the plumbing network, there are clear patterns once you know what you are looking for."

"And you will be able to see those patterns among humans in the great life shield?"

"We will," Belle said. "Especially with a mathematical map worked out by computer first."

"We were experts in structures of networks and computer networks," Nancy said, "when we were alive just a few short days ago."

Belle smiled. "I am fairly certain we haven't forgotten it yet."

Laverne nodded. "I have over two hundred gods and superheroes ready to clean out the dark magic when you two and Jewel and Patty find it. They are all being trained now."

"I understand Patty being our protection against the magic," Belle said. "Is Jewel's part of this for the medical side?"

"No," Laverne said. "Jewel's greatest strength is her ability to focus. She is there to hold you two together and focus and keep you from getting lost in all the data, as you put it. Patty will be too busy to help with that on the exterior shields against not only the massive amount of information from so many people's lives, but in protecting you from the magic and teaching you all to see it in someone."

That surprised Belle and she just nodded.

"Poker Boy and his team will be backing up Patty from his office, feeding her the energy she is going to need to protect herself and the three of you."

Belle looked at Nancy. "Ready?"

Nancy smiled. "Let's go kick some magic butt."

Laverne just smiled slightly and jumped them to Poker Boy's office.

Jewel was already there, standing to one side and Poker Boy and his team were all sitting around the table.

Patty was in the back of the table, with Poker Boy on one side and Stan, the God of Poker, on the other.

They looked very serious and there were no milkshakes or food on the table. In fact, the mood was downright gloomy. No one had died yet, and if this group had anything to say about it, no one would.

Belle leaned over to Nancy and whispered. "For a group that's saved the world a bunch of times, they look pretty darned serious."

Nancy just laughed and everyone looked up at her.

Nancy shrugged and smiled and again Laverne just smiled.

Nancy leaned over and whispered to Belle, "I'll get you for that."

"Is that a date?" Belle asked, smiling at the woman she loved.

"Damn right it is," Nancy said, smiling back.

Thirty-three

"IT'S READY," Stan, the God of Poker said.

Jewel watched as he vanished from his position in the booth, then reappeared a moment later with something in his hand.

The small device he held that looked to Jewel like a funny cube with wires poking out of it like a person who had morning hair. Stan handed it to Laverne, who nodded and held it in her hand. A moment later there was a glow around the device and it vanished completely.

She then turned to Patty. "Ready."

Patty nodded and held out her hand and Laverne touched it across the empty table.

After a moment Patty nodded and closed her eyes.

Poker Boy held out his hand and Laverne touched him as well.

They must have talked about what they were doing before Jewel had arrived, because she had no idea what it was.

Laverne then touched Stan's hand and then everyone else around the table.

Then, almost as one, they all stood.

Patty came over to Jewel and Belle and Nancy. "I have the map of the life connections surface in my mind. You will be able to see it and study it when we are together."

"Do we have an idea where we are starting?" Belle asked.

Patty nodded. "Along with the map, the Bookkeeper has extrapolated the likely spread of the black magic."

"That won't help at all," Belle said.

Jewel was stunned at that statement.

Laverne, who had been talking with Poker Boy, suddenly turned to face them just as Patty said, "Why not."

"Over one hundred years of time is why not," Belle said.

Nancy nodded.

"You said this black magic was buried in people's minds, dormant, right?"

Patty nodded and Laverne just stood there.

"So it spread through their kids and their grandkids as well," Nancy said, "more than likely all over the planet."

Patty looked at Laverne with a slightly panicked look on her face. Jewel felt panicked as well, her stomach twisting into an even tighter knot than it already was in.

"Again," Nancy said, "The system is similar to a computer. When a virus gets into a computer and starts to spread, it has to be dug out of everywhere, not just where it started."

Jewel knew she was right.

Laverne nodded. "So fighting it on a person-by-person level will not solve this problem."

"It will not," Belle said. "In a system of this size, the cure must be systemwide and all at once."

Laverne turned to Poker Boy. "Our plan will not work. Please contact all teams and have them stand by."

Then she turned to Patty. "See if what you were planning will at least work. Report back on the extent of the infection."

Patty nodded as Laverne vanished. Then she turned to Jewel. "Your job is to support these two as much as you can, be their center focus, and be my contact."

Jewel nodded. She had no idea exactly what Patty meant, but she had a hunch she would figure it out quickly.

"Jewel first," Patty said as everyone else in the room stood back and watched.

Jewel moved over to Patty and merged with her. Patty had much of her mind blocked, but Jewel was still impressed that she was inside such a powerful and kind superhero.

She made herself smaller and formed a mental room inside Patty. Then she made a connection to the thought center in Patty's mind and said, "Ready for Belle."

"Ready for Belle," Patty said. Then she shook her head and said, "That was weird. I didn't know I was going to say that."

Jewel stuck her hand and head out of the side of Patty and said to everyone in the room. "That was me. That work for you, Patty?"

"Works perfectly," Patty said.

Jewel could tell that Patty was a little surprised and nervous about this, but Jewel knew Patty would be fine, shortly.

"Now that's the strangest thing I have ever seen," Screamer said, indicating where Patty stood with Jewel sticking her head out of one side.

"I'm doing my best to scrub that image from my mind," Poker Boy said.

Jewel went back inside and made sure her connection with Patty was secure and that there was room for Belle."

A moment later Belle joined her.

"Cozy," Belle said as she settled into the imaginary room that Jewel had made.

A moment later Nancy joined them.

"We're all set," Jewel told Patty. "Unless you want all three of us to stick our heads up through your shoulders to really mess with people."

"I think they are messed up enough," Patty said, laughing.

Jewel could see that everyone in the room just sort of stared at Patty.

"We will return," Patty said.

A moment later they were over the beautiful surface of consciousness that shimmered gold thousands of feet above the planet. Millions of human aura connections were woven through the surface, some touching, some flowing past others, some merging.

The map of the entire surface of the world's consciousness was clear inside Patty's mind and Jewel could see it.

"Hold here," Jewel told Patty. "Let us get our bearings."

"So what are we looking for?" Jewel asked Belle and Nancy.

"We won't see it from up here I don't think," Nancy said. "At least not at first."

"Okay," Jewel said to Patty. "We're going to need to go into your aura connection to this net to find what we are looking for. Can you maintain this position?"

"I can," Patty said out loud to nothing at the high altitude where she was floating. "But Laverne only taught me how to do this flying and teleporting thing a few hours ago, so if I'm a little unsteady, ignore me."

"So hold us together," Belle said to Jewel.

Jewel imagined the room as a small bubble and then she sent the bubble down along the wide, golden stream of Patty's consciousness and into the surface of the world's consciousness.

They hit a spot quickly where she was connected in various ways to hundreds of people. Jewel stopped there before going any farther. It felt like never-ending linked tunnels going off into a thousand directions. She was afraid if she went farther, they would be lost forever inside the surface of consciousness.

Belle said simply, "This isn't going to work."

"I agree," Nancy said. "We are inside the network looking for corruption in the network. We need to be above the system to see the pattern of the corruption, not down in it."

"Back to Patty's mind," Belle said.

Almost instantly Jewel had them back inside the room inside Patty's mind. She felt completely relieved.

"New plan," Jewel said to Patty. "Hold on and we'll figure it out."

Patty only nodded. Jewel could tell that Patty was worried about her ability to stay in the air. This was all very new to her.

This Novel Available Before Christmas
from all your favorite booksellers
in trade paper and electronic editions.

USA TODAY BESTSELLING AUTHOR

DEAN WESLEY
SMITH

HEAVEN PAINTED
as a Christmas Gift

A GHOST OF A CHANCE NOVEL

Jewel quickly went into Patty's mind and calmed her and reinforced what Laverne had taught her earlier.

"That help?" Jewel asked.

Patty sighed. "Yes, much better. Thank you."

"The map is the key," Belle said. "Let's jump to where in the world this originated and see what this black magic even looks like in an infected person's aura."

"I agree," Nancy said.

Jewel told Patty the plan and indicated on the map the area in Europe they wanted to hover over.

Patty understood and a moment later they had jumped to that part of the world.

"Oh, no," Belle said.

Jewel could see the problem. Over Las Vegas the surface of consciousness was mostly all golden threads woven into a shimmering incredible site, like a golden sheet flowing gently in a breeze.

Here, about half the threads were covered in something that looked like a sticky, black tar. The gold threads were still fine, but covered over, like someone had poured some awful black substance over them.

And as they watched, the black substance seemed to crawl and move, as if it was alive.

"We need to get out of here," Patty said.

Jewel could not agree more. She had never been so frightened of anything in her life.

Or her death, for that matter.

"Have Patty take us back over the surface over Las Vegas again," Belle said.

Jewel told Patty and a moment later they were back over the surface of the golden shimmering surface of the consciousness of the people of Las Vegas.

Jewel could feel the relief until Belle said, "Have Patty go right down to the surface of the consciousness directly below us."

Jewel instantly saw what Belle had seen as she told Patty.

One thread there had the black, tar-looking substance crawling on it like a slime monster from a bad movie.

Jewel could feel the panic in Patty's mind start to grow and sent her calming feelings even though she was feeling just as panicked.

"We need to follow that down to the person," Nancy said.

Jewel told Patty and a moment later they were diving toward the surface, following the golden aura covered in black magic slime.

It turned out it was an elderly man sitting at a penny slot machine in the MGM Grand casino.

"Laverne," Patty said into the air.

Belle and Nancy and Jewel crawled out of Patty and stood next to her in the noise of the casino as Laverne and Poker Boy and Stan appeared, followed an instant later by Tommy.

Jewel hugged Tommy. Before the change of plans, he and K.J. were to have been on the teams destroying the black magic, something that had scared Jewel more than she wanted to admit.

Patty pointed to the man sitting at the machine. "Look at his aura and his life connection."

The minute she pointed it out, the black, crawling slime around the life connection became clear.

"Damn," Laverne said. "Just damn."

Jewel had no doubt that if Lady Luck herself was swearing, things had just gone from bad to worse.

Section Five
THE LAST CHRISTMAS STAND

Thirty-four

Belle stared at the black magic slime crawling over the poor man's aura connection to the larger world. More than likely he was a good man who had lived a decent life, since his aura was mostly gold and red and brown. Very little black in the essence of his aura.

But the black magic almost covered his connection to the larger world.

Laverne took the entire group out of time, shutting down all the movement of everyone around them and all the sound as well. To Belle, that intense silence was very unnerving.

"Hold this bubble," Laverne said to Stan. "We need someone who has seen this before."

Then she was gone.

Nancy started toward the man with the black magic on his aura and Belle followed, wanting to stop her, but not saying anything.

"Don't touch that," Stan said as all of them stopped within a few steps of the man.

"It's not moving," Nancy said. "Which means it has a life of sort and is connected in real time."

"Something alive can be killed," Belle said.

"Black magic is very much a living thing," Patty said. "It lives by consuming hosts which is why in darker times those suspected of black magic were killed."

Belle glanced back at Patty and could see the hurt in her dark brown eyes from that statement. Patty had been around many centuries, Belle knew, from being inside her head. More than likely she had seen such awful things happen up close.

"So besides killing the host, what kills black magic?" Poker Boy asked, standing next to Patty and letting her lean on him.

"I honestly don't know," Patty said.

Belle did not want to think about killing all the people infected. That would be millions. She pushed that thought away.

"Well," Nancy said, "if there is something that kills it, we can send it back right here into the larger consciousness layer through this man."

Belle nodded. "Standard system cleaning. Find an infection and turn the infection back on the rest of the infection to clear it out."

A moment later Laverne returned inside the time bubble with a man with a long gray beard, long gray hair, a long deep blue robe that went all the way to the ground, and a colored pointed hat with bright stars on it. He looked like the worst example of a cliché magician Belle had ever seen.

If she hadn't been standing in a time bubble with ghosts, superheroes, and gods, she might have laughed.

Beside her Nancy smiled and shook her head.

The old man said, "Tsk, tsk." Then he stepped toward the black tar frozen around the aura of the poor man at the slot machine and cut off a piece with his knife.

He held the black piece up to look at it. It just looked like a black piece of hard tar to Belle, and she shuddered at the fact that he was holding it.

"I will return," he said to Laverne, who bowed slightly as the man vanished.

Poker Boy asked the question Belle was thinking. "Who was that?"

"One of the ancient ones," Laverne said, shaking her head. "We do not say his name."

Poker Boy nodded and a moment later the ancient one appeared, stuck the piece of black magic back where he had cut it out, and wiped off his hands on his robe.

"Nasty troll magic," he said, sounding clearly disgusted.

His voice sounded deep and raspy and almost echoed in the silence of the time bubble.

"They should be stopped," he said.

"This is hundreds of years old," Laverne said, "and those that planted it inside the heads of the unsuspecting have been destroyed."

"Good," he said, nodding. "So what is it that you need from me if you knew the source?"

"This has infected millions of innocents around the world," Laverne said. "If allowed to progress, this world will cease to exist."

"Well, that can't be allowed to happen," the old man said. "Kill all the infected ones."

Laverne nodded. "We have considered that. But we hope for another solution."

Belle was flat shocked that Laverne had considered mass murder, even to save billions of other lives.

"How can this sort of troll black magic be stopped and destroyed?" Laverne asked.

"Darkness is always destroyed by light," the old man said. "This troll dark magic here will easily fall to a spell of intense brightness."

He looked back up the aura string covered in the black substance. "The light would need to come from inside the human's connection to the great consciousness. I have no idea how you would do that. Better off to kill the humans infected and be done with it."

With that he vanished, leaving the silence even more intense inside the time bubble.

Belle couldn't stand it after a moment and turned to Laverne. "So where do we get a very bright, and very infectious white light?"

Thirty-five

JEWEL JUST FELT STUNNED at the old man in the funny robe and hat. He had looked like someone's grandfather dressing up in a magician's robe and pointed hat for a costume party. She couldn't believe the guy actually dressed like that normally.

And Jewel had felt sick to her stomach when the man had simply said it would be better to kill millions to solve this problem. And Jewel could tell that Laverne had to consider that option.

When Belle asked her where they could get a bright and infectious white light, Laverne had nodded, then said, "Remain here. I will return."

"Could she really think of killing millions to save the planet?" Tommy asked.

Poker Boy and Patty and Stan all nodded.

"Ever heard of Atlantis?" Poker Boy asked.

"Let's not talk about that," Stan said. "And never ask her about that. We need to stay focused on solving this in a better way than what happened with Atlantis."

Jewel and everyone nodded.

Jewel had a hunch she knew what Belle and Nancy were thinking, but she wanted to be sure.

She turned to Belle and Nancy. "So you are thinking we get the light and climb into this guy and kill black goo all the way into the world's subconscious cloud?"

"It would be easier if we could just send the light in like a virus," Belle said.

Nancy nodded. "And let it expand through the network on its own, but I have a hunch it won't be that easy."

Laverne again appeared, this time with two very tiny, pointed-eared women who looked like elves and from what Jewel could tell, actually were elves. Only both were very old, dressed as older women in Vegas would dress, with long dark slacks, sweaters, hats to keep the sun from their faces and hide their ears some, and large black purses.

One carried a coin bucket full of nickels.

Laverne pointed at the black magic surrounding the man's aura connection.

Both older women stepped back and put a hand over their mouths.

"Troll black magic," Laverne said. "Planted a hundred years ago by the Awgwas to wipe the memory of Christmas from all humans."

"They were evil," one short woman said.

"Very," the other said. "We owe the Huntsmen a debt of gratitude for wiping them out."

"I agree," the other said, nodding.

Jewel just kept staring at the two. Between the guy in the hat and these two, this morning was about as strange as any dream she had ever had. Maybe worse.

"So I assume you would like to try to destroy this with elfin light?" one of the tiny women asked.

Laverne nodded.

The woman nodded and pointed at an area above the poor man's head and a white light shot from her finger.

The black vanished from around the core of connection leaving the man's normal golden aura connection for a few feet.

The older woman nodded. "It seems our light will do it just fine. But it will need to be from the inside of the infected person's aura to be effective."

"Can your light, in any fashion, be carried by these four?" Laverne asked.

She pointed to Jewel and Belle and Nancy and Tommy.

"Ghost Agents?" one woman asked.

Laverne nodded.

"It can be," both women said at the same time.

"Can your light be made to be infectious?" Belle asked, bowing slightly first before asking her question.

Jewel was impressed Belle had the courage to even talk to real elves.

"In what way, dear?" one tiny woman asked.

"There are millions that have been infected with this dark magic," Belle said. "We would like to try to put as much white light into the consciousness layer overhead to flood down into every person on the planet and completely wipe out any chance of the black magic surviving."

"Like fighting a computer virus with a cleaning program," one elf said to the other, who nodded.

Jewel was stunned that these two older women, or elves, knew what a computer virus even was.

The two women looked at each other for a moment. "Laverne, please come with us before the great council. We may have a solution."

With that, once again the four ghosts plus Patty, Stan, and Poker Boy remained in the intense silence of the time bubble.

Finally Tommy turned to Poker Boy. "Are all your missions this weird?"

Poker Boy laughed. "Not all of them."

That meant some of them were, and Jewel wasn't sure if she was happy or not to hear that.

Thirty-six

BELLE COULDN'T BELIEVE she had actually had the courage to talk with two elves, but at this point, nothing much was going to surprise her anymore. She and Nancy had only been dead a very short time and everything she had come to believe about the world was tipped on its head, including the entire idea of dying.

How, as ghosts, she and Nancy found themselves fighting to now save millions of lives was beyond her. It would take months before any of this really sank in.

If it ever did.

Suddenly Laverne was back with the two older women. They each handed Patty two golf-ball-sized spheres.

"White light," Laverne said. "Use one to clear the path up through this man's aura and into the consciousness layer. Keep the other for protection."

Patty nodded.

Laverne turned to Jewel and Belle and Nancy. "You three will be with Patty, as you did before. The Great Elvin Council has agreed that all elves, as is needed, will send white light up through their aura connections into the great consciousness layer."

"This is what it will look like," one of the older elves said.

Belle watched as suddenly a stream of white light shot up through her aura connection and through the roof.

"Elves have most green aura connections twisted around with lines of gold," one of the elves said.

Belle could see what they both were saying and that would be easy to spot now that she knew what she was looking for.

"Thank you," Nancy said.

Belle liked this idea a lot. The cure would be coming in from a thousand sources around the world into the network.

Laverne went on. "It is your job to direct the white light sent up to you and ask for more if you need it. Patty, just speak aloud and I will hear you and send more into the area you are in."

Then, before Belle or Nancy could say anything, Laverne turned to Poker Boy and Tommy. "You two will monitor their progress from above the consciousness layer, making sure they do not get lost. Or that they do not miss an infected strand. Tommy, you will be able to hear Jewel's thoughts while this mission lasts. Understood? And connect with Poker Boy so he can hear your instructions as well."

They both nodded.

"I'll show you how to connect," Jewel said to Tommy and he nodded.

"How will we be able to direct the white light into different channels?" Nancy asked the moment before Belle could ask the same exact question.

"White light is a fluid," Laverne said. "Simply damn it with mind shields to the direction you would like it to go. Each of you imagine a clear shield in front of you directing white light at the man who is infected."

Belle did as Laverne said.

Both elf-women pointed at the three of them and white light emitted from their fingers.

Belle made her shield strong in her mind and the white light bounced off like hitting a mirror and hit the man at the slot machine.

Any sign of black magic goo vanished from around the poor man completely.

"Well done," Laverne said, nodding.

Laverne turned to the two elves and bowed "Thank you for your help. We will be ready in a moment."

"This is to save our world and our Nick," one of the short women said. "It is our pleasure to be asked to help this great team save the world once again."

With that, they vanished.

"So this is how you do it," Belle asked, smiling at Patty and Poker Boy.

"Actually," Poker Boy said, "I usually ask more stupid questions."

Both Patty and Stan nodded.

Poker Boy just shook his head. "You didn't have to agree."

Patty kissed him on the cheek. "Yes we did," she said.

Even Laverne smiled.

Thirty-seven

JEWEL QUICKLY showed Tommy how to connect with Poker Boy so they could talk. Then she kissed Tommy and went back over to Patty.

"Ready?"

Patty nodded and without hesitation Jewel stepped inside her and created a safe area and connected to Patty's mind.

"Ready for the other two."

Patty repeated that and Belle and Nancy joined her.

"You hold us together and direct Patty," Belle said. "Nancy and I will create the shields."

"Good idea," Jewel said. Then she had Patty tell Poker Boy and Tommy to jump ahead and get above the consciousness level.

Patty did.

Then she told Laverne and Stan to lower the time bubble.

Jewel could hear through Patty the sounds of the casino smash in around them.

"How do I get inside his aura?" Patty asked, stepping toward the man playing the slots. Jewel could see the black magic goo slowly moving down the man's aura connection.

"Step into him now," Laverne said. "Just as the others stepped into you."

Jewel could read Patty's thoughts about having yet another new power. It seemed she had had the same powers for a lot of centuries until this mission suddenly changed everything.

"Keep me calm, Jewel," Patty said.

"Got you," Jewel said. And gave Patty calming feelings and the memory of how it felt to slip inside a live person.

Patty opened one of the spheres and white light flooded out as she stepped inside the guy sitting at the slots.

Jewel and Patty and Belle and Nancy could all read his thoughts instantly. He was feeling great and having a good day. He was from Michigan, his wife loved to play slots, and he was starting to like them as well, as long as they didn't spend much money each trip.

"He's in a good mood from the white light hitting him," Belle said.

"More than likely," Nancy said.

"Jewel," Nancy said, "We're going to need to keep all of us blocked from the memories and thoughts of all the people in these aura streams."

"Understand," Jewel said. "I'll use my screen for that."

"Form it into a pointed cylinder around all four of us," Belle said.

"Like a bullet?" Jewel asked, laughing.

"Exactly," Belle said, also laughing.

As they started up the aura connection from the man into the clouds, Jewel formed the shield and the man's thoughts went away.

After only another moment, they were in the consciousness cloud. The white light they had directed ahead from the sphere Patty held had wiped out the black magic infection for as far as they could see from inside the aura tunnel.

Around them it felt as if they were in a tube just larger than they were. The tube twisted and turned and joined others and touched others and went off into the distance.

Patty remembered the map of the consciousness and Nancy pointed to a hub area. "We can flood this area with white light from there."

Almost instantly they were at the hub.

Now instead of a tube, they seemed to be in a large golden, shimmering bubble with thousands and thousands of holes in the walls.

The white light Patty still held cleared out a bunch of the black magic threads, leaving the massive chamber white and shimmering gold.

"We're going to have to be careful to not get ahead of ourselves," Jewel said to both Patty and Belle and Nancy.

"I agree," Belle said. "Seems we can travel at the speed of thought in here. I don't want to jump into a nest of that black stuff if we don't have to."

Jewel checked in with Tommy. "Can you see us and hear me?"

"Loud and clear," Tommy said.

"Have the white light sent up from the Las Vegas area and we'll see how this is going to work," Jewel said.

"Be ready," Jewel said to Belle and Nancy.

"I take the north side of this," Belle said.

"Got it," Nancy said.

"Hold us steady," Jewel said to Patty.

A moment later a flood of white light seemed to fill the aura channels and flood into the large sphere around them.

Jewel held all four of them together and kept her shield up solid as Belle and Nancy worked around the large area, sending the white light into every channel.

After a moment Jewel said, "Enough."

The white light stopped.

"Belle, Nancy, you two all right?" Jewel asked.

"We're fine, how are you and Patty?" Belle asked.

Jewel felt fine as well, not tired in the slightest and she could tell that Patty was doing fine as well.

"Any way to tell how much area we flooded from here?" Jewel asked Tommy.

"From what I could tell," Tommy said, and Poker Boy is checking right now as well, that blast covered every person on the western part of the United States. And some areas beyond."

Belle laughed after hearing that. "What's the largest major hub right in the center of the United States?"

"Right over Chicago," Jewel said, checking in with Patty.

"That white light sphere still working?" Belle asked.

Jewel checked quickly with Patty and it was and would last a while.

"Jump us to that big Chicago hub with that white light on," Nancy said.

"Headed for Chicago area," Jewel told Tommy just as Patty jumped them.

The huge central hub above Las Vegas was like a beach ball compared to this central hub. No way could Jewel even begin to imagine the size. Maybe a dozen football field stadiums could fit in this huge sphere.

Or twice that. Impossible to get scale.

"Does everyone on the planet know someone in this area?" Belle said.

"Wow, looks that way, doesn't it?"

The white light that Patty carried kept all the black magic back and shrinking away from them, but Jewel could tell this time the blast needed to be so much larger.

She told Tommy that and Poker Boy relayed that to Laverne and all the elves.

"Hold on," Tommy said. "The white light is coming at full flood."

Jewel braced them all together and got Patty fortified as suddenly white light poured into the vast space from a hundred different directions.

As fast as they could, Belle and Nancy directed the white light back at the millions of aura conduits in the walls, filling the space with intense white light.

The black magic goo just vanished.

This time Jewel let the flood continue for fifteen seconds longer before telling Tommy to shut it down.

Again Jewel checked with all of them to make sure they were all right and they were. This was not even stressing them the way they were shielded.

"How did we do this time?"

"The entire center of the country is clear, almost all of Canada, and most of the upper areas of Mexico," Tommy said.

Jewel could hear the excitement in his voice and she was feeling it as well.

This was going to work.

"How are the elves doing?" Jewel asked.

A moment later Tommy came back. "Laverne says they are enjoying themselves and are ready all over the world."

"Where to next, girls?" Jewel asked after she relayed all that from Tommy.

"There is a hub over Washington D.C. and then we go from there," Patty said.

Belle and Nancy agreed and Jewel had them jump to the huge sphere of merged human consciousness over Washington, D.C.

And as they flooded the sphere with white light, Jewel wondered just how many congressmen and women were going to have a really good day.

Thirty-eight

BELLE HAD NEVER FELT so exhausted and so excited as the moment they arrived back at Poker Boy's office in the sky. Around the office the sun was just starting to come up in beautiful shades of red and orange out over the desert and mountains to the east.

Belle and Nancy and Jewel left Patty. Patty slumped into the arms of Poker Boy and he helped her to the booth.

Jewel went to Tommy and hugged him.

Belle and Nancy just sat on the checkered tile floor. Nancy leaned into Belle and they just sat like that holding each other up.

A moment later K.J. appeared, looking worried and smiling. "You guys are wonderful. Just amazing."

"Did we get it all?" Jewel asked.

Belle had no idea if they did or not, but she knew for a fact they had given it their best try.

Laverne appeared, actually smiling. "We had teams of elves, organized by Nick, following you six around the world making sure nothing was missed and making sure that there were no more black magic time bombs planted in anyone's mind from this."

"So we got it all?" Jewel asked.

"The threat has cleared," Laverne said, nodding. "We will be standing watch for any sign of any outbreak anywhere. But let me simply say you all saved a lot of lives today."

Belle just nodded, not wanting to think about the chance that all those people would have been killed to clear this infection.

Nancy reached around and hugged her and Belle hugged Nancy back. They both needed food and they needed it fast, then a very long night's sleep.

At that moment Madge appeared from the hidden doorway on the other side of the office carrying a tray of milkshakes and baskets of fries. The fries smelled wonderful, but Belle was far too tired to try to get off the tile floor to go to them.

Madge unloaded the tray and then brought a vanilla milkshake to them.

Nancy took the ghost component and said, "Thank you."

Madge put the milkshake back on the table and handed them a basket of fries. Belle took the ghost component of the basket of fries from Madge and took one,

savoring the fantastic salty flavor in her mouth.

Nancy was making oohing and awing sounds while sipping on the milkshake, so they switched.

Madge looked at them. "Cheeseburgers on the way."

"Oh, you are heavenly," Nancy said.

"That's what K.J. said once in his hot tub," Madge said, winking at Belle and Nancy and headed for her invisible door.

Everyone laughed and K.J. just turned a very nice shade of pink that matched his pink suit coat.

Poker Boy's team were all back in the booth. Laverne sat at the end of the table, K.J. sat on a chair beside her, and Jewel and Tommy leaned against the booth.

Belle sipped on the fantastic, cold flavor of the vanilla milkshake, then turned to Nancy. "How did we get so lucky to be a part of this group?" she whispered.

"We died," Nancy whispered, kissing Belle's cheek.

"Lucky for a lot of people that we did, huh?" Belle whispered back.

Laverne turned to them and smiled. "Very lucky."

And when Lady Luck smiles on you, you know it.

Section Six
And Then It Was Christmas Eve

Thirty-nine

It was the night before Christmas and all through Belle and Nancy's wonderful three-bedroom home in the college district of Las Vegas, Christmas decorations and stockings were hung from not only the fireplace, but just about every empty spot that could hold something.

They had gotten a beautiful tree and decorated it with as many ornaments and lights as the poor ten-foot tall thing would hold. It filled a place of importance near their fireplace that at the moment flickered with a wonderful gas flame.

Their home had high ceilings, wood floors, and the most comfortable furniture Belle and Nancy could find.

Nancy had cooked a wonderful ham dinner and Jewel and Tommy and K.J. had joined them, each bringing something special they had liked to eat on Christmas Eve.

Jewel had brought wonderful deviled eggs, Tommy had brought a mincemeat pie that he actually baked himself, and K.J. had brought eggnog that tasted heavenly and had a little bite to it at the same time.

K.J. was dressed in what he called his Christmas attire that consisted of a bright red coat with long tails, white pants, a green scarf, and a Santa hat with fake diamonds in the ball on top. Tommy accused him of taking the hat from a store Santa and K.J. said it wasn't from just any store Santa, but a Tiffany's store Santa.

And the diamonds were real, as much as any ghost element of clothing could be real.

They had finished their dinner and were sitting in the living room enjoying a "nip of the egg" as K.J. called it. Nancy and Belle were cuddled together on the couch, Jewel and Tommy on the love seat, and K.J. in one of the big overstuffed chairs.

Belle had not felt so welcome and with family ever before on Christmas Eve.

Suddenly a voice said, "Knock, knock."

"Come on in," Nancy said, shrugging at Belle.

Poker Boy, Patty, and Stan appeared.

Patty and Poker Boy were carrying wonderful-smelling apple pies and a tub of ice cream and Stan had a plate of sugar cookies he placed near the fireplace on a stand there.

Belle was excited to see them, since Poker Boy and Patty had bought this wonderful home, as an investment, of course, and were letting Belle and Nancy stay in it as long as they wanted.

Patty had helped them furnish it with real furniture and had helped them get real Christmas decorations and the tree. Patty and Poker Boy and Screamer and Sherrie had helped them hang everything. Patty was becoming Belle and Nancy's close friend and it sure never hurt for ghosts to have live friends to do certain things that needed to be done at times.

Belle went with them into the kitchen and after a few minutes of laughter they were all seated back in the living room with helpings of the best-tasting apple pie Belle could remember.

"Since we all saved Christmas," Poker Boy said, "we figured it would be fun to stop and say hi this evening."

"We are so glad you did," Nancy said.

"And you are always welcome," Belle said. "You guys know that. How about making it a tradition?"

"We just might at that," Poker Boy said. "Thank you."

Belle was very, very glad to hear that.

"Where are Screamer and Sherrie tonight?" Nancy asked.

"Spending the evening with friends in Seattle," Poker Boy said.

"Knock. Knock," a voice said from out of the air that Belle instantly recognized as Laverne's voice.

"Got room for two more?"

"I never knock," another voice said out of the air.

A deeper voice.

"Please come in," Nancy shouted as everyone again laughed.

Laverne and a man appeared in the middle of the living room. Laverne was dressed down for her, in jeans, a light blouse and light blue sweater. Her hair was long and down over her shoulders and for a moment she didn't look like the most powerful woman in all of the world.

The very fat man with her was dressed much like K.J. was dressed, in a long red coat with white fluffy trim, black pants and tall black boots, and a Santa hat.

It took Belle a moment to realize that for the first time in her knowledge, she was staring at Santa Claus.

The real Santa Claus.

She was fairly certain her heart stopped and beside her Nancy's hand just gripped her leg.

"I would like to introduce you to St. Nicholas," Laverne said.

"Just call me Nick," he said, bowing slightly to everyone in the room, his voice deep and his smile under his white moustache full.

Belle had no idea what to say.

It seemed that even Poker Boy and Patty and Stan were stunned.

"I wanted to make a special stop here tonight to say thanks to all of you," Nick said. "You saved my bacon."

Nick patted his stomach and laughed. "And I got some rolls of bacon, let me tell you."

Then he spotted the sugar cookies beside the fireplace and shook his head.

"All right, who's the wise-ass who left those there?"

Stan raised his hand and smiled. "But you don't have to eat them."

"Darned toot'n I don't," Nick said.

He waved his hands and a sugar cookie was in everyone's hand.

Belle had one in her right hand. She could feel the sugar crumbs under her fingers.

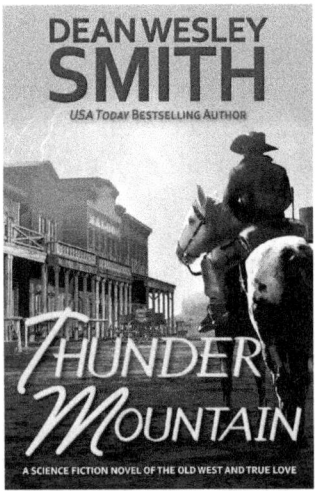

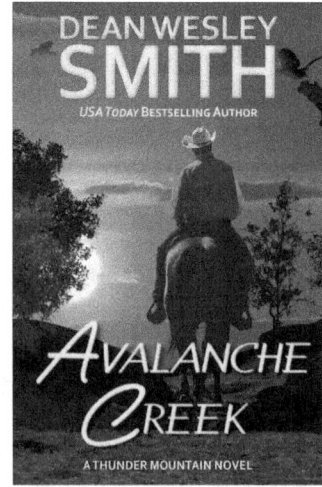

Some Novels Available
From the First Year of Smith's Monthly

Nick had one in his hand as well.

He raised the cookie in the air like a toast. "It took two teams of heroes working together to save me, the world, and a lot of lives. All I can say is thank you. You were all very good boys and girls this year."

He took a bite of the cookie and everyone else did as well.

Then he turned to Laverne. "Got a busy night ahead of me."

She nodded.

"Thank you for the hospitality," Nick said, looking back at everyone. And then he laughed. "And the cookie. You know how many of these things I'm going to eat tonight?"

With that he put the rest of the cookie into his mouth and vanished.

Laverne moved over and dropped into an open chair beside K.J., putting her feet up on a stool in front of the big armchair.

"I hear you make a mean bit of the egg," she said to K.J.

An instant later he was standing in front of her handing her a glass.

After K.J. took his seat, Laverne smiled at everyone. "Thanks also from me. You saved me an ugly alternative I did not want to have to contemplate.

Belle understood as everyone nodded back to Laverne.

Then Laverne took another sip of the eggnog and looked at K. J. "I hear you and Madge are meeting up later in your hot tub."

"She told you about that?" K.J. asked.

Laverne just smiled. "No, but turns out it was a good guess."

K.J.'s face turned as red as his jacket. Everyone laughed.

Belle looked around at the wonderful people in the room, and the wonderful partner beside her, and realized that maybe, just maybe, for the first time in a very long time, she was going to enjoy the holiday season.

How could she not, with friends like these?

Some Novels Available From the First Year of Smith's Monthly

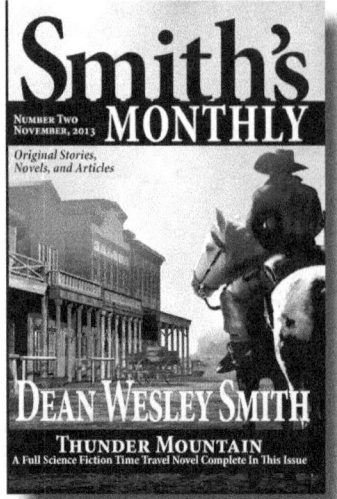

#7... April 2014

#8... May 2014

#9... June 2014

#10... July 2014

#11... August 2014

#12...September 2014

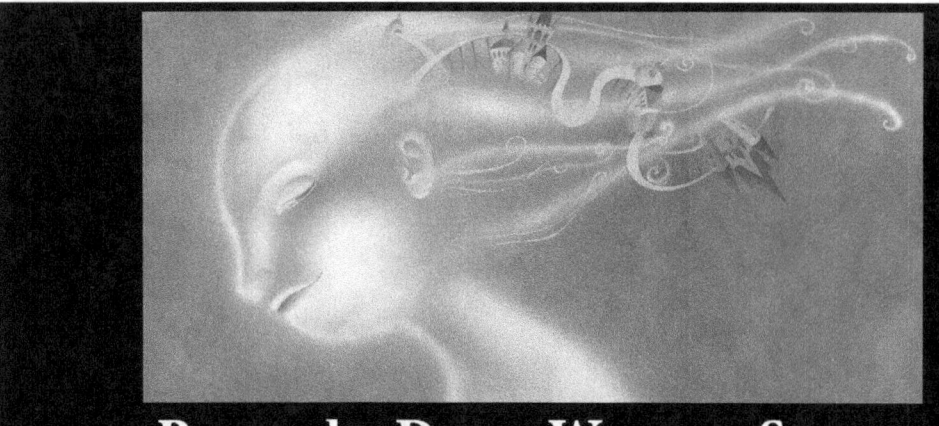

Poems by DEAN WESLEY SMITH

Tasty Morsel

A mother and daughter came
into the restaurant where I was
eating.
You couldn't tell they were related.

I taste my soup
falling in love with the daughter.
She reminds me of Snow White.

Things always taste better
when you're in love.

They sit directly in front.
She's facing me,
smiling.
I ravish my steak, tasting her.

Tender, succulent, medium rare.
My mouth waters at the thought.
The skewer is still hot.

I paused when leaving.
The cashier smiled.
Desert came topped with a cherry.

Things do taste better
when you are in love.

(First published in the 1970s somewhere...)

www.ingramcontent.com/pod-product-compliance
Lightning Source LLC
Chambersburg PA
CBHW081152170626

46813CB00009B/3161